ELLE GRAY | K.S. GRAY

OLIVIA KNIGHT

FBI MYSTERY THRILLER

MURDER ON
THE ASTORIA

PROLOGUE

"WHY AM I NOT ENOUGH FOR YOU?"

Her eyes were wide as he stared her down. *He knows, he knows,* she thought. He advanced on her slowly, backing her up into a corner—somewhere she couldn't escape from.

Even as she was pinned against the wall, she reached up to push her long, curly red hair out of her face and behind her ear. It was a nervous habit that she hated.

"You never trusted me," he snarled, his eyes boring into hers. "You always made me feel like I was doing something terrible to you. But *you're* the one who betrayed *me.*"

She swallowed. Beyond the doors of the cabin, she could hear the party in full swing out there on the yacht. People getting drunk, laughing maniacally, getting wilder than they should. She wished she was among them. Better yet, she wished she hadn't attended the party at all. She was beginning to wish that she'd never let herself get entangled in this crazy world of high rollers, parties, and politics. She'd had enough. She wanted to get away.

But it wasn't going to be that easy now. She was in too deep. She clenched her jaw, glaring at him.

"I don't want to do this anymore," she said. Her voice came out as barely more than a whisper. "I'm done. I'm done with all of it."

She turned her back on her now *ex*-boyfriend and headed for the door, her head held high. The last thing he would see of her was her dazzling red hair bouncing away like the last tendrils of flame. He loved her hair. It was what he always said he liked most about her. And now it would be the last time he ever got to see it.

She thought she'd gotten away with it. She thought she was safe.

Until she felt the hand clenching her wrist.

His grip was so hard that she knew he'd leave a mark on her pale skin. He spun her around to face him. She felt her heart quiver with fear as she looked into his eyes. She saw the anger— saw the fury that lived within his soul.

Anger reserved for her.

"You don't get to walk away now," he snarled. "Not this time."

CHAPTER ONE

A few days earlier...

"CAN I GET YOU ANYTHING BEFORE I HEAD TO BED?"
Brock asked Olivia with a warm smile. Olivia
hugged her knees as she sat on his sofa, making
herself at home. After all, for the past three months, she'd been
living there part-time. It was almost beginning to feel more
like home than her cabin in the woods.

"You don't need to ask me that every night, you know," Olivia
told him. Brock had a relentless urge to take care of her, and
despite being more than perfectly capable of looking after herself,
the feeling his affection brought was unparalleled. Lately, it felt

like their relationship had come to a standstill, but not necessarily in a bad way. Things hadn't moved forward romantically, but there was a sweetness between them that Olivia couldn't deny.

"I know. I just want to make sure you're comfortable here," Brock said, hovering in the doorway to his bedroom and leaning against the doorframe. A smile played on his lips, as it always did when he was around Olivia, but there was a sincerity in his tone. Olivia knew, without having to ask, that Brock really cared.

"I *am* comfortable here. More comfortable than I would be anywhere else," Olivia said softly. Saying it out loud only reminded her of the reason she'd been crashing at Brock's home in the first place.

Every night, she dreamed of her cabin in the woods. She dreamed of the way she found it all those months ago: ransacked, the lock to her front door busted off with some heavy force, half her belongings spilled out all over the floor, glasses and plates smashed and debris strewn everywhere, and everything in utter chaos.

She recalled the way it made her feel. Because whoever had decided to break into her home, to cause chaos there, had wanted her to feel afraid.

And she had been scared. She didn't like to admit that to herself, but the attack on her home had felt so personal. Other than what was broken, nothing seemed to be missing, and she'd searched the place top to bottom four times. It was like someone had gone in and shaken up the house just to rattle her. And someone willing to unleash that kind of chaos was someone that she knew she should have the sense to fear.

Ever since then, she hadn't spent a single night alone in her own home. The first few nights after the break-in, Brock had stayed on her sofa to make her feel better; but Olivia was constantly on edge, wondering how someone might strike at her next. Slowly, she began to accept that her home wasn't safe any longer. She began to sleep on Brock's sofa most of the time when they weren't working a case. Sometimes, she stayed with Emily or Sam, and she'd even spent a few nights with her parents. But mostly, she stayed with Brock. After all, he was her partner. It was his job to have her back, and she knew she'd do the same for him if the tables were turned.

"Well, don't hesitate to shout for me if you need anything at all," Brock said. He hesitated before retreating into his bedroom, and a smile played on Olivia's lips. She knew that the break-in at her house had shaken their foundations a little. They'd been so close to something new—something romantic, perhaps. Olivia couldn't be sure that they would have gotten together if they hadn't been thrown off course by the break-in, but now, it was like those feelings had been swept under the rug. They were still there, but neither of them was acknowledging their emotions.

Maybe they were both hoping those feelings would fade away and they wouldn't have to face up to them. Or maybe they just didn't know how to approach them. But Olivia was glad to put it on the back burner, if only for a little while. It was clear to her that she had some things to figure out before she could commit to anyone or anything. She was just glad to know that it was there to revisit whenever she felt ready.

If she ever felt ready.

There was a good reason that Olivia struggled to sleep every night. Now, as she got herself comfortable on the squishy sofa, she let her troubles replay in her head as she did every evening. Someone out there had it out for her—she was sure of it. But *who*, was the question? It was part of her job to poke the bear, to roll up criminal organizations and put bad people behind bars. Anyone who had ever been involved in one of her cases could be capable of targeting her…

But why now? And why hadn't they struck again since? Was it because she wasn't alone anymore? Did they see her as less vulnerable when she had other people around? The thought irritated her. She could hold her own. If the cowards who ransacked her home ever bothered to show their faces, Olivia would be more than capable of taking them down, with or without Brock's help.

But that was the problem. Olivia had no place to start looking for the culprit. She'd conducted the investigation of the break-in herself, checking for signs of the person who'd done it. But she didn't find a single thing. No fingerprints, no hairs, no DNA to speak of. Whoever had entered her home had been prepared, and that worried Olivia more than anything. She'd dealt with plenty of idiots in her career, criminals who never thought their plans through, but the true psychopaths, the ones who knew how to destroy lives without even leaving a trail behind them… they were the ones to worry about. They were slippery, capable of almost anything, and it required all of her wits to even get close to finding them.

But she was determined to get to the bottom of it. Maybe not that day, or any time soon, but she refused to live in fear of whomever was trying to mess with her. She had no doubt in her mind that someone was trying to shake her up, trying to terrify her into hiding or not doing her job. But she wouldn't give in to them. She would keep working, keep fighting, until she figured out who was trying to ruin her life.

Olivia closed her eyes and put her worries out of sight and out of mind. Whatever was going on in her life, the issues could wait until morning.

When Olivia woke the following morning, it was to the sound of Brock moving around the living area. She sat up groggily, watching him pull on a jacket.

"Everything okay?" she asked him, stifling a yawn. He seemed in a hurry to be somewhere, and his face was creased with anxiety. He shoved his keys into his jacket pocket.

"Ol' JJ wants to see us. I said I'd get us to the office as soon as possible," Brock said. "Throw on some clothes and let's get out of here."

Olivia frowned as she got herself up and grabbed some clothes. It wasn't often that their boss requested to see them in person, and she wondered what was going on. Whatever he had in mind, it must be important. Olivia made herself presentable as quickly as she could and then followed Brock out of his apartment and out to his car.

"Any idea what this is about?" Olivia asked Brock as she strapped herself into the passenger's seat. Brock shrugged.

"Not really. But he did say that it was urgent. I guess maybe it's some time-sensitive case, but I still don't know why he insists on seeing us in person."

"That's what I thought," Olivia mused. The anticipation had her stomach in knots, but in a good way. She'd come to love the feeling of a new case to sink her teeth into. Over the last few months, they'd mostly handled minor things here and there or helped out with the police department in Belle Grove. It would be nice to have some excitement. Not that she was exactly chomping at the bit to take down another horrific monster like The Botanist or The Grim Reaper anytime soon, but at least something to distract from the turbulence in her own life. It helped to have something else to focus on, and as they made the hour-long drive up to Washington, she thought about what Jonathan might have in store for them.

When they arrived, Brock was out of the car in seconds, hurrying up to Jonathan's office. Olivia hurried to keep in step with him, half jogging as they made their way through security and navigated the halls. When they reached the upper levels of the building, they found ASAC Jonathan James already waiting for them outside his office, his face stern as it so often was. He glanced at them both, looking a little surprised to see Olivia there too.

"Knight… I wasn't expecting you to be here too," Jonathan said. Olivia frowned. Since she and Brock had first partnered up, they had come as a package deal. They were joined at the hip for every case they worked. In what world was she not needed there as well?

"Am I not needed?" Olivia asked. Jonathan ran a hand through his hair.

"Well, now that you're here, you might as well hear what's going on. Come in, both of you."

Brock and Olivia exchanged a glance. It was clear that he was just as baffled as she was. Olivia led the way into the office and sat down at one of the two plush wingbacks before Jonathan's desk.

Like the rest of the man, Jonathan's office was, in a word, austere. The mahogany desk was a fine antique, obviously hand-carved by a master in intricate, elegant detail. Behind the desk was a series of simple frames containing nothing particularly interesting: a folded-up American flag, a diploma, and one or two photos of him and his family. To her left, tall bookshelves took up the majority of the wall space, containing a selection of leather-bound antique books that Olivia was certain he'd never even cracked open; and to Olivia's right, tall floor-to-ceiling windows looked over the bustle of downtown Washington DC.

Jonathan sighed as he sank into his desk chair, focusing his gaze on Brock. "By the look on your face, I'm guessing you have no idea why I called you here."

"I'm definitely a little baffled right now," Brock admitted. "I assumed you wanted both Olivia and me here… we've been working cases together for some time now."

"I should have been clearer. This time, I just need you," Jonathan said. He folded his arms over his chest. "I'm sending you undercover in New York. I'm sure you can guess why?"

Olivia glanced over at Brock and caught sight of recognition on his face. Brock let out a long sigh, rubbing at the back of his neck.

"I wondered when this would come back up…"

"Now you understand why this is going to be a solo mission," Jonathan pressed. He turned to Olivia. "You're the only man for the job."

Olivia looked back and forth between the two of them and frowned. "What's this about?" she asked.

"It's about—" Brock started, but a harsh glare from Jonathan cut him off.

"Before you and Brock partnered up, I had him working a case that involved an international crime syndicate that was smuggling drugs, weapons, and possibly even human beings across borders. We've recently received some new intel that could break open this case."

"Does…" Brock hesitated. "Does *he* know about it?" He gestured vaguely with his shoulder out the window.

Jonathan narrowed his eyes. "At this time, we don't believe so. But part of your mission will be to root that out. I don't need to remind you that discretion is paramount here, Tanner. Your loyalty is to the Bureau."

Brock let out yet another sigh. "I know. But it's a really long story." His face softened as he saw the worry on Olivia's face. "It's going to be fine though. I'll be in and out in no time at all."

She didn't really believe him but had no choice but to try. What else could she believe? That this would all be done and dusted in a few days and he'd make it back before the weekend? Or the opposite end of the spectrum—that he'd be gone for months, maybe even years, like her mother?

She couldn't give in to those thoughts. She had to take him at his word. She had to *trust* him. It was all she could do.

Brock broke out into his trademark grin. "And anyway, I thought you'd be more excited to have some time away from me. I won't be around to wind you up for a while."

Olivia smiled sadly. "Oddly, that's something I think I'll miss."

Brock placed a hand on Olivia's arm, and she almost jumped at the sudden contact. Electricity sizzled between the pair of them. It had been a long time since he'd dared to touch her, as if he was worried he might reignite something they weren't ready for. But with his hand on her arm, she felt the chemistry shifting between them once again. She looked up into his eyes and saw familiarity there, but also something new. Something she couldn't place, something exciting. Something she felt like she'd been waiting for.

Heat.

"You'll be fine without me," Brock said gruffly. Olivia quirked her eyebrow.

"Oh, I'm not worried about that. I think *you're* the one that's going to be screwed without *me.*"

Brock laughed loudly, and Olivia managed a smile. The spell between them was broken, but the warmth remained. The thing was … Brock was her best friend. There was no denying that he knew her better than anyone—that he'd been there with her through so much. They spent nearly every hour of every day together, and now, that was going to be ripped away from them. Olivia knew that she'd be okay without Brock, but it didn't mean that she wanted them to be apart.

Brock squeezed her arm gently with a smile. "Hey. Nothing has to change. You're still welcome at my apartment. You don't have to go home, just because I'm not there. What's mine is yours. And when I get back … maybe we can do something fun to celebrate. We never did go out for that dinner, did we?"

Olivia's cheeks heated up. Sure, they'd hit up the diner plenty of times, but it was the first time either of them had acknowledged their almost-date in months. She had wondered if maybe Brock had put it all out of his mind. But the thought of spending some one-on-one time with him when this was all over made her smile.

"I'd like that."

Brock smiled at her. "Good. I'll need something to look forward to after this is over. It's going to be a long few weeks."

You're telling me, Olivia thought. She was already dreading her time away from him. But it was only a few weeks, she told herself. She'd be fine.

And when he came back, perhaps they'd pick up where they left off.

CHAPTER TWO

T HE DRIVE TO OLIVIA'S PARENT'S HOUSE ALWAYS FELT LIKE a long one. Each time she visited, she wondered what the hell she was doing there. After everything that had gone down between them on Thanksgiving, she felt as though she was making a huge mistake by letting them back into her life.

But ever since her home had been broken into, Olivia had begun to lean on her parents a little more again. It felt wrong to be cutting them out of her life when it felt like nothing was promised. She hadn't forgiven them for all the lies and deceit, but at the same time, she hated the idea that they might ever end on bad terms. If something were to happen to any of them and she never got to make things right, then she knew she'd regret it.

And now that Brock was heading out of town, she felt like it was time to see them again. Brock had insisted that she was welcome to stay at his place while he was away, but Olivia wanted to know that she had a backup. She'd stayed with her parents a few times since her home was broken into, and that had helped with rebuilding their relationship, but she still had bridges to build. As much as her parents drove her crazy, she was looking forward to seeing them.

She parked outside their home, trying her best not to think about the explosive argument that had taken place there on Thanksgiving. It had been so bad that all they'd gotten for Christmas was a phone call.

She still couldn't forget the fact that her mom had blatantly lied to her, telling her that she was stepping back from her role in the Bureau when all along she planned to continue with the case that had almost ended her life. The case that had caused her to disappear off the face of the earth for years, leaving Olivia unsure if she'd ever see her again.

Olivia gritted her teeth at the thought. She'd never known anybody to lie as much as her mother, never known anyone to cause as much pain as her. But she had to put that out of her mind if she was ever going to make things okay between them. She had to try and forget the trauma of her past and focus on the future, whatever that may hold.

Everything in Olivia's life was always uncertain. She never knew where the strange path of her life would take her. But the last year had taught her the kind of forgiveness that she'd never expected to be capable of. It had taught her to show kindness even when the people demanding it didn't deserve it. And most importantly, it had taught her that often, the people you love the most let you down the hardest.

She knocked on the front door, feeling an ache in her chest. As much as her family hurt her over and over again, she still felt tied to them. She still felt like she wanted to fix what they'd spent so long breaking. And if that meant hiding her pain, then she was almost willing to do it. If it meant repairing her family, then maybe it would be worth it.

Jean Knight was grinning when she swung the door open. Like nothing had ever turned sour between them. Like she was thrilled to have gotten away with her bad behavior for so long.

Olivia forced a smile back. *Don't start a fight, don't start a fight…* she told herself.

"Darling. You look great," Olivia's mother told her, brushing a light kiss against her cheek.

"Thanks," Olivia replied a little stiffly, sliding her shoes off as she stepped inside. "Where's Dad?"

"Oh, he's working on getting dinner ready. He wanted to cook you something special today. He was so glad when you called and said you were coming over."

Olivia doubted that. She and her father had barely exchanged words in months. He'd always been quiet, but there was certainly a tension between them. Olivia couldn't help feeling betrayed by the ways he'd deceived her about her mother's disappearance, and he hated that she was so unforgiving. As far as Olivia was concerned, she was at a stalemate with her father.

"What's new with you, sweetheart?" Jean asked, ushering her into the living room. "Anything exciting going on? Anything at work?"

"Well… Brock's being sent off on a solo mission soon. He's going undercover in New York, working on some old case that he was involved in before we worked together. So, there's that."

"Are you going to miss him?" she asked with a gleam in her eye. Olivia tried not to roll her eyes. Her mother had always made it her business to be invested in Olivia's nonexistent love life, especially since Brock entered the picture.

"Well, I'm down a roommate for a few weeks, I guess. But maybe the peace and quiet will be nice. And he shouldn't be away for long. It's not like he's not coming back."

Jean chewed her lip. Olivia hadn't intended for her comment to be a dig at her disappearance, but it had certainly sounded like one. Still, that wasn't her fault. As far as Olivia was concerned, Jean was lucky that her daughter still spoke to her at all. Plenty of people in Olivia's shoes would have cut her off a long time ago. She'd lied to Olivia all of her life—about her work, about her intentions, about her lifestyle. It was only a few months ago that Olivia had finally discovered the truth, and it still drove her crazy to know just how deceived she had been.

"Well, I'm sure the time will fly by," Jean said. "Are you sure you're going to be all right in that apartment of his by yourself? You can always stay with us if you need to."

"I'm sure I'll be okay. But thank you for the offer. If I need to, I'll come here," Olivia replied, trying to inject gratitude into her tone. She wanted her mother to know she was being sincere, even after all the difficulties they had faced. As much as her mom had caused her trouble in the past, it seemed like she was doing her best to make up for it now.

Olivia spent the next half an hour making polite small talk with her, mostly allowing Jean to chatter at her instead of making the effort of conversation herself. Then, after a while, Olivia's father called out for them to sit at the dinner table, and Olivia moved to the dining room with a clenched stomach. This was the place where their family had fallen apart at Thanksgiving. This was the place where Olivia had realized just how selfish some people could be. But she tried not to think about that as they gathered around the table to eat a hearty meal together.

"This salmon looks incredible," Jean remarked cheerily, tucking in right away. Olivia glanced uncomfortably at her father, who still had barely said a word. Olivia couldn't decide which was worse: her mom pretending nothing was wrong or her dad making it obvious that there was plenty wrong with their dysfunctional little family. Olivia didn't need to be reminded of the tension under the surface, not when it was so evident at their dinner.

"Olivia, darling... your father and I wanted to talk to you about some things," Jean said with an encouraging nod at her husband. Roger cleared his throat, unwilling to look in Olivia's direction.

"That's right," he confirmed quietly. "We wanted to acknowledge what happened at Thanksgiving. We realize that it was a while ago now, and that we've sort of brushed the whole incident under the carpet..."

"But that's not fair to you," Jean continued. "We're your parents, and you expected better of us. Of me, in particular. I know that I lied. I know that I caused you pain, and that's the last thing that I ever wanted. And I know that it hurt when I told you that I'd be working on my case again. And for all of that, I'm truly sorry."

Olivia raised an eyebrow. She'd heard empty apologies from her parents before, and she wasn't sure how much she trusted them these days. But her mother wasn't finished talking.

"I'm done with secrets and lies," she continued. "It's not fair to you. It's not fair to your father. It betrays all the trust we built over the years. And I know that a lot of that trust is gone now because of me. You have every right to struggle to trust me. But I want to bring this family back together. We've all suffered together. We've lost so much already, and I don't want to lose you too. It was hard enough losing your sister. But I think there's still time to make this right. If you're willing to let me, I'd like to try."

Olivia swallowed. She didn't know whether she could trust her mother's words, but she wanted to. She wanted to believe that her mother truly had the good heart that she grew up believing she had. She wanted to believe that there was something to salvage from the mess they'd made.

"Do you really mean that?" Olivia whispered. Jean nodded.

"I do. All I want is a second chance, sweetheart. Well... maybe a third or fourth chance. I know you've already given me plenty of chances before. But I'm only human. We all make mistakes. And now, I just want to fix this one. If you'll allow it."

Olivia closed her eyes for a moment. It was blissful to picture a life where she didn't have to fight so hard anymore. Where she didn't have to constantly battle with her parents, and they could start taking care of her again. A life where they could at least pretend that they were normal, even if they were far from it.

Wouldn't it be so easy just to take her mom's word for it? That's how it should be, at least. She should be able to trust the woman who raised her. She shouldn't have to fear being lied to. And in that moment, Olivia decided to give her the benefit of the doubt one last time. Because if she was being lied to now, at least it felt good.

"I'll allow it," Olivia murmured.

CHAPTER THREE

"SHE REALLY SAID THAT?"

"Yes," Olivia confirmed, pressing her phone to her ear. She was talking to her best friend, Emily, about her experience at her parents' house. "She insisted that things are going to change. That she won't lie to me again."

"And you believed her?"

Olivia chewed her lip, pacing around Brock's kitchen. "I wouldn't say that exactly. I want to believe her. But trusting her, after everything we've been through? It seems almost impossible."

"Yeah, I get it. I don't blame you."

Olivia sat down on the sofa with a sigh. In some ways, she was glad for a situation in which she wouldn't have to hash this out with Brock yet again. She was used to off-loading her problems onto him, but he didn't know the true depths of Olivia's feelings—

not the way Emily did. He meant well, but when it came to her mother, his advice never quite felt adequate.

In truth, her best friend still held a grudge that nearly matched her own in its ferocity. The two had grown up together, gone to school, and even entered the Academy together. In some ways, her relationship with Emily was much stronger than it had been even with Veronica, her late sister. And Emily had been there for her long before even Brock had.

"I really hope she's telling the truth. I've been waiting for this," Olivia admitted. "All these months have gone by without so much as an apology… I guess I came to the conclusion that I was never going to get one. She's as stubborn as I am, I suppose. But now that she's taken some ownership of the problems she's caused, maybe things can get better. Maybe it doesn't have to be this huge mess any longer."

"I want to believe her too. For your sake," Emily said gently. "Just don't get too comfortable too fast. We both know how she can be so…"

Olivia smirked. "You can say it."

"*Flighty*, was the word I was going to use," Emily said.

Olivia scoffed. "Well, that's an understatement."

"You know, it's weird… when we were kids, I always really looked up to your mom. And I still do, sort of. She's done some really good work for the Bureau. But after all this, I don't know how much I'll ever be able to trust her again. I know that your relationship with her is what it is, but to me? She hurt my friend. I don't like people who hurt my friends."

Olivia was glad this wasn't a video chat so Emily couldn't see her eyes welling up with emotion. She blinked it away as quick as it came though.

"For me it's almost… you know, when you're a kid, you never expect to see an adult that way, right? Especially your parents. We assume that they have their lives completely together and they just know so much. And when you grow up, you kind of realize that they were making it up as they went along. Which is fine. But this is a whole other level."

"Yeah."

"Maybe that's why I find all of her lies so hard to swallow. You never expect to find out that your own mother is morally gray," Olivia admitted. She closed her eyes, a headache forming behind her eyes. "But maybe things will change now. Maybe adults can grow up too."

"I certainly hope so. Or else Sam is in some real trouble."

Olivia laughed. Even if Brock was going away, she was glad to still have Emily. They didn't get to see much of one another ever since Olivia had moved out of Washington. Working for the FBI had its perks, but having lots of free time wasn't one of them. It had put a strain on many of Olivia's relationships over the years, including with her ex-fiancé Tom. But now, maybe she was getting a shot at rectifying that.

"When does Brock leave?" Emily asked Olivia gently. Olivia's breath hitched in her chest. She didn't want to admit that the thought of him being gone made her ache.

"He's leaving early tomorrow morning."

"That's rough."

Olivia couldn't find it in her to respond to that comment. She was really going to miss him. And it wasn't like he was just going away on vacation. He was going off to do something that would put him in danger—something that he might not come back from. It scared her to think of him out there alone, without even being able to cover his back.

She knew he was a perfectly capable agent, and that he'd survived a long time in the field before he even knew her; but now, it felt like they came as a package deal, and she didn't like the idea of them being split up. Perhaps it was immature of her, but she still didn't like to think of him as a single entity when she was so used to being around him.

"Maybe I can do something to take your mind off it?" Emily asked hopefully. "I'm guessing you don't currently have an active assignment?"

"Not at the moment," Olivia admitted. She'd been using her time lately trying to chase down loose ends of the cult of Apep, hoping that maybe something would come to light; but ever since the deaths of Lauren and Amos and the subsequent roundup of most of the inner circle, they were certainly lying low for the moment. Olivia had wondered for a while if maybe they were behind the attack on her home, but she had no evidence to back up that claim, which only left her feeling more frustrated than before.

"Well, I've got my hands full over here," Emily told her. "I've been looking into this big tech company... they're not exactly new on the scene, but they've only just come into big money these past few years, which I always find a little suspicious. Anyway, I'm pretty certain there's something weird going on here behind the scenes. All this money coming in for them all of a sudden... some of their accounts don't seem to add up."

"Has the IRS flagged them or anything?"

"Not quite. But I can't help but feel like there's something fishy going on. I want to dig deeper and check it out, and I could use your help if you're available."

Olivia pondered the details of the case. A big, mysterious organization... a suspicion of criminal activity... plenty of opportunities for fraud... it sounded like the perfect distraction. Murder cases were always intense, but something like this, she could really sink her teeth into. Besides, the details of the case seemed familiar to her.

They made her think of the cult case once again—how they'd used several deft layers of charity fraud to build their financial empire. Somehow, her mind always circled back to that place. It had been a frustrating one. She might have caught the leader, but she knew cutting the head off the snake hadn't been enough to kill it. She'd been waiting so long for something to come up about it, and nothing had happened... maybe this was a chance to investigate a similar case, to get inside the minds of similar criminals. Maybe it would be enough to aid her with investigations of her own.

"All right. I'm in," Olivia said. She heard Emily make a gleeful noise on the other end of the line.

"This is so exciting! We've never worked a case together before, have we? It'll be good to spend some time together too. And having your brain on my side will definitely be of use. I could use a fresh perspective on this whole thing."

"You and I both know you've always been the smarter of the two of us. That's why you're in White Collar and I'm slumming it out here in the field."

"That may be," Emily replied, "but it's nowhere near as glamorous."

Olivia laughed. She was excited too. It was the perfect distraction for her, and Emily was right. It would be nice to work as a partnership. Brock might have been her constant partner for the last six months, but Emily had been her friend her whole life. Olivia was sure that whatever happened, they'd make a great team.

"I'll send you over some of the notes I've made about the case so far," Emily said, diving right in. "I've got some ideas of how I want to approach this already, but take a look and let me know your thoughts."

"I like your style. Usually, it's me coming up with all the bright ideas while Brock just comes along for the ride."

"I don't like your tone," Brock joked as he appeared from his bedroom. He was carrying a single bag in his hand, clearly traveling light for his time in New York. The sight of him getting ready to leave made Olivia's heart hurt. How had it come around so soon?

"I've got to go, Emily. Brock's about to head off to the airport. Send me those documents, and I'll take a look later."

"All right, Olivia, no worries. Tell Brock good luck from me. And I hope you're okay."

"Thanks," Olivia said, her voice barely a whisper. Of course, Emily could sense how Brock going away was making her feel. She never seemed to miss a thing. She was suddenly glad that she was going to have Emily at her side for the next few weeks. Just like when her mom had gone away, Emily was there for her. She loved that about her.

Olivia ended her call with Emily and stood up to face Brock, her heart thudding fast. Anxiety clutched at her chest, and Brock seemed to feel it too. His brow was creased, his usual smile absent from his features. Olivia swallowed.

"You're sure I can't drive you to the airport?" she asked him. He shook his head.

"Best not. It'll be easier to go if you don't."

Olivia nodded in understanding. When she'd gone undercover in prison, it had been hard leaving ordinary life behind. She knew how Brock must be feeling. He would be spending his next few weeks constantly on edge, playing a character instead of himself. It was a dangerous game to play. One slip-up could get him killed.

"I don't want you to go," Olivia admitted out loud. Brock managed a small smile for her.

"Trust me, I'm not over the moon about going myself. But it's only a few weeks. I'll be back before you know it. And hey, I'm sure you'll find something to do while I'm away. You might even get to eat a vegetable for once."

"Oh, that's definitely true. No more trips to our diner until you're home."

Brock's features softened. "*Our* diner?"

Olivia rolled her eyes, though a blush was settling on her cheeks. Because yes, she did see it as their place. Every place they went together felt like it belonged to them. When it was just the two of them, it was like the rest of the world didn't matter, didn't exist. She didn't go to that diner because she liked the food or the atmosphere. It was all right, but at the end of the day, it was just a diner.

She went because when she was there with Brock, it just felt right.

And now, she was saying goodbye to all that. She was saying goodbye to security and her version of normality. Brock had become such an important part of her life that watching him go was like watching a piece of herself leave. She remembered how it had been for her in the prison, feeling the tug of her heart whenever she thought of him. That was months ago, when they weren't half as close as they were now. How would she feel when he was gone this time? When she couldn't contact him, when she had no idea when she'd see him again?

Her throat was tight. She knew if she tried to speak, she'd end up crying. She hated that he had such an effect on her. She hated that he could make her feel things that no one else ever had before.

But she knew that he felt the same. Neither of them wanted to admit it out loud, but they needed one another. And that's why when Brock reached out to hug her close to him, she slid easily into his arms and gripped him hard. She held him so tight that she wasn't sure she would be able to let go. She felt like she could barely breathe, like he was stealing the air from her lungs. How could she let him go now?

But she did. After a long time, they pulled apart silently. Brock's face was solemn, and he didn't seem able to look Olivia in the eye. He cleared his throat.

"I want you to know that you're welcome to stay here if you want. It doesn't matter that I'm not here. This is your home, too, as far as I'm concerned," he said. "I've left a spare key in my mailbox so you can come and go as you please."

Olivia nodded with a tight smile, but she already knew that she'd be leaving the apartment soon after he did. She didn't think she could bear to be in his space without him. She didn't think she could be around so many reminders of him without falling apart. Still, it was nice to know that he wanted her to feel at home. It made her want to smile.

"I'll keep that in mind," Olivia choked out. Brock smiled gently at her.

"I'll be home soon," he murmured. "And the second I get back, I'm taking you out to dinner. That's a promise."

Olivia's heart skipped a beat. He hadn't been so forward with her in months. But she didn't have time to process it because before she knew it, he was planting a kiss on her forehead and heading toward the door. Olivia whipped around to follow him with her gaze.

"Stay safe," she whispered. Brock gave her one last fleeting smile, and then he was gone, shutting the door to the apartment behind him. Olivia felt winded and sat down on the sofa. She couldn't believe what had just happened. Just like that, he was gone.

And he hadn't even said goodbye.

CHAPTER FOUR

O LIVIA DROVE TO HEADQUARTERS ALONE, THE CAR filled with a heavy silence that made her feel uncomfortable. She was used to driving around with Brock in the car, his obnoxiously loud music making her want to scream and laugh simultaneously. She wondered where he was at that very moment. She was certain that he was already throwing himself deep into the investigation. He probably hadn't even had time to think about what he was leaving behind.

But Olivia couldn't get it out of her mind. She was glad to have her case with Emily to keep her busy. She'd been too restless to sleep the night before and had stayed up reading the notes that Emily had sent her. Now, however, she was going to get really deep into the details.

The closer Olivia got to Headquarters, the easier it was becoming to forget about Brock and his adventures without her. He was already well on his way to New York, slipping back into some past she was so curious about. And now there was nothing she could do but try to keep occupied with this case. To fully lose herself in the chaos of it all.

He'll be fine without you, she told herself. *And you'll certainly be fine without him.*

Besides, she was looking forward to seeing Emily. It had been a while since they'd been together in person, but she always found it easy to fall back in sync with her old friend. She was fascinated to see how they would work together. Emily was much more like her than Brock was—methodical in her approach and always using logic to solve her cases. Even though Olivia had been feeling much more impulsive in the past year, she knew she could rely on Emily to rein her in so they could run a smart operation and get things done.

Olivia parked at Headquarters and headed inside, feeling instantly transported back to her early days in the Bureau when everything felt new. It was certainly going to be a different experience working without Brock. She was so used to having him at her side, bouncing ideas off him, sharing her days with him and only him, that it felt odd to be doing anything differently. Still, she found that she was actually looking forward to getting started with Emily.

Emily was waiting for her upstairs, sitting at her desk with two cardboard cups of coffee beside her. She looked up with an enigmatic smile and greeted Olivia with a quick hug.

"Look at us. Raring to go," Emily said, an edge of glee to her tone. "I can't wait to get started. Did you read everything I sent you last night?"

"I did. I think I'm ready to go over everything."

"Pull up a chair, then. Let's get into it."

"I like your style."

Olivia wasted no time getting settled in a chair at Emily's desk. Emily produced a set of notes and laid them out neatly in front of her, examining them with cautious eyes.

"All right then. The company we're looking at is called Infinity. They're certainly not a start-up, but they haven't been on the tech scene for very long either. They've secured several rounds of investment funding, raking in millions, but look." She turned her laptop screen to show Olivia. "Their website is barely anything. No products, no apps, no partnerships... hardly a professional social media presence."

That made Olivia raise an eyebrow. "So what do they do?"

"That's the million-dollar question," Emily said. "What *do* they do?" She shuffled around some of the papers on her desk and handed one to Olivia. "We call them a tech company for now, but look at this press kit they released for investors."

Olivia read the note with a careful eye. "This... this is just gibberish. This doesn't mean anything. 'Bringing innovation in new sectors to maximize the synergy potential of emerging markets'? What the hell does that even mean?"

"Your guess is as good as mine," Emily shrugged. "And by itself, that's not a problem. Investors can waste their money on whatever bullcrap they want, even if it doesn't make sense to me. But what really concerns me is the activities of some of the higher-ups in the company."

"Such as?"

"The works. Corporate fraud, money laundering, scams, the lot."

"Yikes. Sounds like these guys have been busy."

"They sure have. And I'm not pulling this out of nowhere. I've got a whole list." Emily pointed to a spot on the paper. "Point one. An anonymous source informed me of the CEO, Charlie Evans, and his private bank accounts in the Cayman Islands. Now, we all know that there are plenty of scumbags with offshore accounts, raking in big money and hiding it away where they can avoid taxes, but I think there's more to it. My source has reason to believe there's a potential connection to not only money laundering but also funds related to big-time criminal organizations.

"Point two. My source also informed me of some of the habits displayed by the company that might indicate foul play—some stuff that gives us reason to go digging in the first place. Cash-in-hand payments off the books, possible gaps in tax records, which would certainly make sense with the offshore accounts... and then there was other stuff, too. I haven't been able to corroborate much of this yet, but there are rumors of an abusive workplace culture: a high turnover of staff among the lower levels, according to the source, and a very tight inner circle at the top of the company."

"That's not so unusual. Not among rich businessmen," Olivia pointed out.

"Maybe not, but given the rest of the evidence, I'm willing to consider it as suspicious," Emily said. "I had Sam do a little digging too. He's been watching Charlie Evans and the way he interacts online." She opened up a new tab to pull up the man's page on social media.

Olivia frowned. "Oh, I recognize that guy. I don't follow him, but his content is pushed into my feed all the time."

Emily nodded. "He's got several million followers. Half known for inspirational messages and feel-good stories, and half for partying the night away and flashing his expensive lifestyle all over the internet. He's always hawking cryptocurrency, which as far as I'm concerned is a scam in and of itself, and it seems like he's got a legion of trolls and followers who hang on to his every move. There's some big, new charity foundation he claims to be promoting soon, but just like with Infinity, I can't get any hard details on the financials."

Not for the first time, Olivia was reminded of men like Cyrus Lockwood or the Grim Reaper. Men who could command all sorts of people to follow their every command like it was nothing. Men who could inspire some fanatical devotion for a higher cause. She wasn't so sure that Charlie Evans was a cult leader, but the pattern of behavior was similar.

"Do you think it's a matter of Charlie on a personal level?" Olivia asked. "Or is it the whole company?"

"Good question," Emily acknowledged. "At this point, I'm not sure. The finances and activities of both just seem so tightly woven around each other that it's almost hard to tell where the man ends and the company begins."

"Here's to hoping we can find something online... if it's out there."

"That's my hope. I don't doubt there's something out there for us to find. I know these kinds of guys. Big-shot CEOs with more money than sense, jet-setting around the world with their rich buddies, leaving a trail of chaos behind them. And when the cash flow starts to look weak, they resort to criminal activity to keep feeding their lifestyle." Emily shook her head in disgust. "Not the kind of people I have any sympathy for. Maybe we don't have anything solid enough to take them down yet, but I know we can find something. I know this isn't going to be a dead end. I can just feel it."

Olivia smiled. She was used to following her intuition, too, something that often served her well. Brock always thought it was a guessing game, but Emily got it. That was why they were going to be the perfect match for this case.

"So what do you want to do?" Olivia asked. As much as she had her own ideas of how to run the operation, this was Emily's case. She didn't like to take a back seat, but she knew when it was necessary to be the second in command.

"Well, I did think we could do some more digging into Evans and his social media first. I think we can learn a lot about him that way without having to make ourselves known right away. Sam can give us a hand with that, maybe crack his way into some of the more private stuff on his profiles."

Olivia chewed her lip. "So, you don't want to talk to him? Charlie, I mean?"

Emily stopped. "What?"

"You know? Just go in and ask him questions."

Emily gave her a confused blink, looking for all the world like a deer caught in headlights. "This isn't the field, Olivia. This is White Collar. We don't … do that."

Olivia frowned. "You don't go ask people questions? See how they hold up under scrutiny? You can tell a lot about someone by their microexpressions. Their little tells."

Emily shook her head. "Honestly, it's not usually very helpful for us in these sorts of cases. We deal with paper trails, numbers, legal bread crumbs that we track down. We don't want to put any of these people on notice that we're watching them, because then they have all the opportunity in the world to cover their tracks."

"So maybe we cover our backs," Olivia mused. "We could say we're there to double-check regulatory compliance with the company and the opening of the new foundation. You just said that they're working with a charity, didn't you? We can say it's to do with that."

"And you don't think they'll suspect that we're up to something?"

Olivia shrugged. "Maybe. Criminals are always going to have their guard up around FBI agents if they have something to hide. But it could be worth it to get closer to him. Who knows? Maybe a little pressure will make him slip up and say something he shouldn't."

Emily bit her lip, looking nervous. "I don't know, Olivia. That's not how things are typically done around here."

"Well, that's how we do it in the field," Olivia pointed out. "It's your operation, so I won't push it... but I think if we go in there, we can shake things up a little. Besides, if we come face to face with him, we can gauge his reactions, see what he's really thinking."

Emily nodded slowly. "I guess you've got a point. There's only so much we can glean about a person online. And if some of the reports of the workplace culture are true, we might be able to see something..."

She turned it over in her head for a moment, then smiled at Olivia. "I've got to say, you're bringing out a more spontaneous side to me. I wouldn't normally do this."

Olivia almost laughed. She didn't think she'd ever been referred to as spontaneous before. But she knew for sure that her confidence at work had been steadily rising. She was coming into her own, rebuilding herself after all the years of hell that sent her into a downward spiral. She didn't need to second-guess herself anymore. Not when she knew her own worth, knew her own skill set, knew her own ability to get the job done.

And as Olivia continued to discuss the case with Emily, Brock crossed her mind only once. She thought he'd be proud to see how far she'd come if he were watching her then. And as much as she was going to miss him being with her on the case, she knew she didn't need him. In fact, she didn't need anyone.

Having Emily or Brock by her side was a bonus, but she was perfectly capable of going alone. She was stronger than she'd ever given herself credit for. She was smarter and quicker and more dedicated than she even knew. And now, she was going to prove it.

She was more than ready.

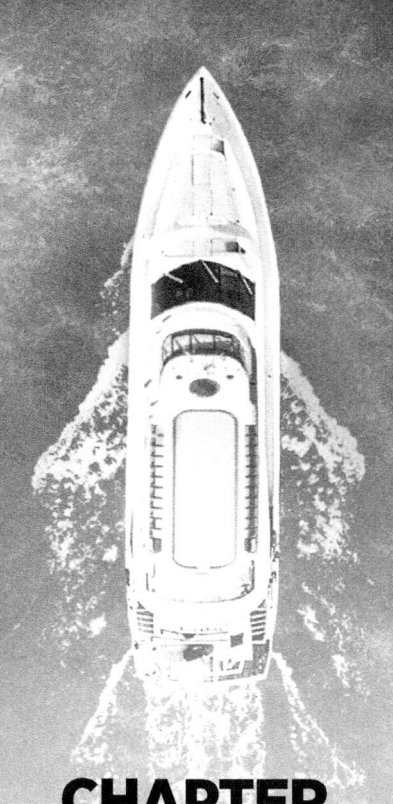

CHAPTER FIVE

"**T**HIS IS IT," EMILY SAID, POINTING TO THE SKYSCRAPER towering above them. "The headquarters of Infinity."

Olivia nodded and turned into the parking lot beneath it. She was stopped by a security guard at the barrier, who requested to see some ID. Olivia obliged, but shook her head as she continued on through to the lot.

"They're not taking any chances, are they? Security in the parking lot?" she noted.

"I imagine normally to protect their intellectual property," Emily said. "But that just brings us back to the question of what exactly are they producing anyway?"

"Or what are they hiding?"

"I guess we're about to find out," Emily replied. "It was nearly impossible trying to get a meeting with Charlie Evans, though. He must have been telling his secretary to say that he's fully booked for months, but I wasn't going to let him get away with that."

"And now we have him locked in for this meeting; he's got nowhere to hide," Olivia said with a smile. She was already getting excited about their meeting with Charlie. She was sure that he was going to be just as slimy as the man she'd studied on social media. She was also sure that he was going to hate every second of their meeting, and that somewhat pleased her. If he was on edge, they'd be more likely to get something useful out of him.

Olivia led the way into the building with Emily trailing behind her. She could tell that Emily was still a little anxious about their brazen approach, throwing themselves straight into the lion's den, but Olivia knew how men like Charlie Evans worked. They were cocky and sure-footed… until someone smarter came along to ruffle their feathers. She was sure that she could get under his skin, make him squirm, and put him in his place. She just needed an hour or so to make him unravel, and then he'd be putty in her hands.

She recognized their target as soon as they walked into the building. He was leaning casually over the reception desk, talking to the receptionist with a cocky smile. She seemed charmed by him, giggling at something he was saying as Olivia and Emily approached. When he finally looked up, his facade didn't slip for even a second. He was as cool as a cucumber, his blond hair styled meticulously to give him an aesthetic of something between a frat boy and a high-flying businessman. He wore a gray sweatshirt and black pants that, at first glance, seemed simple and plain, but had the telltale look of being well-tailored and luxurious. Olivia wouldn't be surprised if the man's shoes alone cost more than her yearly salary.

Olivia could see how a man like Charlie could trick the eye. At first glance, he almost seemed like the kind of effortlessly charming rich man who could wine and dine you with the finest on offer. But then beneath the exterior, she could sense the sleazy, smarmy part of him that made her feel a little sick. It might be enough to fool some people, but she guessed that it was mostly his copious amounts of money that made him seem so appealing.

But Olivia had no interest in his money, unless it was to find out how he had so damn much of it. As Charlie sized them up, he approached with his hand outstretched for them to shake. Emily took his hand first, then Olivia, who lingered a moment to look Charlie in the eyes, shooting him a knowing glance.

I know what you are, her gaze said. He only smirked in return.

"Thank you for coming today," Charlie said, as though it was his personal invitation that had drawn them there. "I've been looking forward to this meeting."

"Is that so?" Olivia said with an edge to her tone. She was sick of him already. Spending even a few seconds with him felt like eating too much ice cream and making yourself feel ill. "Then we're glad to have made it."

"Thank you for having us," Emily said, her tone much more level and polite. Of the pair of them, Emily had always been the one with the patience and poise, not Olivia. She was certainly going to be useful in getting Charlie to cooperate with them. "We appreciate your time, Mr. Evans."

"Please," he waved her off. "Charlie."

Emily gave a tight smile. "Charlie. It's a routine procedure, as I'm sure you know. We just have to make sure that everything is being conducted as it should be. You understand, I'm sure."

"Sure, I do," he said, looking Emily over with a certain hunger in his eyes that made Olivia's stomach clench in anger. He clearly thought his playboy antics would work on her, that he'd be able to charm his way out of trouble if only he could get Emily on his side. But Emily barely flinched at his flirtatious manner, staring him down as though she was completely unaffected.

"Good. Then maybe you could take us up to your office so we can get started."

Charlie's smile wavered for a moment, but no longer. He offered Emily a polite nod. "Of course. Follow me."

As they followed the man to the elevator, Olivia couldn't help but take in the luxury of the office building. She'd never known money like that herself, but she knew enough about that world to know when a place was dripping with money. The floors were made of marble, as though they were in a swanky restaurant or hotel, not a corporate office. The whole place had a sleek, ultramodern aesthetic, complete with spotless glass walls and shining silver surfaces everywhere. The company's logo glowed brightly on a gigantic screen taking up one entire wall.

She thought about what she knew of Infinity, and she couldn't understand how they'd risen to the top so quickly. Not without some illicit activity, for sure. As she stepped into the elevator, choking a little on Charlie's strong aftershave, she knew that whatever he was up to, it was going to be elaborate, and it was going to be hard to pinpoint.

But that wouldn't stop her from doing it.

Charlie and Emily made small talk until they reached his office. It was sky-high and overlooked the entirety of the city from the dizzy height. Just like Jonathan's office, it was sparse as well, but in an entirely different way. Where Jonathan's was rich and warm with a classic—if stodgy—traditionalist appeal, Charlie's was simply a massive desk with a computer screen that must have cost a fortune. To one side of the main desk, tablets and laptops were stacked up, but otherwise, the place was completely devoid of color and personality. Not a single framed picture or a personal knick-knack to be found. Charlie welcomed them with a flourish, holding out his arms.

"Please, make yourselves at home," he said, taking his seat behind the desk. His chair was so big that it could almost be considered a throne, and Olivia was almost certain that Charlie considered himself to be king of the world. "I'm sure we can make this quick, can't we, ladies? I can tell you what you need to know, and then you can be on your way."

"Actually, this could take several weeks, if necessary," Emily said bluntly. "We want to be thorough. But that won't be a problem for you. We won't get in your way. We just need you to answer a few questions for us, dig up some files, and show us what goes on within the company. Then we'll be out of your hair."

"I see," Charlie said. "It's just that I'm a very busy man. We've got a lot of exciting things on the horizon here at Infinity."

"I'm sure you find the time to wind down from time to time," Olivia said pointedly, thinking back to the pictures of him partying all through the weekend plastered on his social media profiles. "But as we said, we don't need much from you. Just cooperation."

Charlie's smile didn't quite reach his eyes. He clearly had plenty of places he'd rather be. He sat back in his chair, keeping his gaze on Olivia.

"I'll cooperate," he said coolly. Something about him chilled Olivia to her core. When she looked at him, she wondered what he was capable of. Were they going to find more than they'd bargained for when they looked deeper into his life?

"Charlie, sweetie, I just wanted to pop in and—oh! I didn't realize you had guests!"

In the doorway to the office stood a beautiful, young woman. She was a little younger than Charlie, perhaps in her mid-twenties, and she held herself like a runway model. She was slim and pale with a fiery shock of vivid red hair and dazzling green eyes. Her hair was gorgeous, cascading down in gentle waves past her shoulders. She smoothed down her mint green suit as though to draw attention to it, since there wasn't a crease in sight. But Olivia knew that a woman like her needed nothing more than a smile to draw the eye.

And what a smile it was. She had an innocent lilt to her lips, and yet Olivia could see the intelligence in her gaze, like she knew exactly what was always going on. She blinked several times and then regarded Emily and Olivia with a warm smile. "Aren't you going to introduce me, Charlie?"

"This is my girlfriend, Darcie Puckett," Charlie said, his tone a little stiff. His smile had once again slipped away, replaced with something darker. Olivia wondered what it was about her presence that was making him so tense. Was he worried that she was going to say or do something that she shouldn't? "This is Agents Boyd and Knight. They're with the FBI."

Darcie raised an eyebrow. "Oh?"

"Just some routine checks of regulation compliance," Emily said smoothly. Darcie's concern eased up.

"Ah," she nodded. "Of course. Well, I'm sure Charlie's giving you all the answers you need."

"I'm trying," Charlie said through gritted teeth. Olivia glanced between the pair of them, trying to figure out where Charlie's hostility was coming from. Why was he being so cold to her? What was he hiding that was changing the mood in the room?

"Anyway, I'm sorry to barge in. Representative Atkins gave me the afternoon off, and I just wanted to pop by."

That sent Emily's eyebrows up. "As in, David Atkins?"

Darcie nodded cheerily. "Yes, I'm a legislative counsel for his office. I was fortunate to get this opportunity just out of law school."

Olivia was impressed. The woman had substance to back up her style. She couldn't help but like her.

"Anyway, I just came to finalize some details for Friday night with you, sweetie."

"What's Friday night?" Olivia asked sweetly, gauging Charlie's levels of irritation, which seemed to be steadily rising. Darcie's eyes lit up.

"We're having a party over the weekend, on Charlie's yacht, the *Astoria*. You know, to celebrate the new partnership with a charity foundation," Darcie told her with a bright smile. "It's friends only, kind of a private affair, but we would absolutely love to have you there. You'll be able to see all the good work Infinity has been engaged in over the past few years. All your hard work is paying off, isn't that right, babe?"

Charlie was shooting Darcie with a look of unhindered anger. "But it's like you said, babe… close friends only."

"Well, I'm sure we can squeeze in some new friends too. I'm sure your friends from the FBI would appreciate some time off after all of their hard work," Darcie said earnestly. She smiled at Olivia and Emily. "Consider yourselves on the guest list. We're sailing out of Virginia Beach, isn't that exciting?"

"It is," Olivia nodded.

Darcie grinned. "Leave your details at reception, and I'll call you. Oh, and the dress code is black tie. Any excuse for us to get dressed up, right, Charlie?"

Charlie didn't even bother to grunt in response this time. Darcie's smile tightened a little before she straightened out her suit once more and left the room with a little wave. Olivia turned in her seat to face Charlie.

"She seems very nice," Olivia said pleasantly. There was a fire in Charlie's eyes as he tried to compose himself, shifting in his chair. The fact that he so clearly didn't want them to attend the party only made Olivia want to attend more. If they got on that yacht, they were sure to see all of the secrets Charlie had under his belt coming into light.

"Yes, she's wonderful," Charlie said with a sniff. "And as she said, you're very welcome at the party, but don't feel obliged."

"Oh, we'll be there," Olivia replied with a wide grin. "We wouldn't miss it for the world."

CHAPTER SIX

"I GOT ANOTHER ANONYMOUS TIP, OLIVIA. YOU SHOULD see this."

Olivia crossed Emily's bedroom to look at the piece of paper she was holding in her hand. Olivia frowned as she regarded the sheet. "This person is sending tips to your apartment? How do they even know where to find you?"

Emily shrugged. "I'm trying not to think about that. I found the last tip shoved under my door, not even addressed. The same with this one. But so far, the intel has been interesting. Take a look at this…"

Olivia read the piece of paper, her heart thudding fast. *"Take care, beware, and focus your stare… this party will be wild, I do declare."* Olivia scoffed at the paper. "Did this guy become an FBI informant because he failed as a poet?"

"Read the rest."

Olivia took a breath and continued. "*If you know where to look, you'll know what they took, these crooks have plenty to hide.*" Olivia shook her head. "This is ridiculous. They're not telling us where to look."

"I guess they're just trying to tell us to keep our eyes peeled. Although… I'm still not sure we should go to this party. We're going to be fish out of water, surrounded by people who move in the same circles as one another. That means loyalty among them. If we run into trouble, it's just going to be the two of us against all of them."

"You've said it yourself though. We have to take risks. We can't afford to miss an opportunity to see these people up close," Olivia insisted, walking over to Emily's bedroom mirror to examine herself. She was dressed for the part that evening in a long black dress that hugged her body. She wouldn't normally wear something so fancy, but she wanted to blend in for the night, to become one of the elite in order to unravel them. Her mind flashed to Brock, wondering what he'd think if he saw her looking like that right then. She had to admit she was feeling good about herself in the dress.

"I know, I know. I'm just being cautious. I guess we'll have to take a leap of faith and pray that it pays off."

"It will. I'm sure of it," Olivia said firmly. She turned to Emily with a smile. "Come on. We can do this. If this guy really is up to something, then this is the perfect opportunity to get him alone where he has no room to escape. And if he's up to something fishy, I'll bet anything that his friends at this little party have plenty in common with him. Maybe we'll end up taking down an entire circle of organized crime."

Emily's lips curved up into a small smile. "Wow. You really know how to entice a girl to a party. All right, I'm in."

Emily and Olivia piled into the car, and they turned into Virginia Beach just as the sky was beginning to darken. By the time they parked up by the dock, Olivia could see that the party was already buzzing. The *Astoria* hadn't even left the harbor yet, but people were drinking and dancing on the deck, and the music was spilling out into the night. Emily puffed out a lungful of air.

"A night surrounded by drunk, rich idiots? Rough," she murmured, fixing her hair in the rearview mirror. She glanced anxiously at Olivia. "How do I look?"

"Perfect as always. Let's get in there before Charlie finds some way of getting us struck off the guest list."

"Are we sure this is a good idea?"

"Yes. No more procrastinating. Let's do this," Olivia said, getting out of the car without another word. She didn't want to miss this opportunity. She was sure that whatever happened that night on the yacht would blow their case wide open.

Olivia strode with as much confidence as she could muster toward the massive ship. Standing on the dock was a woman dressed in a slinky, black dress, holding a clipboard with the exclusive guest list attached. Olivia held her breath as she gave her name, hoping that they were still welcome aboard, but she shouldn't have worried. Without so much as a blink of an eye, she was ushered on board, where a flute of champagne was pressed gently into her hand and she found herself in a crowd of laughing, chattering people dressed in the height of luxury and fashion.

"Welcome on board the *Astoria*," someone said. She couldn't even tell who it was.

The *Astoria* was grand and opulent, even by Charlie Evans's standards. It was a classic multi-level, white yacht that was at least 200 feet long, with enough room behind the cabin area for a large dance floor and a full bar area. Dozens of people milled about in the back as well as the front, in addition to flitting in and out of the indoor areas and on the levels above her. Waiters and waitresses in firmly-pressed white tuxedo shirts and smart black pants or skirts danced in and out of the crowd in perfect rhythm, as if choreographed to an inaudible beat, presenting cocktails and hors d'oeuvres to the guests. Olivia took a shrimp and cucumber round and thanked the waitress, who was already moving on to the next group. It seemed the staff was used to being invisible. She was starting to feel like she was on the Titanic.

Olivia could tell that every single person there was carefully handpicked. As she looked around, she saw some familiar faces among the ranks; politicians, local celebrities, faces she recognized from Charlie's social media accounts. They all had their purpose there: to make Charlie look good, to support him, or to show the world just exactly what he was worth from his connections. Of course, he offered them plenty too: a chance to be considered high-profile; a chance to be among the high-powered, wealthy elite; and a chance to rub shoulders with other like-minded people.

This was no ordinary party. It was where status was decided—where social careers were made or destroyed. There was a palpable tension in the air that couldn't be denied, and Olivia felt a shudder through her body. She had no urge to be famous anyway, but the mood of the party only put her off further.

"I feel so out of place," Emily whispered to her as she joined her on the deck. "I bet these people can tell that we don't belong here. They'll see us as outsiders."

"Then we have to fake it until we make it," Olivia murmured in return. "Let's go try to find Darcie. She seems a lot more loose-lipped than Charlie. Maybe we can get her to talk and slip us something useful."

Emily nodded and Olivia led the way slowly through the crowd of people. Everyone seemed to be packed in together, unbothered by the close proximity with one another. Olivia supposed that maybe they all knew each other well enough for it not to faze them. Still, the heat of bodies and the unusually warm spring night were making her uncomfortable. All she wanted was to find some answers.

But before she could get very far, the *Astoria* began to move, which encouraged a loud cheer out of the party guests. Olivia exchanged a look with Emily.

No going back now, she thought.

Olivia continued to try and push through the crowd, listening in on conversations as she passed. Everyone was talking about the new foundation, the whole reason for the party in the first place. She supposed that many of the guests were supporters and donors. She kept hearing a name being thrown around. *Angus Greenfield. Angus Greenfield…* Olivia had no idea who he was, but if he was a big name around the party, it seemed like he might be someone worth talking to.

Then she heard the clank of a champagne flute being tapped with a spoon. The party fell silent, and everyone, including Olivia, turned to see a massive, muscular man well into middle age perched up on some kind of platform, raising him above the other guests by several heads. He smiled warmly at the crowd through a face that definitely seemed to have taken many bruises over the years.

"Good evening, everyone. For those of you who don't know me, allow me to introduce myself. I'm Angus Greenfield… otherwise known as the life and soul of the party."

Many of the guests laughed hard, as though the joke had somehow been hilarious. He cleared his throat.

"Our host, Charlie Evans, is currently occupied, so I told him I'd make a speech on his behalf. We would like to thank everyone for coming here today to support the new partnership my foundation has with Infinity. As you all may know, I am the director of Bodymind Worx, a charity that gives back to the disadvantaged youth on the streets. It's so great that we can all come together to help each other. We are very lucky to be here tonight and to be able to give back. And that's what this night is all about. Raising some money and celebrating the new collaboration between Infinity and BW. It's our hope that we can continue our mission and help even more people than ever."

The crowd began to applaud, and Olivia joined in quietly, trying not to draw any attention to herself. The man before her seemed genuine, and yet she couldn't help feeling as though it was odd for a corporation like Infinity to collaborate so heavily with a charity. She knew that no corporation on earth had the interests of common people at heart. Their only interests were making money and *keeping* money. What was she missing here?

"What's with his face?" whispered Olivia.

"You don't recognize Angus Greenfield?" Emily asked. "The big MMA fighter?"

"I guess not," she shrugged. "I don't really follow that stuff."

"He's a former champion. Kind of a legend in some ways," Emily explained.

"Seems the type to hang out with a bro like Evans," Olivia noted.

They turned their attention back to Angus onstage.

"As the CEO of Infinity, my good friend Charlie Evans has been going above and beyond to give back to the community. Many of you tonight have worked directly with his company, and you know firsthand the lengths this man goes to to serve his people," Angus continued. "So, tonight, we celebrate not only the foundation, but also Charlie, for his hard work, determination, and kindness."

"Wooo! Yeah!"

Every head turned to see Charlie stumbling his way through the crowd. It was immediately obvious that he wasn't sober. He swayed a little on his feet as he approached Angus, his face a little dopey as he made his unsteady journey. The crowd seemed to part for him, not necessarily out of respect, but as if they already knew he was unlikely to remain steady. Olivia narrowed her eyes in interest. Was such an immature display common for Infinity's beloved CEO? Was substance abuse part of the package deal with Charlie Evans?

Angus began a round of applause, and the other guests politely joined in, though a few of them exchanged glances, clearly amused by Charlie's antics. He joined Angus on the platform and waved to the crowd, his eyes a little clouded.

"Good evening, everyone," he crooned. "Especially to my special guests tonight. You know who you are."

He pointed vaguely in Olivia's direction, and she held back a scowl, keeping her features level. *So much for not drawing attention to ourselves…*

"I'd like to second everything my good friend Angus has just said. We need to be better. We need to give because we already *have,*" Charlie went on, his voice a little slurred. "We have everything we could ever want in life. And sometimes, people envy us for that. They despise our hard work, and they hate that we have everything they don't…"

"Wow," Olivia whispered to Emily. "Is that what he thinks of us? That we're spoiling all his hard work?"

"But that's why we choose to be good people. To give *back,*" Charlie said, nodding once and then continuing as though he were struggling to stop himself. "And that's what this new partnership is all about. To everyone who has supported this venture... thank you. Thank you for choosing goodness. Thank you for being here with me every step of the way. It hasn't gone unnoticed."

"Hear, hear," Angus said, putting an arm around Charlie. Olivia wasn't sure if it was a friendly gesture or a way of holding him upright. "This young man is going to change the world. Long after I'm over the hill, certainly."

The crowd laughed again, and Charlie gave Angus a dopey smile. Olivia checked her watch. It was only just after eight. Was he really that drunk already? It was possible, she supposed, but she suspected there were other substances in his system besides alcohol.

"All right, now here's the fun part," Angus said with a grin at the crowd. "The part where we ask you politely to give us all your money."

"Don't you be skimping out on us now!" Charlie cracked, a wolfish look on his face. "We'll know if you do."

More laughter rose from the crowd.

"We're sending Bishop around to collect your checks, which we *know* you already have written out," Angus added, keeping up the cheeky persona. Olivia saw a hulking, bald man moving through the crowd, accepting the payments and stuffing them into a box. His smile was bright and charming, but the man looked like a linebacker. Olivia wondered if he was more of an assistant or a bodyguard.

"And again... thank you so much for your donations," continued Angus. "If you're still considering how much to give, remember why we're doing this. The kids, the struggling single mothers, the people who have nowhere to go... this is for them. So, give generously, and remember that our lives are fortunate and privileged, compared to theirs. Whatever you give will be appreciated."

Charlie and Angus continued to grin at the crowd as everyone burst into polite applause and began passing their checks to the bodyguard. Olivia folded her check carefully so that no one could see how little she'd offered up. She had no problem giving money to charity, but she wasn't sure she trusted where her money would end up. She certainly didn't want to fund criminal activity, especially if she was yet to figure out what it might be—and it wasn't like she was anywhere near the league of these high rollers anyway.

By the time Bishop the bodyguard had made his rounds, Olivia was sure that everyone's purses were considerably lighter. Angus's eyes seemed to gleam as the funds were handed over to him in a metal box.

"Thank you so much, everyone," he said cheerfully. "These checks will be locked away for the night, nice and tight. So don't even think about coming back to collect them!"

The crowd tittered again, though it was clear that the jokes were running dry now. Olivia watched as Angus disappeared into the interior with the box and Charlie was left alone to rally the crowd once again. He raised a glass to them all, his smile splitting his face.

"All right, now that the boring part is out of the way… let's get this party started!"

The crowd cheered for real this time, likely reminded of the fact that the champagne was free—and flowing freely. If Olivia wasn't there on business, she might have felt the cheeriness seeping into her too. But the fact was that she had a job to do and plenty of mysteries to dig into. She couldn't afford to be distracted by the party mood.

If Brock was there, he would have told her to liven up, to let loose a little. It wasn't often she got to attend a billionaire's yacht party. But Brock wasn't there, and this time, she was doing things her way. This time, it was on her terms.

And it was time to get started.

CHAPTER SEVEN

Olivia and Emily split up to move through the party. Since the big speech, Olivia hadn't been able to pin down any of the people she was interested in talking to the most. She had seen plenty of Charlie, who also seemed to be making his rounds with the guests, but she wasn't particularly interested in trying to approach him. She thought that was a job for Emily, who he'd definitely warmed up to more. No, in his drunken state, she didn't think it was a good idea for her to mess with him. She was more interested in finding Darcie or someone who worked with Charlie. They would be more likely to let something of interest slip.

Or perhaps Emily's anonymous tipper. Whoever they were, they must have been close to Charlie at some point. Perhaps they still were. If that was the case, then they were likely onboard right then. They certainly had enough knowledge of the CEO to tell them about the party. So, who was their mystery tipper? Olivia looked through the crowd, wondering if there was anyone of interest she could spot right off the bat.

Her eyes fell upon a young man. He was dressed as a waiter, but unlike the others that were constantly on the move with trays of champagne flutes, he was empty-handed—and standing perfectly still. He was watching the partygoers intently, and Olivia followed his eyeline to see if there was anyone in particular in his sights.

Of course. Right where he was looking, Charlie was in the middle of entertaining a group of guests, telling some sort of raunchy joke that had the men guffawing and the women gasping politely in shock. Olivia narrowed her eyes. Was the waiter simply keeping an eye on his boss, ready to serve him if needed? Or was he watching him because he was obsessed? Was he perhaps the anonymous tipper, desperate to glean information about him to hand to the FBI on a silver platter?

Olivia knew better than to get lost in speculation. He could simply be watching the party unfold, and Charlie was the host, after all. And it seemed that he wasn't the only person watching Charlie from afar…

As Olivia's eyes scanned the guests, she could see that a lot of people were keeping a close eye on him. Bishop, the bodyguard who had collected the checks earlier, never seemed to take his eyes off Charlie, though he kept his distance from him. Olivia supposed that made sense since he was there for protection.

But there was a woman also keeping her beady, blue eyes on Charlie. She was hard to miss. Instead of an evening gown or a party dress like many of the attendees, she wore a sharp, professional suit. Her black hair was long and perfectly straight, and she wore a pair of wide rimmed glasses that only amplified her gaze. She didn't seem to be with anyone at the party; she was a lone wanderer, but she kept removing her phone and typing on it without even looking away from Charlie…

As though she were taking notes.

Olivia couldn't figure out what any of it meant. There were too many people, too many close acquaintances of the man she was trying to dig up dirt on. So, she pressed on, hoping to strike gold with one of the VIPs. Maybe she'd find Angus somewhere and get him talking about Charlie and his supposed interest in philanthropy.

But then Olivia saw something far more interesting. She made her way into the cabin, which wasn't quite as packed as the outside, and immediately noticed a bedroom with the door ajar. She could hear voices from inside. Angry voices. Olivia moved quietly to get closer, managing to peer through the door from afar.

Inside the room, Darcie was standing with her arms folded, talking heatedly with someone else. Another woman, from the tone of her voice. Olivia stayed as still and quiet as she could manage, waiting to hear what was going on.

"It's not my fault your husband can't keep his hands to himself," Darcie snapped, her arms wrapped tightly around her slim frame protectively. Her hair shook along with her head as she spoke, looking for all the world like a tongue of flame. "I don't want to do this anymore. He's taken it too far."

"You should be grateful for the opportunities you get, young lady. You kids… you all think you're so damn special. Waltzing out of your fancy law schools like you deserve to have the world handed to you on a silver platter. Well, guess what? That's not how the world works. Sometimes you have to do things you don't want to to get ahead. God knows I've had to."

"I worked *damn* hard to get where I am now," Darcie fired back. "I won't have my achievements devalued by a man who claims I'm only in my position now because he wants me there. I get it. He can take it all away from me. Pull the rug out from under my feet. Make me pay for that betrayal. But I'm not stupid. I have power too. Don't you think I can make his whole world crumble if I just tell the world who he really is?"

"You don't have the guts for that, kid."

"Yeah? Just watch me."

"You won't just bring *his* life crashing down. You'll bring yours down too."

"Then it's a good thing I'm made of stronger stuff than most. Enjoy your evening, Mrs. Atkins."

Olivia's heart began to beat a little faster. Mrs. Atkins... that had to be the congressman's wife. Olivia stepped into the shadows out of view as Darcie stormed out of the bedroom, her face flushed with irritation and her hair fluttering behind her. Mrs. Atkins wasn't too far behind her, cursing under her breath as she headed back out to the party.

Olivia remained where she was for a moment, processing what she'd heard. What did it all mean? Had the congressman been inappropriate with Darcie? Had he tried to force her to do something she didn't want to in order to save her job?

It wouldn't surprise Olivia in the slightest. She knew all about the kinds of men who used their power for the wrong things. Usually, older men tried to coerce young, impressionable women into things they didn't want to do, just to advance their careers. Olivia had dealt with a fair few men like that in her life before. She was glad to see that Darcie was standing up for herself.

But whatever drama was unfolding behind the scenes of Darcie's life wasn't really important. It didn't get Olivia any closer to finding out about Charlie and his shady financial dealings. In any other circumstance, Olivia might have reached out to Darcie, to check that she was all right, but she didn't even know the young woman, and it might change the course of her investigation. No, it was better that she didn't get involved. Besides, from what she'd seen, Darcie was perfectly capable of handling herself.

Olivia returned to the party, curious to see how the mood had changed. She saw Darcie storming through the crowd like a tornado, straight in the direction of Charlie. She figured it wasn't the best time to try to approach her for a chat, especially if she was already on edge, but the night was young. She could still try Angus, if she could figure out where he'd disappeared to...

And then a flash of movement caught her eye once more. The woman with the glasses was talking animatedly to an older man that Olivia recognized from many news reports. It was Representative Atkins, and he didn't look happy. Olivia clenched her jaw. She was certain his foul mood had something to do with Darcie and the conversation she'd had with his wife. What else would have him so riled up?

And now he seemed to be taking it out on the other woman, who was giving it right back to him. It was barely ten o'clock, and it seemed that everyone at the party was already swept away by drunkenness, picking fights here, there, and everywhere. Olivia watched as the two continued to square off, their voices low, but the anger in their faces saying it all. Something had happened between them, something serious. When the brunette walked away with a smirk, the congressman was trembling with anger.

Olivia could barely make sense of the party. There was so much going on around her, so many tensions unfolding, that she didn't know where to look. And even as the guests got drunker and the atmosphere became more heated, Olivia still couldn't pin down Angus, Charlie, or Darcie.

It wasn't going as Olivia had hoped. She made small talk with guests for a while, but she lost interest when she began to realize that none of them were close enough to Charlie to be of use to her. She needed someone from his inner circle. Someone who had drunk too many champagne flutes and might be willing to slip her some secrets.

When Emily drifted back to her side, she began to realize that she wasn't the only one having trouble infiltrating the ranks. Emily stood solemnly beside her, surveying the guests.

"I don't think we're going to get much out of these people. Maybe this was a mistake," Emily said. Olivia sighed.

"Maybe. I don't want to give up yet though."

"So, you don't want to drink copious amounts of free champagne instead and get totally wasted?"

Olivia smiled. "As lovely as that sounds, I think there's still something of interest here. I want a clear head just in case."

Emily sighed. "Our first yacht party and we don't even get to enjoy it."

"Hey, when this is over, I'll make sure we get a night out on the town. God knows we'll deserve it after dealing with this bunch."

Emily grinned, and Olivia smiled back. As she suspected, working a case with Emily was turning out to be fun. They might not have gotten any closer to their answers yet, but they couldn't expect to have the case all wrapped up within twenty-four hours.

No, they just needed to stay alert, to track Charlie's movements, to see if they could get inside his head.

When Olivia looked over at him, he was leaning casually against the railing, looking a little worse for wear. His shirt was untucked, and his hair was a mess now; his eyes were red and raw as though he'd been smoking something he shouldn't. Olivia wouldn't be surprised, but that wasn't what she cared about at that moment.

"Maybe we should at least act the part. Start dancing a little," Emily offered. "Everyone else is getting kind of rowdy at this point."

Emily was right. As the night drew on, it was clear that everyone would be knocked off their feet by midnight. The soundtrack of the night had changed from the elegance of classical music into more of an electronic dance music vibe. Olivia wasn't sure if it was just the champagne or whether people were taking drugs, too, but everyone seemed more vacant, more loose, more crazy. Now, Charlie completely fit in because everyone else was almost as drunk as he was, and they certainly didn't care about it. Olivia shrugged.

"If you wanted to dance, Emily, you should have just said so."

"God, that's the last thing I want to do. You know I have two left feet," Emily grumbled, but she was already beginning to move her hips in time to the music, awkwardly shuffling across the deck to get closer to the action. Olivia's feet were hurting in her heels, but she followed and began to dance, closing her eyes for a moment to get into it.

She imagined that Brock was there with her, his arms flailing over his head in an embarrassing fashion just to get under her skin. She knew he was a good dancer, but he would hate to ever be taken seriously. And that's why he'd dance like a mad thing, making the other guests stare and causing Olivia to laugh harder than she ever laughed with anyone else.

He'd have been perfect for this job. But Olivia wanted to put that out of her mind. Tonight wasn't about him. She opened her eyes and smiled at Emily, who looked so uncomfortable that it made Olivia want to chuckle. With one eye on the party and the other on each other, Olivia and Emily danced away, giggling like schoolgirls, finally enjoying the party a bit.

There was something to be said about hanging out with her girlfriend. It had been a long time since Olivia allowed herself to feel like a young woman, to enjoy herself the way other women her age did. But as she danced with her best friend, she felt all the joy of being a young woman rushing back to her. It was rare, and it felt good.

Until she heard the splash.

Olivia stopped dancing. There were plenty of noises coming from the water, and it was sloshing up the sides of the yacht throughout the party, but Olivia was sure that she heard something more. T—the sound of something hitting the water—hard.

Olivia listened, but there was no further sound. Still, she was convinced of what she'd heard, and she wasn't about to let it go. She grabbed Emily's wrist and began to drag her away.

"What's wrong?" Emily hissed in her ear. "What did you see?"

"I didn't see something… I heard it," Olivia whispered. "I'm sure of it."

With Emily following close behind, Olivia rushed to where she thought the sound had come from. It was on the other side of the ship where none of the guests were gathered. Olivia's heart was racing as she made her way to the railing and looked down.

Her heart stopped.

In the water, face down, was a body. Blood was pooling around it, spreading through the water and coloring it like ink. In the darkness, it took Olivia a moment to recognize who it was, but when the clouds shifted and the moon lit up the night, she caught sight of long, beautiful tendrils of bright, red hair, fanning out like flames over the water, and she felt sick.

Darcie was dead.

CHAPTER EIGHT

"OH MY GOD," EMILY WHISPERED. "THIS ISN'T WHAT we came for."

Olivia stared in shock at Darcie's body. Emily was right. They hadn't come here expecting someone to be murdered, but that was exactly what it looked like. From the amount of blood, it didn't seem possible that Darcie had simply slipped and fallen into the water. But there was no one around, and the party was in full swing. How had someone managed to get away with murder and then escape without being seen?

As she was wondering how someone could have pulled this off, Charlie stumbled along the deck toward them. Olivia held up a hand to stop him, shaking her head at him.

"Don't come any closer," she warned him. He scoffed at her.

"This is my ship. I'll do whatever the hell I want. You have no control here," he said, his tongue too thick for his mouth. He moved closer, and then his eyes widened when he saw how serious Olivia and Emily looked. Cautiously, he moved to the edge and looked into the water.

"Mr. Evans—" Emily began, trying to yank him away from the railing, but it was too late.

"Oh my God," he whispered. "Oh my God, Darcie…"

"I'm sorry," Emily said, putting a hand on his arm and trying to tug him away. "But you need to step back now. This is a potential murder scene."

Charlie didn't even seem capable of protesting as Emily pulled him away from the railing and toward the cabin. Olivia was still shaken by what they'd found, but she knew it was going to be up to her and Emily to figure out what had happened. Someone on this ship had a motive. Someone on this ship wanted Darcie dead and had managed to pull it off…

The note. Their anonymous tipper had told them that something would happen that night at the party. Had it been a general guess or something much more sinister? Did they know that someone was going to kill Darcie?

Or were they the killer themselves?

Olivia's mind reeled, and she suddenly found her instincts snapping into place; her brain was moving faster than her body could respond, getting her ready to investigate the woman's death. She may not have been very good at following financial trails, but she was very, very good at solving murders.

And if this was a murder, she would bring the killer to justice.

"We're going to need to talk to everyone onboard," Olivia said, turning to Emily. "No one is going anywhere until we get some answers. But first, we need a copy of the guest list. We need to make sure that everyone is accounted for. We should do a head count, too—make sure there aren't any stowaways here who could have done this."

"Got it," Emily nodded. "I'll handle the guest list. We need to tell people what has happened. And… and retrieve the body. But, Olivia… how are we going to catch the killer? There are so many people here. There's no way we can get an idea of what happened to the victim before we dock. It's not like we can keep them all on board. We're not even sure there was foul play. It could have been an accident. There are so many people we need to interview…"

"Don't spiral, Emily. We're going to solve this. Get the guest list together, and I'll handle the rest of this."

Emily nodded and scurried away. Olivia barely had time to take a deep breath before the chaos continued.

"What the hell is this?" Charlie cried out. His face was contorted with confusion and pain, though no tears shone in his eyes. "Tell me now who did this to her. I have to know."

Olivia narrowed her eyes at Charlie. She didn't trust him for a second. For all she knew, *he* was the one who had killed her. He had shown up quite conveniently just after they had. And he hadn't exactly been warm toward Darcie when she'd shown up at his office. Had he wanted her out of the way? Was she threatening to expose him for who he was?

But then, why do it here? Why risk being caught in a high-profile, public event, where even members of the FBI were in attendance? It didn't make any sense. Was the man so far gone in his drugged haze that he could have done something like this?

"You need to take a seat, Mr. Evans," Olivia said, an edge of ice to her voice. "We'll find out who did this. But for now, you need to back away. We can't have this scene getting contaminated."

Charlie's eyes met hers. "And what exactly are you implying now, Agent?" he snarled. "You got something to say to me?"

"Not at all," Olivia replied. "Maybe you should stop reading between the lines and get your alibi in order. I want to talk to you first."

"This is preposterous. You think *I* killed her? My girlfriend? The woman I love?"

"Now you're just filling in the blanks for me," Olivia said darkly. "Pull yourself together. I want to speak to you as soon as I've informed the guests of what has happened."

Charlie glared at Olivia one final time before disappearing and leaving Olivia alone. She needed someone to help her fetch the body. She thought of Bishop, the bodyguard. He was likely strong enough for the job. She moved through the yacht to see if she could find him, chilled by how the party was continuing like nothing had happened. No one knew the horror she'd witnessed yet. No one knew that there was a potential murderer among them. Olivia's skin crawled as she finally spotted Bishop and tapped his arm urgently.

"Yes?" he asked, his voice a lot less stern than she was expecting.

"You need to come with me."

"I'm supposed to keep watch on the party."

Olivia sighed and immediately started rifling through her clutch. There was no time to waste. She grabbed her badge and flashed it to him.

"FBI. This is urgent. Trust me."

Bishop hesitated for a moment before nodding and following her. Olivia didn't know how to tell Bishop what she'd found, but she led him to the railing anyway, looking up at him with an anxious swallow.

"This may come as a bit of a shock… there's a body in the water. It belongs to one of the guests. I… I need help retrieving it."

Bishop blinked at her several times. "A… a body?"

"Yes. It belongs to the host's girlfriend… he already knows. But I can't fetch her myself. We need to get her out of the water and try to find evidence."

"Darcie?" Bishop whispered, his voice cracking. Olivia nodded slowly.

"You knew her well?"

A look of pure distress crossed Bishop's face. He took a step back as though someone had dealt a punch to his gut. One of his hands clutched his chest.

"Darcie… oh God, Darcie…"

Olivia was about to say something to try and comfort him, but he moved toward the edge and removed his jacket.

"Darcie," he whispered once again. When he turned back around, he had tears in his eyes. Olivia hadn't been expecting that from the hulking bodyguard. It didn't seem like he was just being sensitive… it felt personal… as though he actually knew her and cared for her.

"I'm going to need some rope and a few guys to hoist me back up, once I've got... once I've got the body," Bishop choked out. "Please, hurry. Let's not leave her here. Not like this."

Olivia nodded in understanding. "Of course. I'm so sorry."

"Please, let's just get this over with."

Olivia nodded and rushed off to find some of the other guests to help. By the time she'd rallied some troops and sent Emily along to ensure a chain of custody, someone had cut the music, and the guests were beginning to murmur among themselves, wondering what was going on. As Olivia approached the crowd, she spotted the woman with glasses filming the party, getting everyone's reactions to the unnerving atmosphere. She wanted to tell her to stop, but she had other priorities. She had to tell everyone what happened.

The conversations were starting to boil up into a panic.

"What is going on—"

"Did you hear—"

"What happened to the music—"

"Why are we stopping—"

Their questions overlapped each other like that until Olivia did the only thing she could. She marched up to the stage where Angus had given his speech. She had to do something to corral the chaos before it spilled over into panic. She caught sight of the waiter she'd seen earlier and beckoned him over. He looked confused as she told him to bring her a glass and a spoon, but he agreed, then made his way back through the crowd and returned a few seconds later.

Finally armed with a way of getting the crowd's attention, Olivia took a breath. The entire tenor of the night was about to change.

She rang the glass loudly, several times, until the conversation died down and all eyes turned to her.

"My name is Olivia Knight with the FBI," she announced, holding up her badge for the guests to see. "The party's over. Someone has been killed."

A collective gasp rippled through the guests. It clearly wasn't the kind of disruption they were expecting. Everyone around her looked horrified, but she knew that somewhere among them, someone was guilty of ending Darcie's life. She tried to watch their reactions closely, to see a telltale flash of guilt, but there were just too many people to see in such a quick moment.

"We're going to need to talk to every single person onboard about this," she went on. "This is a serious matter, and we intend to find the person responsible for this. Your cooperation at this time would be much appreciated."

"You really think someone here is capable of killing someone?" a woman cried out, her voice barely a squeak. Olivia nodded.

"This was no accident. That much is clear."

"Who is it?" the woman with glasses shouted from the back of the crowd. "Who is dead?"

Everyone turned to Olivia in horror, waiting for her answer. She swallowed. She hadn't signed up for this.

"Darcie Puckett," Olivia said softly, but everyone heard. She could see the horror crossing every single face in the crowd. She was known, and she was loved. The people here cared for her, and yet, one of them had ended her life.

Olivia's eyes scanned the crowd until they landed on Representative David Atkins. His head was bowed so she could barely see his face. She felt anger surge inside her as she remembered what she'd witnessed between Darcie and his wife. Was he responsible for this? Did he kill her for refusing to do as he wanted her to?

The crowd was in chaos. Behind her, Olivia could hear the sounds of Darcie's body being pulled from the water. The yacht was stationary, no longer cutting against the waves, and the bobbing was making Olivia feel sick. Ideally, they needed to get back to shore and contact the police. They needed to be able to gather evidence before it was too late.

"What now?" a man in the crowd cried out. "How are you going to make this right? How are you going to find the person who did this?"

A collective cheer of approval went through the crowd. Olivia felt like she was alone against the world. But she was strong enough to handle it alone. No matter what happened next, she would be okay. Of that, she was sure.

"If anyone interacted with Darcie tonight, I'd like you to come forward and talk to me. We need to piece together the night and see if we can figure out what happened. Any detail might help us determine what happened tonight." Olivia lifted her chin a little higher and scanned the crowd. "This isn't the time for holding back or keeping secrets. If someone wanted Darcie dead for a reason, I have to know the full story. If you respect her, if you cared about her… come forward and tell me what you know. The sooner you do, the sooner we can get justice for her."

The guests began talking among themselves once again, and Olivia walked away, back to where she'd left Emily, Bishop, and the other guests. She arrived just in time to see Bishop emerging from the water, Darcie's small frame in his arms. His face was streaked with tears. Olivia frowned. Was she missing something that had happened between the bodyguard and the CEO's girlfriend? Whatever it was, he seemed more upset than Charlie had, and that spoke volumes to Olivia. She was beginning to feel that there was a lot more behind the scenes of Darcie's life than she had expected.

Olivia knew it was time to talk to the captain. They couldn't afford to be stuck out in the middle of nowhere with a dead body and a murderer. It was a recipe for disaster. Olivia made her way to the bridge, desperate to get things moving before any further chaos ensued.

But when she approached the captain, it seemed like he was having issues of his own. He was frowning, desperately trying to get the yacht moving, talking in a low voice to some of the crew.

"Excuse me?"

The captain turned to see Olivia standing there. He frowned at her.

"I'm sorry. I'm a little busy right now. Go back to the party."

She badged him and introduced herself. "Special Agent Olivia Knight. There is no party, sir. It's over. We found a young woman dead just off the railing. I need you to get this ship back to shore so we can liaise with the police and find out who did this."

"A woman is dead?" he gasped.

Olivia nodded solemnly. The captain shook his head. He was an older man, with gray coloring his temples and a permanently stern expression on his face. He reminded Olivia quite a bit of Jonathan. The two of them could have been related.

"Something very strange is going on here, Agent Knight. I would love to help you, but we've got another problem: someone has tampered with the engines."

"What are you talking about?" she frowned.

"The engines cut out just a few minutes ago. That's why we stopped where we did. Someone sabotaged us, and I can't figure out how."

Olivia's heart was racing impossibly fast in her chest. What did that mean? Had the killer stopped the yacht in order to carry out the deed? If so, whoever they were looking for was smart. Whoever had done it knew that stranding them in the middle of the ocean would only cause more chaos.

Olivia dreaded thinking about it, but what if the killer decided to strike again? Who would be the next target? If the killer had planned the whole murder in advance, then what else did he or she have planned for those aboard the ship?

"Are communications still up?" Olivia asked. The captain nodded.

"We can still get in contact with the Coast Guard. They've already been contacted for assistance."

"Good," she nodded. "The sooner we can get moving again, the better," she said, though she couldn't help thinking that it would be useful to have the guests all in one place for a little longer. The second they reached the shore, the killer could vanish into the night. If they were stuck on the water, she could conduct interviews, do some digging, and see what she could unearth about the mysterious death of Darcie Puckett before anyone left.

"I'll keep trying to get us up and running until they arrive," the captain told her. "And then I'll join you on deck."

He hesitated for a moment, then his curiosity got the best of him. "Do you know who it was?"

Olivia nodded. "Darcie Puckett."

"Christ," he muttered. "I'm sorry."

"Did you know her?" she asked.

The captain shook his head. "Not particularly. Met her once or twice when Mr. Evans brought her on board. But I never really interacted with her. Bright girl. Great future ahead of her. What a shame."

"It is," Olivia nodded. "I assure you, I'll do everything I can to get to the bottom of this. You focus on getting the engine back up."

The captain nodded. "Can do."

Olivia left the bridge with her head in a spin. She could barely believe what had happened. They were there to investigate fraud, not murder. But now that Darcie was dead, she couldn't help thinking that there was more to her death than met the eye. A young, beautiful, successful woman like her didn't seem like the sort to make enemies… and yet she was beginning to see the cracks in the perfection of the night. Charlie and his drunken ways, the bodyguard who cared a little too much, a disgruntled employer with too much to lose…

Olivia could see how any number of people might have had a reason to want Darcie dead. She might not have done anything wrong, but that didn't mean she wasn't on the wrong side of some people.

Maybe examining the body would enlighten her. As she headed back onto the deck, she found a small crowd of people gathered around the scene. Emily had enlisted Bishop and a few others to keep the crowd back, but there was only so much they could do against so many people. A few even had their phones out and were taking pictures, which set Olivia's blood on fire.

"Back away," she demanded, pushing her way through the onlookers. "All of you. Now!"

The crowd murmured in embarrassment as she turned to face them. "And if you're taking pictures, I suggest you delete those right now," Olivia barked. "Don't make me charge you with tampering with evidence. Now all of you get out of here and let me work."

Most of them put their phones away and began to filter out, clearly chastened by her words, but the black-haired woman in glasses kept snapping away.

"I said *now,*" Olivia growled. The woman finally seemed to get the hint and put her phone away, but she hung back, lingering around with a few others instead of returning to the dance floor.

Olivia glared at her, but she didn't have time for this. She had to investigate Darcie's corpse.

Olivia stepped forward and knelt beside Darcie's body. She didn't want to touch her because she didn't have gloves to put on, but she let her eyes scan Darcie's body.

Her skin was pale and glistening in the moonlight, and her hair, once so vibrant and beautiful, clung to the side of her head.

It didn't take her long to spot the bruising on Darcie's wrist. The blossoming purple ring around her wrist looked relatively fresh, like it had happened just before she died. Olivia was sure of it: someone had grabbed Darcie. Hard.

Perhaps it was the same person who had gotten angry and thrown her overboard. Perhaps the same person who had caused the wound on her head, the one that had surely killed her. Blood was still crusted to the side of her face, and her face was badly bruised. Had someone hit her? If so, with what?

"Poor girl," someone murmured in the crowd behind her. "She was stumbling around half the night. Clearly wasted. She probably slipped and fell over the side before she could stop herself. What a waste of a young life."

Olivia gritted her teeth. She didn't believe that for one second. She knew there was more to it. There had to be. Someone had hurt her deliberately. The bruising on her wrist told her that. Someone had wanted her dead.

And she was going to find out why.

CHAPTER NINE

"**G**OD, HOW ARE WE EVER GOING TO TALK TO ALL OF these people?" Emily groaned, observing the rabble of people that had formed outside the cabin. The captain had allowed Olivia and Emily to use it as a place to interview the guests while he and the bosun tried to figure out what was wrong with the engine.

But Emily was right. Between the guests, the crew, and the two of them, there was a total of fifty-seven people onboard, and it seemed like all of them were clamoring to speak to Olivia and Emily. Olivia took a deep breath.

"We just need to prioritize who we talk to. Let's start with Charlie. Where did he go?"

"As I was coming in, I saw him smoking a cigarette," Emily answered." He said he'd be with us in a moment."

"Of course, he will," Olivia muttered. She didn't trust Charlie for one second. It seemed obvious to her that he was stalling, trying to buy himself more time to make it look as though he had nothing to do with his girlfriend's death. As the minutes passed by, Olivia felt more and more strongly that Charlie had something to hide.

When he finally entered the cabin, there was no sign of grief on his face. The smell of cigarette smoke followed him into the cabin, and he took a seat opposite Olivia and Emily before lighting another cigarette right in front of them. When he caught them staring at him, he offered them both a cruel, yet dopey smile.

"Oh, how rude of me. I should have offered you one."

"We don't want your cigarettes. We want answers from you," Olivia said coldly. "This doesn't look good for you, Charlie. Your girlfriend is dead and you haven't shed a tear. You waltz in here like you'd rather be in the spotlight than help us out. You—"

"People grieve in different ways," Charlie cut in, taking a long drag from his cigarette. "I don't have to explain myself to you."

"Actually, you do. Because this is your party, your yacht, your partner lying dead in the ocean water. If you don't start talking, then maybe we'll start thinking you have something to hide."

"You're trying to put words in my mouth, aren't you?" Charlie snapped at Olivia, his voice a little slurred. "You would *love* for it to be me, wouldn't you? That would suit your little narrative that you've written in your head about me. Don't think I don't know why you're here. Trying to dig up dirt on me, trying to throw me off so I say something that you want to hear. Well, that's not going to happen because I've done nothing wrong. There's nothing I can say to you that will put me in a bad light."

"If that's the case, then why don't you cooperate with us?" Emily said gently. "We're not trying to antagonize you, Charlie. We're trying to find out the truth. You don't need to be playing defense. That is, if you have nothing to hide, right?"

Charlie muttered something under his breath, and Olivia took a moment to examine his face. He was looking a little worse for wear. His skin was pasty, and there was a sheen of sweat covering his forehead. His eyes were milky but bloodshot. His hair was tousled, and his state of dress had deteriorated even more since the beginning of the party. The man was clearly wasted, but the question was, how much?

"Why don't you start telling us about your night, scene by scene?" Emily pushed. Charlie ran a hand through his hair.

"I want my lawyer here," he muttered half-heartedly. Emily raised an eyebrow.

"Surely that's not necessary, Charlie? You said you had nothing to do with what happened to Darcie."

"I *didn't*."

"Well, all right then. But in any case, it's going to take some time to get your lawyer here. We're out in the middle of nowhere," Olivia countered. "Don't you want to get to the bottom of this as soon as possible?"

Charlie sniffed absently and then shrugged his shoulders, sitting up a little straighter.

"Fine. I guess I don't need a lawyer. But we're doing this interview *my* way."

Olivia exchanged a glance with Emily. Clearly, he wanted to feel like he was in control, even if his slurred words and drunk demeanor suggested otherwise. Olivia gave Emily a slight nod, silently communicating that she was okay with it. She'd let Emily take the lead on the interview too. She didn't want to say anything that might make Charlie clam up again.

"All right then, Charlie," Emily said gently. "Whenever you're ready."

Charlie folded his arms and slumped down in his chair like a naughty school kid. He was avoiding eye contact with the pair of them and murmuring to himself. Olivia could barely recognize him as the man she'd met the day before—the cocksure, confident man who had been completely on his game. Something had happened to him at the party; she was sure of it. Even with his reputation for partying, this didn't seem like a person who had simply gotten a little drunk.

He was completely destroyed.

"I got here at five-thirty to do a little pregaming with Darcie," Charlie said vacantly. "We haven't had much time together lately since she started her new job, and I wanted to spend a little time with her. But she was all on my case, telling me that I drink too much, that I party too much, that I'm embarrassing myself at my age... she always acts like I'm supposed to be boring and stuffy just because I'm successful and over the age of twenty-five. Anyway, she didn't want to drink, so we didn't. We just sat and talked until the guests started showing up. And then, I guess I had a few drinks after that. I mean, who wants to go to a party stone-cold sober?"

Emily nodded along with what he was saying, as though sympathizing with his struggles. Charlie let out a dramatic sigh, shaking his head.

"I've got to admit, the drink kind of hit me out of nowhere. I can handle my alcohol most of the time, but tonight, it was like someone hit me over the head with a brick. That champagne must be off or something. I feel sick to my stomach."

"The other guests don't seem to be taking it so hard," Olivia pointed out. "Perhaps you drank more than you thought, Mr. Evans."

Charlie gritted his teeth. "I didn't. Three glasses, I told myself. I had two at the start of the party, and then half of another glass. Then everything is a little hazy. Like I said, something must've happened to the champagne. I don't know. It curdled or something."

"Can you be sure that you only had three drinks if the night became more blurry?" Emily asked. "I'm not accusing you of anything. I'm just curious to know."

"I told you. I didn't drink anything else," Charlie insisted, even though his eyes were clearly having trouble focusing and he could barely speak without messing up his words. Emily cleared her throat.

"All I'll say, Mr. Evans," Emily began, "is that you seemed... you seemed to be the life and soul of the party. Perhaps you were a little drunker than you thought. When you went up to do your speech, Angus mentioned that you were otherwise occupied. Where were you at that point?"

"Smoking a cigarette," Charlie said, almost too quickly. "Is that a crime? Darcie hated that I smoked. Hated everything I do, probably. I was trying to be good and drink less, for *her sake,* so who could deny me a cigarette? It's a party, for God's sake. Is a man not allowed a little fun?"

"It seems to me that you saw Darcie as someone who dragged you down," Olivia poked. "Like she was always getting in the way of a good time. Would you say that's true, Mr. Evans?"

"You're putting words into my mouth," Charlie snapped. "I did my best to please her, but it was never enough. Women like her want the world on a silver platter, and when you don't hand it to them, they act like it's *you* that's in the wrong. And then they go looking elsewhere for all the things you can't provide."

Charlie took a long drag of his cigarette, and Olivia caught Emily's eye. Did he know something he wasn't mentioning about Darcie? Olivia thought about Darcie's argument with the congressman's wife. Did Charlie know about what happened there? Did he believe that Darcie was looking at other men for the things she wanted?

"And did she get those things?" Emily pressed. Charlie looked like a kicked puppy when he raised his eyes to meet hers.

"Who knows? Maybe she was never satisfied. Maybe that's what got her killed."

"You don't seem to be very sympathetic," Olivia said, anger flashing through her. "Your girlfriend was just killed. Don't you care?"

"Don't try and tell me what I care about and what I don't," Charlie shot back. "Of course, I care. But really, you should be asking if *she* cared. You might think she was this beautiful, sweet little creature, but I knew her better than anyone. I know that she had secrets that could get her killed. I know she hurt people who might want to hurt her back. But that doesn't mean I had anything to do with it, all right?"

Charlie's face softened a little. "I was angry with her. I still am. But I didn't wish her dead. If I could bring her back, don't you think I would? Jeez, you people. You assume because I'm rich, because I live a certain lifestyle, that I'm cold and unfeeling. That's how you see us, don't you? You think we're morally corrupt because we dare to make money and love it. But I'm telling you now, Darcie mattered more to me than any of that. So, before you judge me, maybe you should consider the fact that *I'm* the one that lost something here."

Olivia had no idea what to say to Charlie and his little speech. He was right, on some level. She did see him as a different kind of man, but not necessarily the kind capable of killing in cold blood.

And yet, Charlie's speech only made him seem more guilty to her. It was like he'd thought about it too hard—like he knew what she saw in him because it was all there, laid out before her. It was like he was dissecting his own personality for her, laying himself bare in front of her so she could pick him apart for real.

Still, he seemed to be sobering up now, and maybe that was why emotions seemed to be seeping back into his face. He took a shaky breath, almost like he was exhausted by his little outburst. He glanced up at Emily and Olivia, regret in his eyes. He'd said too much, and he knew it.

"Why don't you fill in the rest of the blanks for us?" Emily asked, choosing to gloss over his moment of madness. "After the speech. You said you had half a glass of champagne."

Charlie nodded slowly. "And then Darcie took the rest. She knocked it back so I wouldn't touch it. We bickered about it. She tries to control me, and I won't let that happen. I told her that. I told her to let me live my own life. And then she stormed off. Typical woman, can't stand her ground in a fight. She just walked off and expected me to go running after her again. But no. Not this time. I told myself… screw her. I took another drink, but that's when I started to feel sick. And then, I don't know what happened. The alcohol and the stress must have just hit me… and I blurred out the rest of the night."

He blinked several times, as though he was trying to hold on to his own reality. "I remember finding you, finding Darcie… but the rest…" Charlie closed his eyes and shook his head. "It's hazy. That's all I know."

"So, what you're saying is… you don't have an alibi for the time of death," Olivia pointed out. She recalled the moment that Darcie must have died. The sound of her body splashing into the water. In just a few seconds, her life had come to an end. And now, Charlie, their most likely suspect, was telling them that he didn't remember anything leading up to that time?

"That's … that's not what I said," Charlie backtracked.

"Yes, it is. You said everything was hazy until you found me and Darcie's body. Which means that you can't tell us what you did during that time. And if you were, in fact, as intoxicated as you seem, then perhaps you were capable of something more than you expected. Something dark."

Charlie's eyes were wide. "Now hold on a second—"

"If you can't recall what happened to you during that time, then you're a potential suspect. We'll just have to see whether others can vouch for you," Olivia said pointedly, looking away from Charlie. "I think we've heard enough from you."

"You're twisting my words again! I want my lawyer!"

"Your lawyer isn't here, and we're stuck here until we can get the *Astoria* moving again," Olivia said. "I suggest you lie low and hope that someone else on this yacht can get you in the clear."

Charlie's face flitted between anger and confusion. Clearly, he didn't know how to get himself out of this one. But he rose to leave the room regardless, his cigarette dangling from his lip as he thundered out of the room.

Emily let out a long sigh and glanced over at Olivia. "Well. That was certainly interesting. Do you think he did it?"

Olivia shrugged. "He's in too much of a state right now to glean anything useful from him. I think if he did do it, he wouldn't even remember. But from what I can see, he clearly has an alcohol problem, anger issues, or both. Does he really think he can get away with pretending he's not absolutely wasted? It was obvious. And if he's a seasoned drinker, then three glasses of champagne wouldn't be nearly enough to have him looking like that. Something's not right here, but we have a lot of people to talk to. I think until he's sobered up, we have other priorities."

Emily nodded. "Agreed. Maybe we can get some answers from the next person we interview."

"Let's hope so. Time's ticking. And we still have a killer on the loose."

CHAPTER TEN

OLIVIA FELT LIKE SHE NEEDED TO TAKE A BREATH BEFORE she went on to the next interview. She went outside onto the deck and took in the fresh air. It was colder now, perhaps because the party was no longer in session, generating heat around them. Everyone seemed to be keeping to themselves, huddling in small groups, watching everyone else suspiciously and talking about where they'd been when Darcie died. Olivia couldn't blame everyone for being on edge, not when Darcie's blood still stained the deck even though her body had been moved. Not when they were still no closer to answers.

Olivia was waiting to talk to the congressman and his wife. She'd asked for them to attend an interview with her under the pretense that they wanted to speak to Darcie's employer. The pair had no idea that Olivia had overheard Darcie talking to Mrs. Atkins about how her husband had made her feel uncomfortable. Olivia was hoping that her element of surprise would catch them off guard. If it was true that the congressman had acted inappropriately, then he certainly had a motive to want Darcie out of his way.

In her quiet moment of contemplation, Olivia thought about how friendly, how genuine Darcie had been. She had so much to live for. She'd worked so hard to get through law school, made deep connections, become her own person, and refused to be anyone but herself. Olivia hadn't known her well, and yet she knew all of this was true. She didn't know if Darcie was a good person or not, but she knew that she was full of life, that she had a lot more to give, and that she would be missed. Her absence would be felt like a gaping hole, and Olivia knew all too much about that.

In some ways, Darcie reminded Olivia of her sister. Of the young woman struck down before she really had a chance to live. It made Olivia's heart ache to think of all the young, ambitious women who were killed for being too present, too much for the men around them to bear—like they took up too much space or didn't deserve to make such an impact on the earth they walked.

It was sickening, really. Olivia was tired of seeing lives lost for no reason at all. She was sure that whoever killed Darcie did it out of jealousy, or spite, or insecurity. A life had ended, and whoever had done it was sure they would get away with it. But Olivia wasn't going to allow Darcie to be swept under the rug.

As she was about to head back to the cabin, Olivia caught sight of the dark-haired woman in glasses once again in the distance. Whoever this woman was, she kept turning up. And she wasn't alone.

Representative Atkins was standing close to her again, talking in a low voice. There was no sign of his wife, and Atkins himself seemed just as agitated as he had earlier. The woman had a confident smirk on her face as Atkins spoke to her, like she was certain that she had the upper hand in their circumstances. Olivia narrowed her eyes, wondering what the pair of them still had to talk about. Whatever it was, Atkins clearly didn't want anyone finding out. He kept shooting looks in different directions, like he was terrified of being watched. But he didn't see Olivia watching his every move.

She'd seen him before in television interviews, and she had never quite trusted him. Politics was a game she didn't get too heavily involved in, but she knew a snake in the grass when she saw one. He had always seemed sly to her, and now that she'd seen him in the flesh, she was even more convinced that he was. Even as he walked away from the woman, he seemed to slink by so no one would see him—so no one would realize that he was clearly attempting to hide something.

The question was … what was he hiding?

She quietly headed back to the cabin and sat down beside Emily just moments before Atkins and his wife showed up. They were putting on a united front, her arm threaded through his and their faces blank of emotion. Despite their act, Olivia could feel the tension between the two of them due to her body being stiffly positioned as far as possible from his. It was like they could barely stand to touch one another, and Olivia was almost relieved when they sat down and dropped the facade.

"It's a pleasure to meet you, Congressman Atkins," Emily said, schmoozing just a little. Atkins held out his hand and took Emily's in his, reaching forward to kiss the skin of her knuckle. Olivia shuddered. Did he respond this way to all young women? It certainly seemed that way.

"The pleasure is all mine," he replied smoothly. Olivia was certain that she caught his wife rolling her eyes at him. "Please, call me David. And this is my wife, Rebecca."

"Thank you both for coming to speak to us," Olivia said, trying to keep her tone light. She didn't need yet another person to be uncooperative with her. "We appreciate your time. Of course, the two of you likely knew Darcie well, with her having worked for you."

"Yes, she was a sweet, young thing," Atkins said. He genuinely looked a little upset, which Olivia could understand—upset to have lost his young plaything. He sighed, scratching at his white, stubbly beard and hitching his glasses up his nose. "What can I say about her? She was hardworking, gentle, funny, a joy to have around … brilliant, too. Everyone in the office loved having her around. She just lit up every room she walked into."

"I'm sure they've heard enough of your *touching* eulogy," Rebecca snapped. She was a severe-looking woman with a beaky nose and a blonde bob that was obviously from a bottle. She slouched forward in her seat, fiddling with her handbag. "They don't want to know how wonderful she was. They want to know who would do something so stupid as to kill her."

Olivia was a little surprised. Rebecca Atkins was clearly much smarter than her husband. She lifted her gaze to meet Olivia's and held it for almost too long before diverting her eyes once again.

"Did you spend much time with her tonight?" Olivia asked them both. "We're trying to put together an idea of how she spent her evening, who she spoke to, whether anything triggered the events that happened tonight … anything you can tell us might be helpful."

Rebecca remained in stony silence, which Olivia found interesting. She knew for a fact that Darcie and Rebecca had spent time together, because she'd seen it. She'd heard it. And it seemed at the time that Darcie was implying that Rebecca's husband was up to no good. Was Rebecca being quiet because she was covering her own back? Did her conversation with Darcie trigger some pent-up anger within her—anger at her sleazy husband, maybe? Did she snap and take Darcie out to regain some control?

And then there was Congressman Atkins. If he had in fact been inappropriate with Darcie, then he certainly wasn't in the mood to admit it aloud. He sniffed a little, playing the part of the grieving boss who had lost his fondest employee. But Olivia didn't buy it. She knew too much to trust either of them.

"I barely saw her," Atkins insisted. "You know how it is … young women don't want to hang around with their stuffy old boss, do they? She was out making connections, which is how it should be. I guess I saw her here and there, but she was barely on my radar tonight. Wouldn't you agree, Rebecca?"

Rebecca didn't respond, threading her fingers together on her lap. She clearly had some things that she wanted to say to Olivia from the way she kept looking at her, but she clearly wasn't going to say those things in front of her husband. She shrugged.

"I barely know the girl. What David does at work and who he falls in with is none of my business... apparently," Rebecca said. There was venom in her tone, which told Olivia everything she needed to know about their marriage. It was practically over.

So, what part did Rebecca play? The united front was clearly Atkins's idea, his way of saving his own skin as he navigated the interview. But if she didn't care for her husband, then why was she holding back? Olivia knew she knew more than she was letting on—not just because of the conversation she'd overheard, but from Rebecca's entire demeanor. Something wasn't being said, and Olivia was desperate to know what it was.

"Mr. Atkins, could you perhaps fetch me a glass of water?" Olivia asked him with a warm smile that felt wholly unnatural. "A gentleman like you surely wouldn't mind?"

"Absolutely," Atkins nodded, clearly not understanding that he was being manipulated. He stood up from his seat and winked at Olivia. "I'll be back in just a moment."

He left the room, and Olivia leaned forward in her seat to meet Rebecca's gaze. The older woman stared back at her.

"You shouldn't take advantage of his stupidity like that," Rebecca said with a flicker of amusement in her expression. Olivia folded her arms.

"I think you have something you want to tell me—something you don't want your husband to overhear," Olivia replied. Emily frowned at Olivia in surprise, but Rebecca remained unfazed. She glanced around to make sure no one was listening before leaning closer as well.

"You're right. Now, to be clear, I'm sharing this information with you, but I don't want it leaving this room if it is not absolutely necessary. Is that clear?"

"Yes," Olivia nodded, though she knew she couldn't promise that if Rebecca was hiding something important. Rebecca cleared her throat, clearly enjoying her little moment in the spotlight.

"Well, if there's one thing you should know about my husband... it's that he likes younger women. He says it's not a crime. That women get older and they lose their looks and their charm. I've been aware of his habits for years, of him trying to woo younger women before enticing them with money into some kind of relationship. You wouldn't believe the number of times I've met these girls just making themselves at home under my roof. Hell, I should have left him years ago, but he's always provided for me, and I can't just start again. This life suits us fine. We have an arrangement. But now, I'm concerned about what he might have done."

"Meaning?" Olivia pushed. Rebecca sat back in her chair.

"Meaning that I know he tried to take things to another level with Darcie. He's had his eye on her for a while, I could tell. He's been taking her out to dinner, buttering her up, pretending he's interested in advancing her career and giving her a perfect life. He probably told her that he could get her into the White House or something. Well, it all came out today. He switched it up on her, and she wasn't happy about it."

"I can imagine," Emily commented.

Rebecca's eyes darkened. "He tried to make a move on her and she said 'no.' She made a big scene, apparently. She was furious. She went on and on about how he treated her as some plaything rather than a woman with thoughts of her own and a career to pursue. But David never cared about any of that. He never does. Hell would freeze over before he'd actually help a woman achieve her dreams. She was going to quit. But boy, did he try and convince her that it was worth sticking with him. He promised her a promotion if she slept with him."

Olivia had been expecting as much, but for Rebecca to so openly admit it came as a shock.

"But still," Emily pressed, "wouldn't something like that getting out ruin his career?"

Rebecca's lips twisted into a cruel grimace. She scoffed at Emily. "Politics is an ugly game. You do what you have to do to get ahead," she said. "Look at the world we live in now. Nobody would care."

Olivia fervently disagreed, and the outraged expression on Emily's face mirrored her own. But they had no time to pursue this line of questioning. They weren't here to interrogate a pattern of sexual harassment. They were here to investigate a murder.

"So what happened after he propositioned her?"

She sighed, but Olivia got the impression that it was out of frustration with Darcie more than it was with her husband. "He overplayed his hand. He knows the value of discretion, but I suppose some sultry redhead crosses his path and he can't help himself. Men are all the same. A woman like Darcie… she was never going to let him demean her like that. She stormed off, came and found me herself. She told me all about it, expecting me to be surprised… but nothing that man does can shock me anymore. And personally? I think she overreacted. It's like I told her. We all do things to get ahead. She could have just said 'no' and moved on. But I think she wanted to make him suffer. I think she planned to take him down. And that was the mistake she made."

Rebecca's gaze sent a shiver down Olivia's spine. "And perhaps she paid for it," Rebecca added.

"You mean to say that you think your husband might have hurt her?"

"Don't ask me. I can't say I know the man anymore. He's like a stranger to me. But it seems like a coincidence, doesn't it? The day they fight she ends up going overboard, her life snatched away from her. I think my husband would do plenty to keep his dirty secrets from getting out. He's paid me off for years. I've done my fair share of keeping my trap shut." She paused. "But that young girl… she didn't deserve what happened to her. I couldn't be silent about what I know. I don't want to believe that he could be so cruel… but I had to be honest for once."

Olivia nodded in understanding. "We appreciate your honesty."

Rebecca nodded slowly. "I don't know if any of this will help your case. Maybe it means nothing. But there's one more thing. I keep seeing my husband with a woman. She has long black hair and glasses."

Olivia knew exactly who she was talking about. "You think he is already moving on?"

Rebecca shook her head. "No. The dynamic's not the same. I've been watching them all night, and she seems to have something on him. I think maybe you should speak to her. Maybe she knows something that I don't. And please, like I asked, keep this on the down low. The last thing I want is the paparazzi hounding us in our home... not unless he's guilty."

It was at that moment that the door reopened and Atkins returned with a bottle of water in his hand, smiling like he had no idea how exposed he had just become. Olivia didn't raise a smile as he placed the bottle in front of her. She knew too much now to pretend to like him. He seemed to notice because he looked uneasy as he sat down once again.

"Is everything all right?" he asked. Rebecca sighed and rose to her feet, glancing at Olivia with a bored expression.

"Am I free to go?"

"Yes, Rebecca. You can go."

Rebecca cast a cold glance at her husband before storming out of the room. Atkins let out a light chuckle, though it seemed forced.

"You'll have to forgive my wife. She has a flair for the dramatic," he said. Olivia didn't reply. She was trying to figure out how to play him. Should she let him know she was on to him—see if he would panic? Or should she play innocent for now?

The second option seemed preferable. She wanted to speak to the woman with black hair. She was cropping up too often to not be important. And she didn't want to anger Atkins until she was certain that his relationship with the victim was relevant. She looked him up and down.

"Why don't you tell us a little about your relationship with Darcie Puckett?" she asked, leaning forward with a blank expression painted on her face. Atkins's forehead crinkled, and he scoffed.

"Well, she was my employee. Nothing more to it."

"So, you don't form any close connections to your staff?" Emily pressed carefully. "We heard that you often take your legislative staff out for dinner... including Darcie."

Atkins's face darkened. They'd said too much. He knew that they were on to him. He straightened his tie and coughed a little. "Well, yes, I did on occasion spend some time alone with her... but it's hardly relevant. I would do the same for any one of my employees. Now, I think I'd prefer to say nothing more until I have my lawyer present."

Olivia winced. So much for keeping him on their side. As Atkins stood to leave, Emily shot Olivia an apologetic look, but she knew it wasn't her fault. Clearly, he had plenty to hide, or he wouldn't be acting so edgy about the whole thing. Whether he killed Darcie or not, David Atkins clearly had plenty of skeletons in his closet.

But at least they had a lead now. Olivia knew that the next step had to be talking to the mysterious woman who seemed to be watching everything. She'd put herself on Olivia's radar earlier that evening, and she wouldn't be leaving until she coughed up something juicy for Olivia, that was for sure. They had to keep up the pressure, keep up the momentum, and keep finding the juicy tidbits that would lead them to Darcie's killer.

Olivia only hoped they were quick enough to stop the killer from striking again.

CHAPTER ELEVEN

"**W**HAT DO YOU THINK OUR NEXT STEP SHOULD BE?" Emily asked Olivia after David Atkins made his dramatic exit. "Who do you think is most important for us to talk to?"

Olivia examined the guest list that Emily had gotten from the party planner, but the names on the list were pretty meaningless to her. She didn't know who among the guests was close to Darcie or even who had interacted with her that night. All she could think of was the congressman and the mysterious woman talking in low voices and acting shady. She was even more convinced after speaking to Rebecca that Atkins had something he was hiding from them, and she wanted to get to the bottom of it.

"How would you feel about splitting up?" Olivia asked. "I want to follow the lead of that woman Rebecca told us about. I think she has some things she could tell us. But we'll get more done separately. You could keep talking to the guests who are willing to offer up their thoughts while I try to dig some stuff out of those less willing to talk to us."

"I'm good with that plan. You're much better at digging than I am," Emily nodded. "I'll see how far I can get through the backlog. There are still so many people to talk to…"

"I'll be quick," Olivia said, standing up. "I'd be surprised if I came up empty-handed though. I think Representative Atkins is trying to cover his tracks, but if he is, it won't stop me from figuring out what he's up to."

"Good luck. You've got this," Emily said to Olivia's retreating figure. Olivia put on her sternest face as she headed out to the deck. It wasn't often she went solo anymore, but she felt ready for it. Anyone tagging along with her would only slow her down. She needed to handle this one on her own.

The guests were still on edge, most of them not even talking now. They cast anxious glances at Olivia, as if they hoped that she might have solved the case already. *I'm working on it,* she thought as she tried to draw less attention to herself. She needed to see if she could catch the woman off guard. Or better yet, catch her talking to Representative Atkins himself.

Whoever this woman was, she seemed significant. She kept popping up everywhere, and her unusual demeanor only drew attention to her antics. Olivia wasn't sure what her involvement could possibly be, but she was sure it was important.

It wasn't long before she spotted her target. She was impossible to miss, especially in the company she kept. Once again, she appeared to be bargaining with the congressman. Since his interview, he appeared to be even more on edge, his head twitching from side to side as he spoke. The woman smirked at him, clearly enjoying the fact that he was in distress. It made Olivia frown. Who was she, and what relation did she have to the congressman? And why did she feel the need to play with him? Did she know something that no one else did?

She needed to get closer. Despite the stillness of the night and the absence of noise from the party, she couldn't hear what either of them were saying from so far away. The pair was talking near a set of cocktail tables by the bar, so Olivia slipped casually to the bar for a drink, straining her ears to hear anything juicy.

"It's simple, *David*. I can sink you anytime I want. All I'm asking is for a small favor in return. What is there to think about?" the woman asked, a tinge of amusement in her voice. Atkins huffed in frustration.

"I did what you asked me. You just always want more, don't you? How can I trust that this will be the last time?"

"You can't," the woman replied, laughing fruitily. "But put it this way, congressman. If you do as I ask, then you can guarantee I'll keep my lips sealed. And if you don't... well, then I have no loyalties to you anymore, do I? Which means that I might just slip up... and let *all* of your dirty laundry come spilling out of the basket."

"You're pure evil. Has anyone ever told you that? What have I done to deserve this kind of treatment?"

"I'm sure you can guess," the woman said darkly. "If you hadn't done anything wrong, then this little game we're playing would never work anyway. If you were innocent, I'd have nothing to dangle in front of you, would I? So consider this a kindness on my part. I could tell the world who you really are. But I won't. All I'm asking for is a little cooperation."

Olivia sat silently, listening to the whole thing unfold. Clearly, the two were involved in some kind of underhanded deal. It didn't surprise her, but she still needed to know more. She needed to get the woman alone and figure out what she knew. Whatever she was blackmailing the congressman with, it had to be something big. Angry as he was, he clearly had no intention of allowing his secret to get out.

"Fine. You win. I'll see it done."

"Good boy," the woman said smugly. Olivia heard footsteps as he retreated, humiliated enough for one evening. Olivia knew it was her chance to get the woman alone and find out what she knew. She turned on her barstool to look at the woman, who was nursing a cocktail with a grin on her face. She seemed pretty pleased with herself, but Olivia knew that wouldn't last for long. Not with the plan she had in mind.

She approached the woman, who looked up at her with a slow smile. She looked Olivia up and down, sizing her up, trying to figure out whether she was a threat or not.

"Look who we have here," she crowed. "Little Miss FBI. Made any progress on Darcie's death?"

Olivia's eyes flared. "How can you be so flippant at a time like this?" she demanded. "A young woman is *dead*, and the killer is still at large on this very ship!"

The woman gave a limp shrug. "That sounds like your problem. Not mine. It's a tragedy what happened to that poor girl, but what do you want me to do about it?"

"You can start by telling me what exactly you and Representative Atkins have been up to all evening," she pressed. "It seems pretty serious to me."

"I don't have to tell you anything."

"Don't waste my time," Olivia snapped, prepared for another round of the woman's lies. "You've been on my radar all night. I don't know who you are or what you want, but I suggest you take me seriously. I've been pointed in your direction plenty of times tonight, and I want to know why. I could arrest you right now for blackmail charges. So, start talking or there will be a cell with your name on it."

The woman looked a little taken aback by Olivia's attitude, but she was no longer playing nice. It never got her anywhere, and she was sick of people trying to pull the wool over her eyes. Now that she was doing this alone, she had nothing stopping her from playing the game her own way.

And it felt damn good to be in control.

"Chill, lady. Jesus," the woman relented, but she looked chastened by Olivia's outburst. "My name's Devyn Ward. I'm a reporter for *The Hot Take*."

A paparazzi. Wonderful, Olivia thought with a roll of her eyes.

"I often get invited to these big parties to give some good press on the big names here," Devyn continued. "Except that these people are rotten to their core. Every last one of them. It's getting harder and harder to find nice things to say about these people, and when I don't come up with the goods… I don't get paid."

"So, you decided to resort to blackmail?"

She paused, meeting Olivia's eyes. "So, I decided that there might be a way for me to make some extra cash. God knows I need it in a cutthroat industry like this. I thought I'd let these people know that I can ruin them any time I like. I have all their secrets. They spill them so easily when they've had a lot to drink—which is often. So, when I find something good, I ask them for a small... *donation* in order for me to keep their secrets."

"So, you know something about Congressman Atkins? Something no one else knows?" Olivia pressed, keeping her gaze hardened. She didn't want the reporter to know how desperately she needed her information.

Devyn, however, clearly knew when there was a bargain available to be made. She folded her arms over her chest, her confidence returning.

"I do. But I'm not giving it up until I'm granted a free pass for my... indiscretion. Look the other way, and I'll gladly tell you what I know."

"Fine," Olivia replied through gritted teeth. She had bigger problems than some smarmy journalist anyway. She was certain she'd get her comeuppance sooner or later regardless. "But I want to know everything. No details left out."

"Okay, okay," Devyn said, putting her hands up defensively. She took a dramatically deep breath, her eyes closed. "Okay. So, I overheard something earlier tonight. Something that could get him into trouble. He was talking to Darcie."

"You're sure of this?"

Devyn nodded and pushed her glasses up on her face. "She was clearly upset. He was asking her to calm down, trying to touch her and stop her from leaving, but she was really put off. He said that she should really be grateful to him because he had offered her so much... all in exchange for sex. She was furious. She said she felt betrayed. She'd trusted him, and now she knew that it was all a lie."

Olivia nodded impatiently. Apart from a few extra details, this was all stuff she already knew. She was going to need more if the information was going to be useful to her.

"That's when the mood changed between them," Devyn continued. She wrapped her arms around herself as though she was suddenly cold. "He began to see that she wasn't willing to cooperate with his demands. He grabbed her and turned her around, making her look him dead in the eye. She looked frightened, and in all honesty, who could blame her? He called her some horrible names. He said that she was flirting with him the whole time, practically begging for his attention. And then he said something else: he said that if she tried to tell anyone about what had happened between them… he'd end her."

Olivia's blood ran cold. "End her? As in her life?"

Devyn sighed. "I don't know. People like him are always making empty threats like that. It was the heat of the moment, I imagine. Maybe he just meant that he'd end her career… but I knew I could use it. When Darcie got free from him and left, I made my move."

"So, you demanded a payout for your silence?"

She shrugged. "How was I supposed to know she would end up dead a couple of hours later?"

"Why didn't you come forward when we found her body?" Olivia asked.

"Honestly, I didn't know what to do. I knew that Atkins looked guilty. But I knew that if I tried to say anything against him, I might end up dead too. So I took another approach…"

"You capitalized on her death to get *more* money," Olivia finished for her, her voice low and trembling with anger. She was disgusted by the woman. How had her first thought been to try and make some cash when a young woman was dead, possibly murdered simply for rejecting sexual advances?

At least Devyn had the good sense to look a little guilty. "Look, I obviously regret that now. It's not a good look for me, I know."

"You think?"

"But if I could go back, I wouldn't do it."

"Now that you've been caught, you mean?"

The woman could barely meet Olivia's eyes. Olivia thought about the implications of what the congressman had said. If it was true, then it implied that he'd thought about hurting Darcie in one way or another. He'd promised to "end her" if she spoke to anyone else about what had happened… did he know about her conversation with Rebecca? Did he know that she was going to tell anyone that would listen about what he had done?

Olivia knew it was a good enough reason for him to kill her, but she still didn't have any evidence to back it up. Other than the word of an ethically compromised paparazzi, of course. Olivia knew that she wouldn't be able to build a case against the congressman without more solid information…

And then she remembered something. She'd seen Devyn snapping away all night, taking notes and watching the attendees like a hawk. Maybe there was something in those pictures and videos that might help Olivia piece the night together. If there was some evidence of foul play in those images, then maybe she could take the congressman down for good. Olivia turned back to the reporter and held out her hand.

"Give me your phone."

Devyn's eyes widened. "What? Absolutely not."

"It's not up for debate. I need to see the photographs you've taken tonight. They might help me in my investigation."

"You can't just take my phone. That's my property!"

"Is this your personal phone or your work phone?" Olivia demanded.

Devyn blinked. "Well… my work phone."

"So it's not your property, then. Hand it over."

"You can't just—"

"In your position, I suggest you do what I say," Olivia snapped. "I don't want to have to tack on obstruction of justice to your charges. You've caused enough damage already. Hand over the phone, or I'll be forced to do something more drastic."

Devyn hesitated a moment longer before handing over her device. Olivia raised an eyebrow at her.

"Aren't you going to tell me the password?"

With a frustrated scowl, she quietly relayed the number that would unlock the phone. When Olivia was in, she nodded to the bespectacled woman.

"You can go now. I'll look through these and give it back when I'm done with my investigation. Tell your boss at *The Hot Take* to get in touch, if he's so inclined. But if I catch you causing any more trouble, you'll have *me* to answer to. Don't speak to anyone unless it's necessary, and certainly not to David Atkins. You can forget about your payout too. Even if he is a killer, you can't just blackmail people like that. I'll be keeping an eye on you."

"When can I have my phone back?" she asked hopefully. "I'll need to contact my editor…"

"Get out of here!"

Devyn finally retreated, and Olivia sighed, shaking her head. *The nerve of some people,* she thought to herself.

But thanks to her, she was finally getting somewhere. She clicked on to the photo gallery and began to scroll through the night's images, hoping for something of interest. Unfortunately for her, there were hundreds of images. It would take her the whole night to look at them all in detail. She tried to skim past some of them where she didn't see any familiar faces, but it still left her with far too many to examine alone. Olivia cursed under her breath. There was such a thing as too little evidence, and then there was such a thing as *too much.*

Olivia slid the phone into her pocket and pondered her next move. She knew that they still had plenty of interviews left to conduct before they could get a clear picture of what happened that evening. Even though there was no one around at the time of Darcie's death—that they knew of—Olivia was willing to bet that others had seen Darcie interacting with people who were angry at her. And since Devyn Ward had proved to be a useful witness, maybe some of the other guests overheard or saw something that would help her out. The whole party scene thrived on gossip, so Olivia was certain that if Darcie had been fighting or arguing with someone, then somebody on that boat may have overheard it. Now, she just had to hope that the witnesses were reliable enough to pin down the killer and end the investigation before anything worse could happen.

Olivia felt like she needed a stiff drink. Being stone-cold sober at a party where a murder had taken place was certainly not the best way to spend an evening, especially when the rest of the guests seemed so hazy. It then occurred to Olivia that the drunken guests might not be as much help as she had hoped. How could they reliably tell her what had happened that night when they could barely stand up straight?

And worse still, there were so many threads to pull to get to the truth. It was becoming clear that Darcie's life was not as perfect as it had first seemed. She clearly didn't shy away from trouble, and she was clearly on the rocks with plenty of people at the party. So far, Olivia already had two strong candidates for the killer: Congressman Atkins and Charlie Evans. What else would she discover on her path to the truth?

Did everyone on the damn boat have a reason to want Darcie Puckett dead?

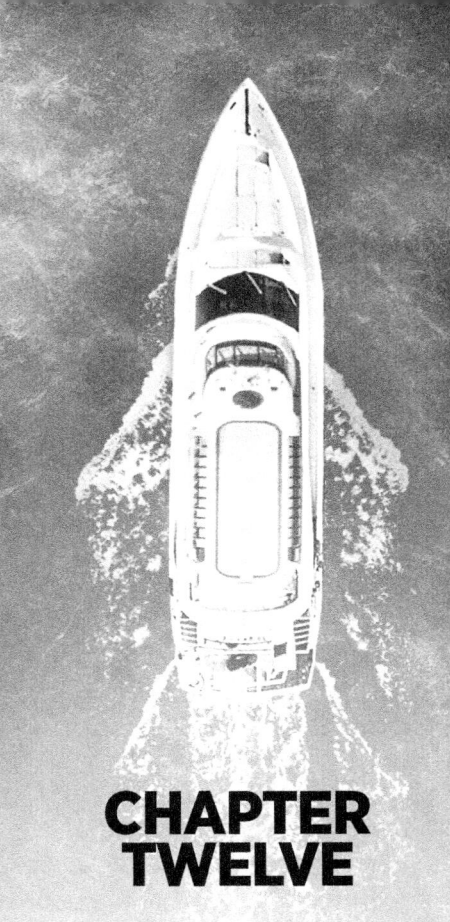

CHAPTER TWELVE

O LIVIA RETURNED TO THE CABIN AND FOUND THAT Emily was just finishing up talking to someone, a tall woman with afro hair and a friendly smile. Olivia slid into the chair beside Emily, watching the woman leave.

"How's it been going?" Olivia asked. Emily cast her a tired glance, shaking her head.

"Not good. These people are more interested in finding out the gossip than telling us anything useful. Honestly, that last woman was just desperate to know our thoughts on the case so far. My thoughts? That all these awful people are more interested in a story than finding justice for a young woman."

Olivia nodded in understanding. There was something sinister about the people who had been in attendance that night. She hadn't spoken to most of them, and yet she felt like knowing one of them meant you knew them all. Every single one of them seemed to harbor dark secrets. Every one of them appeared to be at least a little morally gray. And every single one of them was there for themselves and no one else.

"Unfortunately, I agree with you," Olivia said, her voice low. "I found out something of interest from the woman that Rebecca tipped us off to. Devyn Ward. She's a paparazzi from *The Hot Take*, and she came to the party scavenging for news to write about. What she found instead was Congressman Atkins and Darcie arguing. She overheard him saying that he would, quote-unquote, 'end her.'"

Emily's eyes widened. "God. Are we sure he meant it that way? That's a pretty big statement to make…"

"I'm not sure, but he's looking more and more guilty by the hour. He was willing to pay her off to cover his back. He didn't want the press to find out about their conversation, and that was before she wound up dead. Now, according to Devyn, he's trying to put a lid on it entirely. I don't know how much he was willing to pay her to keep quiet, but I'll bet it wasn't pocket change."

"Damn… so we might have found our killer already. He's got a motive, for sure. And everyone we've spoken to so far had something negative to say about him. To think, his own wife was so fed up with him that she was willing to throw him under the bus… that says a lot, don't you think?" Emily paused, chewing her lip. "We just need something more to get him for this. If only we had evidence of the conversation he had with Darcie. He's a politician. He's likely got all sorts of ways that he can wriggle out of this without the evidence we need."

"Well, I'm hoping that I might have a solution to that." Olivia handed Emily the phone she had taken from Devyn. "This belonged to the reporter. She was taking photos and videos all night. I haven't found anything yet, but hopefully there's something usable on here. If we can see any pictures of Darcie on there, we might be able to place where she was and when based on the timestamps and the locations."

"That will definitely be useful," Emily agreed, nodding as she handed the phone back to Olivia. She checked her watch. "Already past eleven. I wonder how long it's going to take for the engine to get back up and running? And the Coast Guard still isn't here…"

"Let's see it as a blessing in disguise. We need more time to talk to the guests. Have you managed to whittle down the numbers at all?"

"A little. I got through a few time wasters pretty quickly, but I did find someone of interest too. I don't know if you knew this, but Charlie's business partner is here tonight. He was dating a close friend of Darcie's, so I imagine they knew each other pretty well. I thought it would be good if we could talk to him."

"What's his name?"

"Luke Shaw. From what I can gather, he's not really on the party scene as much as Charlie. When I looked through his social media, Luke was barely ever there. I get the feeling he's more of a behind-the-scenes guy. But still, he must have known Darcie, and, in theory, he might have some dirt on Charlie for us. Hell, he might even be involved in some of these financial irregularities we were looking at in the first place."

"Sounds like the kind of guy we want to talk to then."

"I'm glad you think so," Emily continued. "I tracked him down before my last interview. He said he'd come and speak to us soon."

Olivia nodded. She was keen to meet the man who had formed a business with Charlie Evans. She was picturing a guy similar to him: cocky and self-assured in a sort of sickening way. But when Luke Shaw turned up a few minutes later, Olivia was pleasantly surprised.

Charlie's partner was nothing like him. He was dressed simply in a white shirt and black pants, his attention to detail clearly not as sharp as Charlie's. He had a mop of brown curls that were a little too long, and he slicked them back off his face as he entered. He also wore a pair of thick glasses which had left red ridges on either side of his nose. His shoulders slumped forward a little, and he gave a shy wave to the pair of them as he came to sit with them. Luke might be rich and semi-famous, but he carried himself like an average guy, and Olivia found herself warming to him much more than she had to Charlie.

"Hi. I'm Luke, nice to meet you both," he started, with an awkward invitation to shake his hand. Both the women obliged, and Olivia ignored that his palms were a little sweaty. When he sat back in his seat, his posture was stiff, and he looked so uncomfortable that Olivia wondered whether they were making him nervous. If they were, good. She wanted him to feel vulnerable. She wanted him to tell them everything that might get them closer to answers.

"We appreciate you coming to talk to us," Emily said. "After what happened, we're trying to talk to anyone who might have interacted with Darcie before she went overboard. Given that you're dating one of her friends and she's your partner's girlfriend, I assume you were friends, or at least acquaintances?"

Luke nodded slowly, but also shrugged at the same time. The gesture was so awkward that in any other circumstances, Olivia might have found it funny. "We knew... we knew of each other. I don't see a lot of Charlie these days. He kind of runs the business end of things, and I mainly work on the technical side of the company. So... yeah. I wouldn't say that I was close with Darcie. But I was very sorry to hear of her passing."

Olivia resisted the urge to frown. She refused to believe that he had almost nothing to do with his business partner's girlfriend. Even if he wasn't a hard partier like Charlie, they'd still have to attend meetings together, go out for business lunches, the works. And in what world would two best friends such as Darcie and Luke's girlfriend not force their boyfriends to hang out all the time?

"So, you don't spend much time with Charlie then?" Olivia pushed, intrigued by the apparent rift between the pair of them. Luke blinked behind his glasses.

"Well, I wouldn't say that. But I work mostly in the Los Angeles branch, while he stays at the headquarters in DC. Of course, we're close. We always have been. We started this company together—but we go back way farther than that, back to college. But you know how it is. Life gets busy. He had his life, and I had mine. That's just the way things go." He paused. "I feel bad for him. He really cared about her a lot."

That made Olivia raise an eyebrow. From what she'd seen, there was plenty of tension between Charlie and Darcie, and not the good kind. Charlie had said it himself: they were in a rocky place. According to him, she always picked out his flaws and found solace in other men. So, if that was the case, why was Luke insisting that everything was going well?

"They were in a really serious relationship then?"

"Of course. They were joined at the hip," Luke said a little absently. "They were head over heels for each other, right from when they met. It was like one minute he was single, a bachelor for life, and then Darcie came along and changed him. She was the only woman capable of locking him down, and she knew it. I think she demanded the best from him because she knew she deserved it. Charlie hated the criticism, but there's no denying it … she made him a better man."

Olivia took a moment to take in everything he'd said. For someone who claimed not to know Darcie well, he seemed to have a very high opinion of her. In fact, he seemed to know a lot about her. Plus, she was finding it hard to understand how he had so many positive things to say about Darcie, and yet the one thing he'd said about his lifelong friend was that his girlfriend made him a better man. That didn't sound very positive to her.

"Like I said … she always seemed nice," Luke continued. "And my girlfriend Lucy just adores her. They've been friends a long time, too, and they talk all the time, even when we're traveling or out of the country. She said she'd be happy to talk to you later, but she was very upset when she found out what happened to Darcie. I think she needs some time before she's ready to talk."

"Of course," Emily said kindly. "So, you came here tonight with your girlfriend?"

"That's right. I suppose we're joined at the hip too," Luke said with a tight smile. Somehow, Olivia wasn't sure that was true. There was no enthusiasm to his comment.

Honeymoon phase over then, I assume? she thought to herself.

"And presumably, Lucy spent quite some time with Darcie tonight? I guess this was a good opportunity for them to catch up. And since you're joined at the hip, as you said … I can assume you were there too?" Emily asked with an innocent quirk of her eyebrow. Olivia held back a smirk. Damn, Emily could be sneaky when she wanted to be.

Luke shifted in his chair, his brow furrowed. "Well, no, actually. On any other night, I would have expected that to be the case. But we mostly kept to ourselves tonight. I mostly came because I support the foundation. These parties are usually the last thing I want to attend. But Charlie really wanted to have me here, even if he and Darcie were too busy schmoozing to come and say hello. A wasted trip, if you ask me. But… I guess it did give Lucy one last evening with her friend, even if they barely saw one another."

Olivia chewed her lip. Something wasn't adding up. Luke seemed a little fidgety to her, never quite looking her in the eye. At first, she'd assumed it was just nerves, but now she wondered if there was something he wasn't saying out loud. Something about the four of them didn't sit right with Olivia. How could they all be so close and yet avoid each other entirely at a party? How could Luke and Charlie possibly be as close as he said if they barely saw one another, despite running a business together? And what kind of best friends got to see each other in person for the first time in months and barely even hung out?

"Can you think of anything else about tonight that might help us with our investigation?" Olivia asked. "Did you see Darcie talking to anyone in particular? Where were you around the time when she went overboard?"

"Lucy and I were dancing," Luke said almost immediately. Olivia couldn't imagine him dancing, but she didn't argue the point. "And, no. Like I told you, I barely saw her tonight. She was probably flitting all over the place, making connections, whatever it is that people do at these functions. I'm sure she was too busy to say hello. As for people of interest… I saw her a few times with Charlie, maybe once or twice with her boss, but that's it. I couldn't possibly tell you anything more."

"Well, thank you anyway," Emily said, offering her hand for Luke to shake again. "We won't keep you from Lucy any longer. I'm sure she could use your support right now."

"Thank you. If I can do anything further to help, please let me know," Luke said stiffly, but he was already halfway out of the room at that point. Olivia glanced at Emily as the door shut behind him.

"What do you think?" Olivia asked. Emily frowned.

"Of what? Of Luke?"

"Don't you think his story is a little strange?"

"How so?"

"All that stuff about him being close with Charlie, but he barely ever sees him? And their girlfriends don't either? I don't know… it seems a bit off to me."

Emily shrugged. "I hadn't picked up on that. I figured it was just like he said. Life gets busy. You stop having as much time for your friends." She paused, looking up at Olivia. "It's just the way life works, right?"

Olivia felt heat crossing her cheeks. Was Emily referring to *their* friendship? Was she implying that Olivia didn't have time for *her* anymore? She knew she wasn't always the best at keeping in contact, but she hated to think that Emily thought she didn't make any effort. Olivia felt herself deflate a little. They'd had such a good day together so far, working in tandem, finding little moments to laugh and have fun together… but was that enough? Did Emily need more from her?

Olivia was about to address the moment when someone appeared at the door. It was Angus, the charity's director, smiling pleasantly through the window of the door. Emily ushered him inside, and Olivia tried to forget the uncomfortable moment they had just shared. It was just going to have to wait a little longer.

"Hi. Angus, isn't it?"

"That's me," he nodded, taking a seat opposite them. "I thought I'd offer up a few minutes of my time for you. I don't know what I can tell you about what happened tonight, but I figured you'd have the questions, and I could provide the answers."

"Sure," Emily said, a little taken aback by his direct approach. "I won't say 'no' to that. So, um, did you know Darcie well?"

"I knew her a little. She was always pressing Charlie to set up the foundation. She got involved where she could, and we interacted in that manner. She seemed like a lovely young woman. It's a shame that her life ended so quickly. I was very sorry to hear about it."

"So, you only knew Charlie and Darcie in a business capacity?" Olivia asked. "They're not friends of yours?"

"Oh, well, I wouldn't put it that way. Any friend of BW is a friend of mine," Angus said brightly. "I started the charity after I retired from MMA fighting. I wanted to give back to the community, to really help these kids who grow up in underserved communities."

Olivia raised an eyebrow. "You teach them mixed martial arts?"

He chuckled and shook his head. "Not for fighting. For discipline. For a structure in their lives that they may not have at home. We also help them with homework, with educational opportunities like field trips, and we have a facility for them to come to if they need to find somewhere to go. These are kids. Troubled teenagers. It keeps them off the streets and points them to more productive pursuits. Teaches them to be strong in mind and body."

Olivia had to admit, that was a surprise. She wasn't sure what she'd been expecting from the muscle-bound man, but he seemed genuine. "Did you ever work with Darcie?"

He shrugged. "Not so directly. Mostly in the way she influenced Charlie to put together these funds. I'm not sure how much Charlie has ever really cared for charity work, but Darcie was a good influence on him, I suppose. Most women know how to bring out the best in a man, don't they? Especially women like Darcie."

"A lot of people have been saying that about Darcie," Olivia mused. It hadn't escaped her notice that a lot of the men she'd spoken to seemed to have a soft spot for her, no matter the age gap between them. Olivia wondered if it was simply because she was a young, beautiful, and intelligent woman… or whether she had encouraged some of the advances. It would explain why there was so much tension among her peers. But Olivia didn't want to assume that the victim was at fault. She just had to explore every possible avenue. If Darcie had, as Charlie implied, flirted with other men and enticed them, then perhaps it was one of the things that had led to her death, one way or another.

"Did you see much of the victim tonight? Before her death?" Olivia asked, clearing her thoughts for a moment. "We're trying to figure out where she might have been just before it happened, but so far, we're drawing a blank."

Angus scratched his chin. "Couldn't tell you. I don't recall seeing her much at all, actually. It was a very busy night, and I had a lot of donors to catch up with. She wasn't particularly a priority of mine tonight. Didn't she have some friend come in? Lily or Lacy or something?"

"Lucy," Olivia supplied.

"Right," he shrugged. "I dunno. I barely knew Darcie. Maybe you could try her."

Olivia nodded. Angus hadn't been particularly useful to them, but she was glad to have spoken to him. His thoughts on Darcie had fueled some of her own opinions further, and she was ready to dig deeper.

"Thank you, Angus. You've been a big help," Emily told him. He offered them a warm smile as he left the room. Olivia rubbed her eyes, feeling tiredness clawing at her. She felt a gentle hand on her arm and glanced over at Emily. She was smiling softly, her own expression a little faded too. It had been a long night so far.

"Coffee?" Emily asked Olivia. She smiled properly now. She and Emily might not be as close as they used to be, but they knew each other so well. Olivia reached for her friend's hand and squeezed it in return.

"Nothing could sound better right now."

CHAPTER THIRTEEN

Armed with cups of coffee, Olivia and Emily returned to the deck to see if they could find anyone else of interest to talk to. They'd decided to abandon the idea of talking to everyone and narrow down their people of interest.

"I definitely want to talk to Lucy," Olivia mentioned to Emily as they walked. "Not only because she's Darcie's best friend but also because I think maybe she can shed some light on the relationship between Charlie, Darcie, and even Luke. I get the feeling Luke wasn't being entirely honest with us."

"I think we might be overthinking it, but Lucy is definitely important regardless," Emily agreed. "I guess we just have to find her now. I might be able to pinpoint her from photographs on Darcie's social media."

While Emily scrolled through Darcie's profile, Olivia scanned the guests again. She spotted Charlie, slumped down in a corner, sitting on the deck instead of a chair. He looked a little worse for wear, but no one seemed to be interested in helping him out. Then there were David and Rebecca Atkins, talking hotly in low voices on the other side of the deck. No doubt Atkins had figured out what his wife had been saying about him.

Luke was standing alone, too, as far away from Charlie as he could possibly manage, which Olivia noted as odd. Only Angus appeared to be showing signs of normality, humming quietly to himself as he approached the bar.

The atmosphere of the night wasn't improving. Olivia couldn't help wondering why the Coast Guard hadn't shown up yet. The ship still showed no signs of moving, though the captain and the bosun had been discussing it for a long time and examining the engine as the hours dragged on. Olivia was just glad that nothing else had happened yet. It seemed that everyone was on high alert, and the guests were afraid to be alone. It was a good thing. At least their fear was keeping them safe from any kind of ambush.

At least, that was what Olivia hoped.

"Here," Emily said, pointing to a picture on her phone. It showed Darcie with another young woman. She was pretty and young but also wholly generic, like every other Instagram model Olivia had ever seen. Her hair was dark brown, and she had thick eyebrows that stood out against her pale skin. Olivia couldn't recall seeing the woman that evening, but she wasn't a particularly memorable looking person, which didn't help her case.

"This is Lucy. Have you seen her at all tonight?" Olivia asked. Emily shook her head.

"I don't recognize her at all. I've started to recognize people around the ship, but I don't recall her."

A perfect trait for a killer, Olivia thought. *To be so forgettable that no one suspects what you're doing when you lurk around in the shadows…*

She blinked the thought away. She had no evidence at all that Lucy might have wanted to hurt Darcie. In fact, if Luke had been telling the truth about how distraught she was, then she might be the person who cared most on the entire boat. The other guests were shockingly devoid of emotion, clearly more interested in their own safety than pinpointing a killer. These people, who claimed to be Darcie's friends, had barely even shed a tear for her death.

Olivia hoped to never feel so insignificant in her own life.

"Let's go find her," Emily said, leading the way back to the interior. Olivia followed her, glad for the warmth of the cabins. It took them a long time to figure out where Lucy might be, but when they heard the muffled sobs of a woman in the ladies' bathroom, they immediately knew they'd found the right person.

Olivia and Emily stepped cautiously into the bathroom. They could see a woman kneeling inside a stall, her feet visible through the base of the door. Olivia glanced at Emily, who nodded in response. It was clearly a task for Emily, the more sensitive of the two of them.

"Lucy Dillard? Is that you in there?" Emily asked gently. They heard a loud sniff from within the stall.

"Yeah… this is Lucy. Who's asking?" Lucy croaked. Emily swallowed.

"I'm Emily Boyd, with the FBI. I'm here with my partner, Olivia Knight. We're so sorry about your friend. But we're working on trying to find out who did this to her… and anything you can tell us might help us catch her killer."

Lucy fell silent for a moment, but then she got to her feet. She flushed the toilet and then came out of the cubicle. Her face was blotchy and pale and her hair a mess. Her makeup had run over her cheeks, leaving her looking more than a little worse for wear. She dabbed at her eyes with the sleeve of her dress. It was hard to imagine her beside Darcie because the pair were so different, but clearly, the loss of her friend had hit her hard.

"Are you all right?" Emily asked quietly. Lucy swallowed, avoiding her gaze.

"I don't think I can be right now, can I? I just… I just lost my best friend." She sniffed again, her eyes red and filled with tears. "But I want to help. I don't want to just sit and cry all day when I'm sure I can be of use."

"You think you might know something?" Olivia asked. Lucy chewed her lip.

"I... I don't know," she admitted. "I don't think I can picture anyone on this boat doing that to her. But I know these people... I know everything that they did to her, every single word they ever spoke to her. Darcie used to tell me everything." A flash of emotion crossed her brown eyes. "Darcie always asked me to keep the things I told her secret, but secrets are no good to her now. Just promise me one thing... please don't repeat anything that I tell you. No good can come from it."

"Of course," Emily said kindly. "Would you like to come upstairs with us? Maybe have some coffee?"

Lucy nodded meekly and Emily put a hand on her shoulder, guiding her out of the bathroom. Olivia took the opportunity to head back to the cabin and prep for the interview. More than anyone, Olivia was excited to talk to Lucy—to find out what she knew. She was almost certain that Lucy would tell them one hundred percent of the truth. She was the person she felt they could trust most on the *Astoria*, and she hoped that whatever secrets she knew would help them solve the case.

When Lucy and Emily returned, Lucy looked a little calmer, her hands wrapped around a warm, steaming mug. When she sat down, she took a deep breath with her eyes closed, preparing herself for the moment. Olivia leaned in eagerly, interested in what she was about to say. Lucy's eyes snapped open.

"What I'm about to tell you is something I never told Darcie. Something that I always felt hung over our relationship. I regret not telling her about it... but I was left with no choice," Lucy said. She took another heaving breath and then let it go, her chest rising and falling. She looked Olivia directly in the eyes. "I've been in a secret relationship with Luke for the past year. He's the partner in her boyfriend's business. Charlie and Luke have been working together for years, and—"

"Wait a second," Emily cut in. "*Secret* relationship?"

Lucy blinked several times. "Yes. Luke asked me never to tell anyone about it. Not until he was ready..."

Olivia and Emily exchanged a shocked glance. Had Luke slipped up by telling them about the relationship, and then had to go with it? Had he lied to make it seem as though Charlie and Darcie were aware of who he was dating?

If that was the case, then why?

"Luke asked you to keep it a secret? Why?" Olivia asked. Lucy chewed her lip.

"Before we met... Luke had a bit of a thing for Darcie. I say a bit of a thing... he was in love with her. I hate saying that out loud. It's so weird that he loved my best friend before he loved me, but that's the truth of it. He was head over heels for her. And at the time, Charlie and Darcie were only just starting out. They'd been dating a few months or so, and at the time, the three of them did everything together. That was before things became really complicated between them all..."

"All three of them?"

Lucy nodded. "I guess the whole thing got a bit messy. I think Darcie knew how Luke felt about her. She's always been kind of flirtatious, and I guess maybe she took it a little far and feelings got involved. Not on Darcie's end—on Luke's. By the time Charlie figured out what was going on, well, it all fell apart. Charlie blamed Luke for obsessing over her. He thought Darcie could do no wrong. They fought, and Charlie said he wanted Luke out of the business. Luke refused to sell up, even though he never really cared for the business in the same way that Charlie did. Instead, he said he would go away for a while. Take a step back, you know? So, he went to LA and handled things out there. I happened to live in LA already, so that's when he and I began dating. He told me all of this after a while... after he'd gotten over it all. I guess you could say I'm his rebound, but I know all those feelings have gone away now. He and I really care for each other."

"So, why keep the relationship a secret?"

Lucy tilted her head back and forth. "He just... he was just never ready to let Darcie and Charlie know. Everything between them was so fragile... and honestly, I didn't want Darcie to know either. I think she would have told me that I could do better than one of her old flames..." Lucy forced a small laugh.

Olivia tried to process what she was hearing. If Lucy was telling the truth, that meant that she'd been lied to, mostly by Luke. Not only had he implied that he and Charlie were as close as brothers, but he'd also pretended that Charlie and Darcie knew all about his relationship with Lucy—not to mention the fact that he claimed he barely knew Darcie, and yet he'd known her well enough to fall in love with her.

And what reason did he have to lie about that? Was he simply hoping not to dig up the past once again and cause trouble? Or did he have something more sinister to hide? Perhaps a motive for murder?

Olivia could see how easy it would be for Luke to become consumed by hatred for Darcie. She'd led him on, destroyed his lifelong friendship with Charlie, and then forced him to live a secret life so as not to cause any more damage.

And then there was Lucy. Sweet, vulnerable Lucy. Had Luke truly fallen for her, or did he choose her to get back at Darcie? Did he despise the fact that he'd been so close to winning Darcie, only to be left with her best friend, a girl who would do anything for him, but who paled in comparison?

Olivia hated making those assumptions. Lucy seemed like a lovely young woman. And yet she knew how the male mind worked. How they pitted women against one another in their minds, always looking to upgrade, never downgrade. Luke hadn't seemed particularly enthused about Lucy when he spoke of her. Instead of comforting her, he'd been standing out on the deck since his interview, avoiding her entirely. Olivia couldn't make sense of it. Luke had weaved such a web of lies that it had changed everything.

"You said that Charlie tried to cut Luke out of the company...." Olivia prompted, brushing her other thoughts aside for the moment. "Why didn't he, in the end? Surely, he's still angry?"

Lucy shrugged, sniffing a little. "I couldn't tell you. Luke doesn't like to talk about work, which I understand, given the way that things are now... but I assume that he realized that he didn't have the power to get rid of him. So, things have just stayed the same. But they barely talk anymore. They sometimes meet up together, for appearances, I guess, but their relationship is in the tank. It's just dead in the water."

Lucy closed her eyes, shaking her head. "I wanted to tell Darcie so badly. This is the one guy I've ever really been serious about. I'm used to being overlooked, especially with Darcie as my best friend. Everyone was always so interested in her that they never took a second glance at me. But Luke understands me, and he loves me. I wanted Darcie to know. But now she's gone… and I'll never get a chance to tell her."

Olivia felt sorry for the young woman. Anyone could see that she wasn't meant for this life, full of cutthroats and betrayals and revenge. But what she had told them changed everything. Olivia glanced at Emily.

"You stay here. I'm going to talk to Luke," Olivia told her. She had to know why he lied. She had to know if he was more dangerous than they had first realized.

While Emily soothed Lucy with comforting words, Olivia went to find Luke. He hadn't moved from the last time she'd seen him, staring out at the ocean with no emotion on his face. He seemed to sense Olivia coming and glanced up as she arrived next to him. He stared her down, clearly unaware of the slipups he'd made. Olivia raised an eyebrow at him.

"Is there anything you want to tell me? The truth, maybe?" Olivia asked him, their voices mostly disguised by the waves around them. Luke broke his gaze away from hers.

"I don't know what you're talking about."

"So let me get this straight. You're *not* in a secret relationship with Darcie's best friend? And you weren't in love with Darcie at one point in time, destroying the relationship between you and your business partner? Your best friend, or ex-best friend? You told me that everything was great between you all, but now I know you're a liar, Luke. I just want to know why."

Luke continued to look out over the water, his expression unchanged. "It's all ancient history now. I didn't want you to think it mattered."

"How can you be so sure it doesn't matter? And how can I be sure that your lies weren't to cover your own tracks?"

"You think I'd kill the woman I love?" Luke snapped. Olivia raised an eyebrow.

"*Love?* Present tense?"

Luke winced at his own words. Olivia folded her arms over her chest, staring him down. He shook his head at her.

"Fine. I still loved her, all right? Is that what you wanted to hear?" he asked. "How was I supposed to stop… even after she pretended like I didn't mean a thing to her. You met the woman. She was incredible. And I cared for her. But I care about Lucy too. That's why I tried to keep it all a secret. I knew it would only make things messier between the four of us, and I didn't want Lucy to have to deal with that... not when she already felt like she was playing second fiddle."

Luke ran a hand through his curls. "I know it doesn't look great... lying to you about it. But I'm not thinking straight. A woman I cared for is dead. I'm out of my mind with grief. Not like Charlie... more interested in getting wasted than mourning his girlfriend. It's ridiculous. I may not be a good person, but I would never hurt anyone. I would never kill Darcie."

Olivia found herself believing him. She could see the pain in his eyes now. He had never truly left her behind. And now, he was suffering for it. As much as she didn't like the man before her, she didn't think he was the killer.

But she wasn't so sure about his ex-best friend.

"And what about Charlie?" Olivia asked. Luke sighed.

"Look... we fought. It happens in the world of business," he stated. "There's a reason they tell you not to work with your best friend. It ruined our friendship, but we're over it now. It is what it is. We're just colleagues now. I couldn't tell you a thing about his life with Darcie. I stay out of his way, and he stays out of mine. It suits us well. Now, if you don't mind, I'd like a moment to myself. I'm trying to grieve."

Olivia knew better than to push further and cause a scene. Walking away from Luke, she felt frustrated. It was like they'd taken a step back. Lucy's information had only proved that Luke was even less likely to have been the killer. Olivia didn't trust him, but she also didn't think he was capable of ending Darcie's life....

... which circled Olivia back around to where she'd been before. Charlie and Representative Atkins. The two main suspects thus far. The question was, who was truly twisted enough to end Darcie's life?

And what was in it for them?

CHAPTER FOURTEEN

THE HOUR CROSSED MIDNIGHT, AND THE *ASTORIA* WAS still stationary in the middle of the ocean. With no signs of the Coast Guard coming for them, Olivia knew that they were in for a long night. It struck her as strange that no one had arrived to help them, but every extra minute she had to interview the people onboard was a bonus for her.

And there were still plenty of people to talk to. Olivia's head was spinning at the possibility of how many people might have wanted Darcie dead. She had clearly ruffled a few feathers when she was alive, whether intentionally or not. She was starting to think that almost every single person on board had some sort of motive.

What she needed was evidence. Without the right equipment to carry out her investigation, she was forced to rely on witnesses.

But who could she trust? It felt like everyone she'd spoken to was hiding something, or at least trying to. She couldn't be sure how honest anyone was being with her, and that was only going to make her job harder.

She headed down to the last room on this level, which was comprised of living quarters. Darcie's body had been placed there under lock and key, and she'd deputized Bishop, the bodyguard, to stand watch over the door. The chain of evidence had been broken long ago, but there was nothing she could do about it. It was far from an ideal situation, but with no other way to keep her body secure until they had an opportunity for rescue, she had no choice.

She paused for a moment to watch the hulking man. He'd reacted oddly to the news of Darcie's death. Even now, after the worst of the immediate emotion had passed, he seemed to be struggling more than even Charlie Evans had been. It hadn't been the shock of finding out someone had died, nor even the loss of his boss's girlfriend—no, this was something personal. Olivia stood there for a moment, contemplating what connection he could possibly have to Darcie.

Was this yet another man in love with her?

"Any news for me?" she asked, pressing a cup of coffee into his hand. He accepted with a grateful nod and took a sip.

"Been quiet. No one in or out, like you said."

"Thanks, Bishop. You've been such a big help. Mind if I go in and take another look at her?"

The big man looked down to the ground and back to Olivia, like he was ardently trying not to even catch a glimpse of Darcie's body through the tiny window in the door.

"Um, yeah. Sure." He reached behind him to unlock the door and allowed Olivia in, then quietly slid the door shut behind her as she entered.

Olivia's heart broke yet again to see Darcie spread on the bed, her fiery tresses spreading out behind her like a halo. She wanted to tell herself that Darcie was just asleep, but couldn't convince herself of even that. There was too much blood staining her face. Her porcelain skin had turned a cold shade of blue, and her eyes were wide open, frozen forever in an expression of shock and fear. The sight sent a shudder down Olivia's spine.

She didn't deserve this. Nobody did, but especially not such a brilliant, vibrant young woman with her whole life ahead of her.

Olivia had barely even met the woman. She'd known her for all of one day. And yet, part of her felt a kinship with her, like in another life they could have been friends.

"I'm sorry," Olivia whispered.

She pulled on a pair of latex gloves from a first aid kit that someone had brought into the room, already knowing they wouldn't be of much use. Even if she did find something, it would be hard to prove since the evidence had been tainted from the beginning.

Olivia knelt down next to Darcie's motionless form, squinting to take in every detail—every tiny, minute thing that could possibly give her answers. Unfortunately, there simply wasn't much to go on. Darcie had extensive bruising on her wrist, and close examination revealed that she also had bruises on her upper arms. But Olivia was no doctor, she couldn't tell just by looking what the injuries meant or how they'd been inflicted upon Darcie. All she could tell was that someone had hurt her.

And she had to find out who.

With a sigh, she stood back up and tossed the gloves in the trash can. This was a waste of time. She wasn't likely to find anything with an examination of the body until they got to shore and transferred it to a medical examiner's office. In the meantime, she had to focus on interrogating everyone she could while she could.

She made her way to the en suite bathroom and washed her hands with soap and water, then exited the room. Bishop stood a bit away from the door, his eyes rimmed red as if he'd broken into tears in the short time since Olivia had seen him last. She wondered again why he seemed to be taking this so personally when even Darcie's boyfriend hadn't.

She waved him over to lock it behind her, and he nodded. Now was her chance to catch him off guard and see if she could wrestle some honesty out of him.

"How did you know her?" she asked.

Bishop sniffled and turned the key in the door lock with a click. He rested his bald head on the window and closed his eyes for a moment before seeming to compose himself.

"We were very close," he said in his deep, rumbling voice. "I can't believe she's gone…"

"You loved her, didn't you?" Olivia pressed sympathetically. It seemed that Darcie had that effect on many men in her orbit.

The sound Bishop let out was halfway between a chuckle and a sob.

"Yeah. I really did. But not in the way you might be thinking. She is—was—one of my best friends. Like a sister to me," he explained. "Our families grew up together. I've known her since we were in the first grade."

He looked out over the water, watching the stars reflecting off the infinite expanse of the sea. "Darcie was the only one who supported my decision to go into the military instead of college," he began. "Everyone said I was stupid. Throwing my life away. But I never woulda made it in school. That's not me. I knew what I wanted to do, and she was the only one who believed in me. And then when I got medically discharged, she was the first one by my side. She was the one who recommended me to take this job in the first place. She changed my life, and I can never thank her enough for that."

It was odd seeing the big man suddenly so overwhelmed with emotion. Of all the men she'd spoken to that night, Bishop was the only one who seemed truly broken by Darcie's death. Even Charlie and Luke, two men who claimed to be in love with her, didn't seem nearly as fazed.

"She's… she was such a great person," he went on. "Kind. Full of life. She was at the top of our class in high school, but she never let it get to her head. She spent so much of her time volunteering and tutoring people like me who couldn't get good grades. And when she was in college, she always sent me care packages when I was stationed out in Kuwait. And then she got inspired to become a lawyer so she could help people. She volunteered all the time. She saw veterans, the homeless, disabled people, orphans… she saw how all those people were treated, and she wanted to fight for them."

"Sounds like she was an amazing person," Olivia said.

"She really was."

Olivia knew that everyone grieves differently, of course, and that Darcie's death had come as such a sudden shock that she couldn't necessarily tell anyone's true guilt or innocence by their immediate reactions. Still, though, only Bishop gave her the impression that he truly cared about Darcie as a person at all— not just as someone who could give him something.

"I'm truly sorry for your loss," Olivia said.

"Thank you," he said.

A long beat of silence passed between them. In the distance, she could still hear the party guests gossiping up a storm on some of the other levels, but right now, all she was concerned with was the immediate moment.

Bishop cleared his throat then said, "Can you promise me something? Can you promise me... that whoever did this... you'll find them? You'll put them away?"

Olivia hated making promises she wasn't sure she could keep.

"I promise I'll try my best. I promise I'll do everything I can to find out who did this to Darcie and bring them to justice."

Bishop nodded solemnly. It was all she could promise, and he knew that. Olivia just hoped it would be enough.

CHAPTER FIFTEEN

O LIVIA LEFT BISHOP, WHO RESUMED HIS POST BY THE door guarding Darcie, and headed back down toward the engine room where the captain and bosun were hard at work trying to get things back up and running.

Olivia still found it odd that someone had managed to tamper with the engine. She didn't know how she would even begin to do something as complicated as shutting down an engine, especially without putting everyone onboard in danger. Whoever had come to the party intending to kill Darcie had clearly thought of everything.

And that worried Olivia even more.

"No luck with the engine?" Olivia asked the captain and the bosun. The captain shook his head.

"Nothing yet. Harry here is an expert, and he still hasn't been able to figure out what's going on," he said, nodding to the bosun. Harry offered Olivia a slight smile. He was around her age with a handsome face. His eyes crinkled at the corners as though he smiled a lot, and his slightly static, brown hair gave him a dazed look.

"I can't make head or tails of it," Harry added with a shake of his head. "I'm so sorry about this. I should have had it fixed by now."

"It's all right," Olivia said. "Being stuck out here actually gives me more time to try and figure out who did this."

Harry nodded, his expression grave. "I guess that's true. I still feel responsible. This is practically my ship. I just inspected the whole engine yesterday in preparation for this trip... and then for something terrible like this to happen..."

Olivia didn't see how it was Harry's problem that things had taken a turn for the worse. He was there to keep the ship running and not much more. But Olivia could see that he was distressed, so she offered him a smile.

"I don't think anyone could have predicted this," she reassured him. "What happened to Darcie was terrible, but no one could have stopped it. I think the killer had this planned for some time."

Harry bowed his head. "I just don't understand. I can't understand at all why someone would want to do that to her. Everyone loved her."

"Did you know her well?" Olivia asked, a little surprised. She wondered what business the bosun had getting chummy with his boss's girlfriend. Harry shrugged.

"We became friendly, I guess. I come to a lot of these parties just to keep an eye on the ship... sometimes, Darcie liked to get away for a bit. She'd come and sit with me on the bridge and have a chat. I got the feeling that despite being a part of this rich man's world, she didn't really belong here. She was just a normal girl."

Olivia didn't miss the tone in his voice when he spoke about her. He clearly had a soft spot for her, and given the number of romantic affairs that the victim appeared to be having, she wouldn't be surprised if she'd roped Harry in with her charms too. Olivia glanced at the captain, who had his eyebrow slightly raised.

Something told her that he knew more about Harry and Darcie than he was letting on.

"So, you became good friends, then?" Olivia asked, not wanting to ask outright about the nature of their relationship. She got the feeling Harry might be a little defensive about it. He sighed, rubbing the back of his neck.

"I cared deeply for her," he said carefully. "Yes, we were friends. I felt I knew her pretty damn well."

"And can you think of any reason why tonight might have been different? Why someone might have chosen to hurt her?" Olivia pushed. If Harry was as close to her as he said he was, then perhaps he might know something useful. She'd overlooked the captain and the bosun as suspects, but the deeper she got into her investigation, the more she realized that every single person on the ship appeared to be linked. It was the kind of tight-knit community that had everyone nosing into each other's business. That meant that everyone knew everything about everyone...

Any one of them could have done it.

Harry shrugged. "Well... she did seem a little different tonight when I saw her. A little frazzled."

"She did?" Olivia pushed. She wasn't taken by surprise by that revelation—after she argued with half the party guests, of course she'd have been frazzled—but maybe Harry knew something that she didn't yet. Something that might point her in the right direction.

"Well, yes. See, the thing is... she wasn't much of a drinker, but she seemed to be pretty out of it tonight. It shocked me when I saw her stumbling around. I mean, most of the guests at these parties usually get wasted, but not Darcie. She'd always have a glass or two of champagne if it was offered to her, but I don't think she ever really enjoyed being drunk. And yet tonight... she was unsteady on her feet, slurring her words, saying things she wouldn't normally say..."

"Like what?"

Harry blushed. "Oh, nothing of massive importance... I think she was just being more honest than normal. She'd implied before that her relationship was on the rocks... but tonight, she told me that she was thinking about leaving Charlie for good."

Olivia stood up a little straighter. Interesting. Charlie had implied that the pair of them argued, but he hadn't mentioned that Darcie planned to leave him. She supposed it made sense. Her night was already in turmoil, emotions were high, she had a bunch of other men waiting for her on the sidelines… she could see how it would be easy for Darcie to just slip away and leave Charlie and his crazy world behind.

"And she came to you directly to tell you that?" Olivia asked. Harry's cheeks continued to redden.

"It's like I said… we got to know each other well. I think she trusted me because she knew I wouldn't talk to the other guests about it. The gossip mill here never stops. If she told anyone else, I guess her secret would have spread like wildfire. And she wouldn't have wanted to put Bishop in that situation."

Interesting, Olivia noted. It seemed the web of connections went farther than she thought.

"So, as far as you know, she didn't tell anyone else?"

"As far as I know. But things got a little hairy after that, so I didn't get to see her again before… before…" Harry lowered his head. "Well, you know."

"What do you mean, things got 'hairy'?"

Harry swallowed. "Well, I was trying to be a good friend. A shoulder to cry on, you know? I was hugging Darcie, trying to comfort her… and Charlie showed up."

Here we go, Olivia thought. *We're finally getting down to the nitty-gritty here…*

"He came into the bridge. He was pretty out of it too. I guess they'd both been hitting the drink hard after their argument. He was angry when he saw the two of us together. I think he thought I was being inappropriate. I tried to calm him down, explaining that my intention was only to make sure she was okay, but he was furious. I thought he was going to hit me, or even her. He was getting up in my face, saying he couldn't trust anyone with Darcie. He accused us of having an affair."

Were you having an affair? Olivia wanted to ask, but she kept her mouth shut. It didn't matter either way if they were, she figured. Harry was clearly head over heels for her, and Charlie could spot that a mile off. It didn't make sense for Harry to have wanted to hurt her, not when things were finally going his way. But Charlie? If Darcie was being unfaithful, straying from him once again, then it gave him even more motive to want her dead.

"I told him to calm down. I didn't want any trouble. I mean, he's my boss, technically. He bought out this yacht and the crew, so we technically belong to him," Harry said, his eyes darting around to check no one was listening in. "But I think after tonight, I might be getting fired. He was so angry with me."

"Does Charlie have a tendency to get aggressive when he's intoxicated?" Olivia asked. Harry puffed out air, nodding.

"Let's just say this isn't the first time he's flown off the handle," Harry shared, "but never like this before. I was honestly a little scared. But I was more worried about Darcie. She could always hold her own in those scenarios, but I still didn't like leaving her with him. But I had no choice. Charlie told me to leave and stick to doing my job. He said he wanted to talk with Darcie alone. I refused at first, but she told me it was okay to go. So I left."

Harry swallowed, his eyes a little misty. "And I didn't see her again after that. I kept looking out for her, right up until the moment she was dragged out of the water." Harry wiped a tear away from his eye, trembling a little. "I'm sorry… I told myself I wouldn't do this…"

"It's all right, kid," the captain said, patting Harry's shoulder. "Tonight was quite a night. Why don't you go get some fresh air? Looks like we won't be moving any time soon anyway."

Harry nodded, gulping in air as he turned and walked off toward the bar. "I'll, um… I'll call the Coast Guard again. Don't know what's taking them so long."

"You do that," said the captain. He offered Olivia a small smile.

"Sorry about him. He's having a tough time coping with this. I think he had a soft spot for the little lady."

"I can see that," Olivia said, shaking her head. It seemed like every man aboard the ship did. She chewed her lip. "Can I ask… you were often here at these parties, too, right? Did you ever notice all of these things going on? All of these undercurrents. Because from what I've learned tonight, it feels like everyone has tension. Everyone is having affairs or harboring secrets or doing things that they shouldn't. Do you see it happening?"

The captain sighed. "If there's one thing I know about these people… it's that they are young, beautiful, and filthy rich. They get bored easily. They do these things to bring excitement back into their lives. When everything is handed to you on a silver platter, things get a little predictable." He shook his head slowly. "I've seen a lot of things during my career. I've seen how corrupt money makes people. But I've never known anyone to get killed before. Tonight is different from everything else I've experienced. But to tell you the truth, agent, it didn't shock me."

Olivia felt a cold shiver run down her spine. There was too much going on for her to comprehend. With everything going on, she'd almost forgotten the real reason she was there in the first place. But the more she learned, the more fingers were pointing in Charlie's direction. What if he was more than just a fraud?

What if he was a killer as well?

CHAPTER SIXTEEN

OLIVIA FOUND EMILY CHATTING WITH A FEW OF THE guests on the deck. She had so much to tell her, and it felt like time was starting to run out. They'd been stuck in the middle of the ocean for hours now, and Olivia was sure that they'd eventually make it back to shore. She wanted answers before then, and she'd do anything she could to get them.

And now she had yet another clue that could lead her to the truth. Emily noticed the urgency in Olivia's gaze, so she excused herself and approached Olivia. Emily wrapped her arms around herself. The cold was starting to seep in now as the night drew on and the waves crashed more insistently against the hull.

"What's going on?" Emily asked, searching Olivia's face for clues. "Did you find something?"

"Just had an interesting conversation with the bosun," Olivia whispered. "Another of Darcie's conquests, it seems. But he told me some things I didn't know. First, Darcie had solid plans to break things off with Charlie. That's a motive right there. And second, he told me that Darcie doesn't usually drink, but that she seemed drunk tonight. I wonder if that played a part in her death. Apparently, she was a lot more loose-lipped than usual tonight.

"Do you think maybe she said something that provoked the killer?" Emily asked.

Olivia nodded. "It's a possibility."

Emily furrowed her brow in thought. "But aren't we assuming that the killing was pre-planned? After all, we have the anonymous tip implying that something would happen tonight, and then there's the fact that someone tampered with the engine. Why would someone do that if it was an accident or a spur of the moment thing?"

Emily had a point. The truth was, Olivia wasn't sure that her conversation with the bosun brought her any closer to the truth at all. They'd had suspicions about Charlie from the start, given his attitude toward Darcie and the fact that he was the focus of their investigation in the first place. The only new lead that they had was that Charlie tended to be belligerent when drunk, which was entirely believable based on what Olivia had personally seen. However, that didn't prove he was a murderer.

They needed to speak to Charlie again. They needed to press him further and see what he'd spill. He'd been in a foul mood when they spoke earlier in the night, but perhaps that might work in their favor. If Olivia could get him to crack, then she might even be able to get him to fly off the handle and show his true colors. And if he did, Olivia would be ready for him. There was no way that a man like Charlie could evade the truth from two experienced FBI agents. Olivia felt glad that she had her gun stowed away in her bag; she was ready for any unforeseen reactions from Charlie or anyone else for that matter.

"I want to grill Charlie again," Olivia said. "He's still our best bet right now. He and Representative Atkins have the strongest motives so far, especially Charlie. It seems like there was tension building up between him and Darcie for a long time. I don't think we can afford to overlook him, and I'd rather speak to him while his defenses are still down."

"All right. Do you want me to approach him first? He seems a lot calmer around me," Emily offered, but Olivia was already shaking her head.

"No. I think we need him on edge. I think we need to poke the bear if we're going to get anywhere with him. The bosun said that he's prone to aggression and that he gets angry easily. That's when his guard will be down the most and when he might be more likely to slip up in front of us."

"Got it," Emily nodded. "I'll follow your lead."

Olivia led the way to find Charlie. He hadn't moved far from where she'd seen him last. He was still slumped in his corner, but this time, he had a fresh glass of champagne in his hand. Against his better judgment, he'd clearly decided that it didn't matter how wasted he got anymore. It wasn't like Darcie was around to tell him not to.

"Hello, Charlie," Olivia said as they approached. His face turned from neutral to a cruel sneer as he looked Olivia up and down in apparent disgust.

"What do you want now? I told you, I don't want to talk to you until I've got my lawyer present."

Olivia said nothing, her eyebrows raised. She was sure that would aggravate him further. He seemed a little lost, unable to put his own thoughts together fast enough, and she watched his face contort as he tried to piece himself together.

"Didn't even want you here in the first place. Why did Darcie have to invite you?" Charlie muttered, slurring a little. Olivia glanced at the flute in his hand.

"I see that you're having another drink."

"So what? It's my party. I can do what I damn well please," Charlie snapped, swigging from the flute again. Olivia shrugged.

"Well, that's true. I've just heard a few things about you tonight, that's all."

Charlie's gaze snapped up to meet Olivia's eyes. "Oh yeah? And what is it that you've heard?"

"Just that you can be a little belligerent. Like you're being now. And that it's usually after you've had a lot to drink. Which you have."

Charlie tossed aside his glass, which miraculously didn't smash as it rolled away. He got to his feet unsteadily and squared up to Olivia. He was close enough that she could smell the acrid aroma of the fizzy wine. Still, she didn't flinch. She didn't want him to think for a single second that he was capable of intimidating her.

"What I do or don't do is none of your damn business," Charlie snapped. Olivia kept herself steady as she glared into his eyes.

"It is when there's been a murder aboard your yacht. You seemed keen to remind me that it was *your* party, after all. And don't you have plenty of motive to want her dead, Charlie? You see, I've heard other things tonight too. Like the fact that Darcie was *this close* to dumping you," she said, putting her measured finger and thumb in his face. "Is that true? Did I get that right?"

The anger in Charlie's eyes was at a boiling point, but he didn't lay a hand on Olivia. He had more sense than that, clearly, even in the state he was in. And the comment had stung him. That much was clear. He finally turned his face away from her, murmuring to himself. He slumped back down onto the deck as though in defeat.

"Maybe," he muttered. He wiped the back of his hand over his entire face, though no tears were falling from his eyes. "Maybe, yeah. She was mad at me. She was always mad at me. I guess it was only a matter of time before she gave up on me entirely." He laughed to himself, a hollow sound that made Olivia's heart squeeze a little.

"Is that why you wanted her out of the way?"

Charlie's hands curled into fists, but it seemed like the fight had gone out of him. His head lolled back against the wall, his eyes vacant. He shook his head very slowly, seemingly unaware that his movements had become so sluggish. Olivia watched him carefully. He didn't just look drunk. There was something more to him. She'd noticed it before, but it was painfully obvious now. What had he taken to make himself so erratic?

"I was trying so hard," Charlie slurred. "I wanted to show her that I could be who she wanted me to be. I barely drank a thing. I told you that already. And then … boom. It hit me."

Olivia and Emily exchanged a look. Olivia was sure they were both thinking the same thing. If this wasn't Charlie's typical behavior, then maybe something was different. Maybe they'd been missing something all along.

And then another thought struck Olivia. She turned her attention back to Charlie.

"I've been told that Darcie didn't drink much … is that right?"

Charlie nodded his head sluggishly. "She was such a Goody Two-shoes. She barely touched the stuff."

"But tonight was different, wasn't it? You noticed too, right? That she was pretty wasted?"

Charlie frowned deeply, his head lolling once again. "I don't know… I don't remember…"

"Think, Charlie. Did you see her drinking?"

Charlie blinked several times. "I guess I saw her sipping champagne at the beginning, but then after that… I don't think so? She snatched half of my drink away and drank it herself, but that was before she got really rowdy…"

Olivia's heart skipped a beat. "Which means that you both took a drink from the same glass."

Emily frowned at Olivia, unsure of where she was going with her train of thought. Olivia took a few steps toward Charlie and bent down to his level. She could once again see that his eyes were red and his skin was pasty. He barely seemed to notice how close she was to him, and his entire body was moving at half tempo.

"If there was something in that glass… something that was meant for one of the two of you to consume, but you only had half each… then perhaps it explains why you were both so out of it," Olivia wondered aloud. She straightened up again. "I think your drink was spiked, Charlie."

Charlie looked up at her slowly, and then, after a moment's delay, he began to laugh. He shook his head, his chest heaving with the effort of laughing. "Spiked? Why would anyone want to spike me? Or her?"

"That's the question," Olivia replied. She observed Charlie for a moment longer. If someone had tried to spike him that night, did that discount him as the killer? Maybe. Maybe not. Perhaps there was much more at play than Olivia had realized. What if Darcie wasn't the only target of the night?

Or what if she was never the target in the first place?

Olivia's mind was whirling. "Charlie… do you remember where you got that glass from? The one that you and Darcie shared?"

He frowned like he didn't understand the question. "From a tray, like every other drink I had tonight. There's waiters wandering around everywhere, handing them out. Where else would I get it from?"

"Did you pick the glass yourself? Or was it handed to you?"

That question seemed to confuse him even more. He huffed as he tried to scour his brain for the answer, but he seemed to draw a blank. Olivia sighed. She was sure she wasn't going to get much more out of Charlie in this state, but she had to try.

"Was it after that drink that you started to feel worse?" she pressed. "You were complaining of feeling sick earlier?"

Charlie nodded. "Yeah, I was, but I drank the sickness away. And now I feel fine."

"Do you feel *drunk*, Charlie? Or something else?"

He had his eyes closed, and he smiled dozily. He was barely clinging to consciousness. "I feel… good," he shrugged, drawing out his final word until his body finally gave up and he fell into sleep. Olivia checked his pulse to make sure he was okay, but it seemed he was just sleeping.

Olivia glanced at Emily. Concern was written across her friend's entire face.

"I think he's okay. But I also think he's lucky. If he was spiked, and the drug in that drink was intended to knock him out, or worse… then he's very lucky to be alive right now," Olivia said. "This complicates things. We can't be sure that Darcie was ever a target in the first place now. Perhaps she was just in the wrong place at the wrong time. Hell, maybe the drug even caused her to slip and fall over the edge…"

"Doubtful. The railings are still pretty high. She'd have to have one hell of a fall to launch herself over the railing, especially if she was wasted," Emily pointed out. "Maybe the drink was intended for Darcie?"

"If it was, then the killer wasn't very smart about it, were they?" Olivia stated. "Anyone that knew her would know she didn't drink much. Granted, she broke the pattern tonight, but it still wouldn't make sense to spike a champagne flute for her. I think the drink was meant for Charlie. And if that's the case, then maybe there are two entirely separate things going on here."

"So, Charlie was the target all along? But then why would somebody have injured Darcie? You saw how badly she was bruised."

Olivia chewed her lip. "Good point. In any case, this has turned out to be much bigger than we first thought. And we don't know what drug was used to spike Charlie. Maybe it wasn't intended to kill him, though it's certainly done a number on him. I don't know. There are so many variables, so many possibilities… what have we gotten ourselves into here?"

Emily shook her head. "I don't know. But perhaps we need to see if we can get Charlie some help. He's not in a good way right now. Is there a medical professional onboard?"

"You could ask the captain. I'll stay with Charlie and make sure he's all right. And then, once we've got him all set, we can go and find answers."

"Agreed," Emily said, her voice barely a whisper. As she walked off, Olivia felt the weight of the evening come crashing down on her shoulders. There was so much going on that it was hard to keep up. All of the lies were tangling up, getting lost in one another. Were they even close to the truth? And did they have any clue who their killer was at all? It seemed like they didn't— not when their main suspect had also suddenly become a victim himself.

Olivia felt more confused than ever. If she was going to get answers, she was going to have to push through the confusion. Maybe when Charlie came around, she'd get some real sense out of him. But until then, she had to go another route.

Time was ticking. The night was getting colder and darker. And Olivia was determined that their killer wouldn't get off that yacht without handcuffs on.

"So, the plot thickens," she murmured.

CHAPTER SEVENTEEN

"**A**LL RIGHT. IF WE'RE GOING TO FIND OUT WHO SPIKED Charlie's drink, I guess we'd better start with who had access to the drinks in the first place," Olivia started as she and Emily reconvened. A nurse onboard was seeing to Charlie, though he'd been sleeping since he passed out mid-conversation with them. "Which means kitchen staff, right? The waiters and the chefs who cooked the food. No one else would be able to get into the kitchens."

"There's the servers at the bar, but I think they're doing custom drink orders only," Emily mused. "I think we can rule them out. Charlie was drinking champagne, as was Darcie, from what we can tell."

"I agree," Emily said. "Better to focus our attention on the waitstaff and chefs. Let's see if any of them have anything to say for themselves."

Olivia and Emily headed to the lower levels where a cramped kitchen space was filled to the brim with employees. The change in temperature from outside sent a shockwave through Olivia's body. The sheer number of bodies was generating a lot of heat in the small space, creating a suffocating atmosphere. Olivia wondered if they'd been instructed to stay down there after what had happened, shooed away like servants in an old mansion house.

"Great working conditions," Olivia remarked as she glanced around the kitchen. There were three chefs, all of them huddled by the stoves on one side of the room, while the dozen members of the waitstaff grouped on the other end of the kitchen. There were still trays of champagne waiting to be taken out to the guests, but they'd been long abandoned now.

"Who do we want to speak with first?" Olivia murmured to Emily. Emily nodded toward the chefs.

"I think the chefs. They'll be the ones in charge of the kitchen. They should know what goes on around here."

Olivia nodded in agreement, so they approached the chefs. There were two women and a man, all of them very similar in looks, as though they were a family unit. They had the telltale dark hair of Italian heritage, and the women had sharp cheekbones and piercing eyes that made them intimidating to approach. However, it was the man, the eldest of the three, who folded his arms and gave them a disapproving look.

"Have you fixed the damn boat yet?" he snapped.

Olivia shook her head. "The captain is working diligently on it. I don't have any updates for you yet. We're still trying to find who killed Darcie Puckett."

He snorted. "Yes, yes, it's all very tragic. What does it have to do with us?"

"An innocent woman was murdered, *sir,*" Olivia spat, suddenly feeling rage boil up in her blood. "It would advantageous for you to cooperate with us if you want to clear your name."

The man's own eyes flared in anger, but one of the women grabbed his arm and held him back before he could explode on Olivia.

"Control it, Frank," she murmured.

Olivia wasn't worried, though. She took mental note of the chef's propensity for aggression and pressed on. "We're here because we need your help."

Frank took a few deep breaths and nodded. "Fine," he relented. "What does this have to do with my kitchen?"

"Hopefully nothing," Olivia said. "But we believe that the victim, as well as her boyfriend, may have been drugged. We know that they both drank from the same glass, and they both suffered from side effects afterward. The victim, who was not a big drinker, was said to be very out of it; and your boss, Charlie, claims he drank very little but still became very intoxicated. I've observed him, and he's clearly being affected by something far more potent than alcohol."

The chef glared at Olivia. "And what exactly are you suggesting?"

"We were hoping you might be able to shed some light on this. The glass that they both drank from came from the selection of champagne flutes served from your kitchen," Emily said. "And therefore, we believe that whoever drugged the victim and the host had access to this kitchen."

"I run a damn clean kitchen," the chef growled, glaring at them. "We don't have drugs here."

Olivia held back a sigh. The man's defensive attitude wasn't helping to speed the investigation along. "We're not placing the blame here, sir. We're simply interested to know whether you can tell us anything about the staff here. Or perhaps you saw something out of the ordinary. Whatever you can tell us, we'd appreciate it."

Frank considered this for a moment, his brow furrowed. He glanced over at the waitstaff, who appeared to be trying to eavesdrop on the conversation, but they looked away when they were caught.

"Honestly, I don't know how helpful I would be," he told them. "We're so busy down here in the kitchens we don't even get a chance to come up for air, let alone go up on deck."

Olivia could believe it. She didn't think that the chefs would even have had a chance to slip away from their workstations for any illicit activities, so she was sure they weren't the problem. Committing murder or trying to poison the guests would be too time-consuming for them, and their absence would be felt in the kitchen far too much. As far as she was concerned, they were in the clear.

"The waitstaff," one of the women said to Olivia in a lower voice. "We typically serve the parties ourselves, but during large events such as this, the waitstaff is contracted out. They don't work for us."

That made Olivia's eyebrows shoot up. Was there someone in the waitstaff with a grudge against Charlie? Could one of them have done it?

"Are there any of them you can vouch for?"

The woman nodded. "We have worked with some of them in the past, but as with anything, there is turnaround."

"Yes. Yes, she's right … the staff here come and go so often that we barely bother to remember their names," Frank added. "We have six new waiters tonight. All the others I can vouch for, but I don't know these new ones. They were brought in on a contract."

Olivia looked over to the group of waiters huddled in the opposite corner.

"Would you be able to point out the newer staff members to us?" she asked.

Frank nodded and squinted. "Those two on the left, the three in the chairs, and then that guy over in the corner by himself."

"Anything you can tell me about them?"

Frank shrugged. "I don't know, but … that man looks familiar to me. I'm sure. Maybe I've seen him before … maybe not. It's been a long night."

Olivia turned her gaze fully to the man Frank pointed out to her. And when her eyes landed on him, she instantly realized that she recognized him. He was the young waiter who had been staring at Charlie earlier that night, standing around instead of working. The same one who'd looked utterly shocked when she'd asked him for help. A coincidence, perhaps, but at this point, she wasn't given to believe in coincidences at all. She didn't want to dismiss anything that might be important.

"You," she said, nodding to him. "What's your name?"

"T-T-Tim," he stuttered. "I'm Tim Sweeney."

"Is this your first night working here?"

"It's his first night," Frank confirmed. "But like I told you before… he seems familiar to me. I can't place where I know him from though."

Olivia narrowed her eyes at Tim. She thought it was suspicious that the chef recognized him, given that she had singled him out earlier too. Intuition told her that he was the one they needed to speak to.

"Come with us, please."

"N-n-now?" Tim gasped. "Why me?"

"We just want to talk, Mr. Sweeney," Emily said reassuringly. "You'll be back here in no time."

Tim glanced around at his fellow staff members, but all of them were avoiding his eyes. It was as though they knew what had happened, but they weren't willing to say anything to support him. Tim swallowed and then followed Olivia and Emily out of the stuffy kitchen area. He was clearly nervous to speak to them, and Olivia wondered whether that was because had something to hide or whether he was just a nervous person. He was skinny and twitchy, and his eyes darted back and forth nervously. Was this their poisoner?

They took him up to the cabin and resumed their seats at the table. Tim stood close to the door, twitching anxiously. He'd hidden his hands in his sleeves like a child, and there were damp patches of sweat on his white shirt. He'd looked smart earlier in the night with his uniform, but now, he looked like a school boy who'd just been rejected at prom.

"Sit with us," Emily started, nodding to the seat opposite her. "We just want to have a little chat with you, that's all."

Tim hesitated a moment before sitting down with them. Olivia kept a steady eye on him, and he began to squirm under her gaze. She was sure if he was hiding something, it would be easy enough to break him and have him spill his secrets. He looked as though he might already be close to giving in.

"So, tonight is your first night working an event like this," Emily probed gently, "but some of the staff say that you look familiar. Did you know Charlie Evans before tonight? Is there a reason you came to work for him, or did the staff get it wrong?"

Tim swallowed. There was a bead of sweat on his forehead, and it trickled slowly down his face and over the bridge of his nose. He winced as it dripped off the end; he glanced up at the two women, his movements jittery and unpredictable.

"I… I don't know."

"You don't know whether you knew Charlie Evans before tonight? It's a straightforward question," Olivia said, feeling a little impatient. She could feel that he was holding back on them. She needed him to crack. Tim sniffed, avoiding their gaze.

"I… err… I knew him. He hired me for tonight."

"How did you know him before?"

"I… I… I used to work for Infinity," he stammered. "I was in IT."

"What the hell is an IT professional doing waiting tables on the yacht of his former boss?"

Tim looked struck by the implication of her question. "I needed the cash. I haven't worked for Infinity for a while. I… I think he forgot about me… but he had to let me go."

"He fired you from Infinity?"

"Not exactly," Tim struggled to say. "He let me go. He paid me a little to leave."

"Why?" Olivia pressed.

"I… I don't know. He just said he couldn't have me at the company any longer."

A lie, Olivia thought. This was all far too convenient. Her mind went back to the reports Emily had received of the grueling workplace culture at the company. She had no doubt that Charlie Evans had been a bad boss if his behavior elsewhere was any indication. But she didn't believe Tim's excuse for a second.

"It's time to be honest with us," Olivia said, staring him down. "Why did he make you leave?"

Tim gulped, his forehead beginning to sweat again. He looked down and sighed. "I took off work early a few times without permission. My mother is very sick. I was leaving early to take care of her and fudging my reports to make it look like I was at work. Eventually, it caught up to me. I've been just stringing jobs together ever since."

"So, what led you to working here tonight?"

The nervousness slipped, and the terror in his eyes turned into more of a sullen shame. Olivia felt a pang of sympathy for the man, but quickly had to shut it down. He could be their killer. While it was truly unfortunate that he'd been placed in this situation, she had to keep the pressure on to make sure his story checked out.

"I needed the money," he went on. "She has a very expensive, very difficult treatment, so I've been taking whatever jobs I can. I work during the day in tech support, and I wait tables at night, all in between taking care of Mom when I can. I heard about the party tonight, and I contacted him. I told him I'd do anything for a job, even waiting tables."

"And so, he hired you?"

Tim looked down, avoiding Olivia's gaze once again. "He laughed in my face," he admitted. "I told him who I was, what had happened… he'd forgotten about me entirely. And he laughed at me."

"He laughed at you?" Emily asked. Tim nodded glumly.

Olivia could see her taking pity. Yes, Charlie was cruel. Yes, it didn't surprise her that Charlie had acted so cruelly toward an employee who only cut work in order to care for his sick mother.

But Olivia also knew it gave him a motive. A motive to kill. Olivia stared right at Tim, watching him twitch, knowing there was more to the story than he was saying.

"But he still gave you the job tonight?"

Tim nodded. "He… he said that he could take a little pity on me. He said I could make myself useful."

"And you did, didn't you? When you slipped a drug into his drink."

Tim's eyes opened wide in horror. "What? I don't understand…"

"You understand me perfectly well. You put something in his drink tonight, didn't you? You knew you had access to the drinks, that you could hand one directly to him without risking someone else having it," Olivia said. "You were angry about what he did to you. And rightly so. So, you tried to humiliate him the way he humiliated you. You tried to hurt him, didn't you?"

He opened his mouth, then closed it, then opened it again, looking for all the world like a fish. "I—I…"

"You…?" she prompted.

Tim rubbed his eyes and finally looked up at them. "I didn't mean to hurt anyone."

"But you did have drugs on your person, didn't you? Drugs that you bought to slip into your former boss's drink."

"I just wanted to embarrass him—that's all!"

"But you didn't know what they were capable of, and you didn't expect Darcie to consume them too, which is why neither of them got really sick. They only took half a dose each, causing their erratic behavior and throwing them off balance. So, your plan didn't work, did it, Tim?"

"I didn't mean to!" Tim protested. "I just wanted to make him feel as bad as he made me feel. I didn't want anyone to get hurt, I swear to God! I didn't know those drugs would hurt anyone. I didn't think anyone would wind up dead…"

Olivia sat back in her seat, staring at Tim. He was falling apart right before her eyes, a complete mess of a man. He'd barely taken any convincing to give up the truth. But what was the full truth?

"Did you kill Darcie?"

"No!" Tim sobbed. "I didn't even know that she'd had any of the drink, I swear. Not until you told me… I thought someone else had thrown her overboard. But if she was sick… oh, God, that's my fault. Maybe if I hadn't done it, she might still be alive now. No, no, no…"

He put his head in his hands and groaned.

Olivia chewed the inside of her cheek. She was inclined to believe that he hadn't committed the murder, at least not intentionally. But it wasn't looking good for Tim. He'd essentially poisoned two of the guests and perhaps caused the death of one of them. Charlie was lucky he hadn't taken the full dose—Olivia was sure he would have wreaked all kinds of havoc for himself otherwise. But it still left her with more questions than answers. If Charlie was out of it because of the drugs, and Tim wasn't the killer… then who was?

"Did you see Darcie die?" Olivia asked darkly, but Tim just kept shaking his head, his body trembling and his voice merely a whimper now. Olivia could understand why he'd done what he'd done. Charlie had embarrassed him, had left him without work, and had disrespected him in more ways than one.

But it didn't explain anything. Here they were, with a man confessing that he'd spiked his former boss's drink, but it didn't make sense of anything else they knew. They still didn't have any idea who had hurt Darcie and pushed her off the railing into the sea, not to mention they still hadn't gotten any closer to their suspicions of corporate fraud that had started this whole thing. All they had confirmed was that Charlie had a vicious, cruel streak, and that Tim was stupid enough to not cover his tracks.

And yet his confession had come so easily. Olivia couldn't believe how quickly he'd given himself up. Was there more at play? Was she missing something? She wasn't sure. It was so late now, and she was beginning to lose focus of what was true and what wasn't. How were they supposed to find the truth in such a tangle of lies?

"I'm so sorry," Tim sobbed, rocking back and forward. Olivia sighed. She was going to have to place him under arrest for what he'd done. Her best hope was to somehow get out of him the truth about what had happened to Darcie, but she was becoming more doubtful by the minute. Tim wasn't there for Darcie; he was there for Charlie.

So, who had wanted Darcie dead?

CHAPTER EIGHTEEN

T HE ENGINE FINALLY ROARED BACK TO LIFE AT 1:30 A.M., and the guests aboard gave a half-hearted cheer. Olivia was on her third coffee in as many hours, staving off sleep until they made it to shore. As the *Astoria* began to make its way back to the harbor, she called for everyone to form a line and leave their names and details.

"Don't leave town. We may need to speak to any of you at any point," Olivia reminded them as the guests grudgingly offered up their contact details and flashed their IDs. Olivia was glad to already have one person in custody, but it wasn't much. Tim Sweeney would go down for what he'd done, but she knew that someone else onboard was likely the reason Darcie was dead.

It would be nice to believe that Tim had accidentally caused Darcie to fall from the boat and hit her head after she was drugged.

That would truly tie the whole case up neatly with a ribbon. But unfortunately, Olivia was almost certain that wasn't the case. Though she believed that Darcie's intoxicated state might have contributed to her death, she didn't for a second believe that she'd fallen overboard of her own accord. It just didn't add up. Which meant that when they got back to shore, a potential killer was going to walk away from them, at least temporarily.

But there was nothing that could be done. Not until Olivia and Emily had found more evidence. It would take a few days for them to get the autopsy of Darcie's body completed, as well as a thorough sweep of the yacht. Olivia wasn't sure what either investigation would find, if anything, but she hoped that things would be clearer once the searches were completed.

By the time they actually made it back to shore and everyone was disembarking, even the moon had set and the sky was covered in inky blackness. Olivia felt a sinking feeling in her chest, knowing that they hadn't caught the culprit yet. She reminded herself that it was rare for a case to be solved so quickly, but it felt like no matter how much she'd unearthed in her investigations, she still didn't have a clue what had happened to Darcie that night. She just wanted answers. She wanted justice. And if she couldn't get those things, then maybe she couldn't solve the mystery of Infinity either.

Olivia watched, arms folded, as each guest passed by her. Last of all was Charlie himself. He looked a little rough, but at least he was sober. He had his hands dug deep into his pockets as he sauntered off the deck.

"Good luck with your little investigation," he muttered. "If you think you're capable."

Olivia wasn't sure if he was referring to the murder investigation or the investigation into his company, but either way, her skin prickled at his tone. She was more determined than ever to solve both cases—and she'd do it quickly—before Charlie even had time to plant his stupid smirk back on his face.

Emily appeared with Tim Sweeney in tow a few minutes later. He was handcuffed, ready to be taken into custody for drugging Charlie Evans and Darcie Puckett. His face was mournful, like he actually regretted what he'd done, and Olivia believed him. But she also knew that anger drove people to do crazy things. Tim must have been pretty angry to practically poison someone, nearly killing two people.

"Let's get him down to the station. Then we can rest and recuperate," Olivia murmured to Emily. "It's been one hell of a night."

"It sure has," Emily replied with a yawn. "That's the first time I've been up past ten o'clock in a *long* time."

Olivia chuckled. She had to admit, despite the turbulence of the night, she'd enjoyed working the case with Emily. They were so often on the same wavelength that working in tandem felt easier than breathing. Brock was great, but he often had different ideas from Olivia, and that sometimes frustrated her more than she'd care to admit. Still, she felt a sharp pang in her chest at the thought of him. At least this case had been a welcome distraction from his absence... so far. She couldn't help wondering what he was doing, where exactly he was, and whether he was doing okay. She felt disconnected from him, like she'd been watching his life pan out on a TV screen and someone had suddenly just pulled the plug. She'd be glad when he was home and safe, and then at least things could go back to normal a little.

"Let's get a motel. I'm beat," Emily said as they made it back to the car. The local police had already carted Tim off to a holding cell for the night, and now that the adrenaline had subsided, both of them were running on fumes.

Olivia let out a yawn. She was much more tired than she'd thought. "Good idea. There's no point going back home. We'll have to talk to Tim again tomorrow."

"To ask him what?" Emily asked, a tinge of grumpiness in her tone as they clipped in their seatbelts. Olivia knew Emily well enough to know that she did not do well when she hadn't slept enough. "He already told us what happened. If he was going to tell the truth so easily, then surely he's told us everything we need to know, right? I don't know how much more we can get until the autopsy's done."

"I thought that... but there's got to be way more to his story than this," Olivia mused. "I don't think we've heard everything from him yet. Since he's the best lead we have, we might as well sit down with him and see what else we can find out."

By the time they checked in to the motel and got all situated, the sun was already starting to peek over the eastern horizon. Olivia groaned, pulled down the blackout curtain, and tried to force sleep to come.

The sun was already well into the sky when she woke up with a groggy feeling and a buzzy headache behind her eyes. A quick glance over at the clock confirmed it was already past noon. She sighed. *Too much coffee and not enough sleep... hello, old friend.*

She took a shower and threw on the extra set of clothes she usually kept in the car. Emily stirred not long after and got ready while Olivia poked around at the coffee maker.

"Back to instant coffee," she muttered. Over the last few months, Brock had finally broken her dependence on the stuff, insisting that if she was going to be downing a pot a day, she might as well invest in the fancy stuff. She'd hated to admit it, but he was right. She took a sip of the dusty old stuff and winced at the bitterness, wondering how she ever stood it in the first place.

Emily emerged from the bathroom looking tired, but ready to get started on their day.

"What a night," she groaned as she pulled on her clothes. "So... how are we going to handle this? We don't even have any leads other than Tim, and there's nothing indicating he even did it."

Olivia nodded. "He's our only lead as of now, though. We've at least got him for assaulting Charlie and Darcie. I don't get the feeling that he's a murderer, but I'm not sure how else to proceed from here. I just feel like there's some bigger picture we're missing."

"What if we press on where he got the drugs?" Emily offered. "And of course, we still don't know who left the anonymous tip at my apartment."

Olivia nodded. "Right. Which makes me think it's less likely to be Tim. He wouldn't have concocted this whole conspiratorial thing if his goal really was just to make Charlie Evans look like a fool on his big night. Somebody specifically wanted us there on the *Astoria*. They wanted us to see what happened. But why?"

Emily sighed. "Your guess is as good as mine."

Olivia chewed her lip for a moment. "This whole time… everyone we've spoken to has had nothing but wonderful things to say about Darcie. She was an amazing, kind, perfect angel. She spent her time volunteering, she pushed Charlie to get into charity, she was the kindest, sweetest, most beautiful soul you've ever met. And we met her ourselves; she was very nice. But are you thinking what I'm thinking?"

"Nobody could possibly be so perfect?" Emily supplied for her.

"Right. What if there's something in Darcie's past—something bigger than just the various men she'd been fending off—that could have led to this? Everyone has secrets… what were hers?"

"If you go and interview Tim, I can stay back and do a deep dive into our victim," Emily offered. "Social media accounts, backgrounds, previous associations… there's got to be something there we can follow up on."

Olivia nodded. "If you have time, would you mind looking more into some of our suspects as well? Charlie, Representative Atkins, all those we spoke to."

Emily nodded. "Absolutely."

When Olivia made it to the station, Tim was sitting on his bed with his arms wrapped around his knees. He looked almost glad to see Olivia for some reason, and Olivia wondered how the hell a guy like him was going to last in jail. After all, that was exactly where he was headed.

"Good afternoon, Tim. Do you feel like talking to me for a while?"

Tim nodded, almost a little too enthusiastically. Olivia spoke to one of the officers who agreed to let him out of the handcuffs. They headed to a small office room down the corridor where Olivia was allowed to conduct her interview. In sharp contrast to his completely nervous demeanor the previous night, Tim looked entirely too peppy for her liking. She would have to make sure to do something about that.

"Mr. Sweeney, I hope you know that what you've done is a serious crime," she began, threading her fingers together and placing them on the table. "No matter your intent, you drugged two people, which means that you possessed dangerous drugs in the first place, and then used them to harm."

"I didn't know what the drug would do," Tim replied, his eyes imploring. "I asked for something strong, something that would make the victim suffer. I didn't... I didn't think too hard about what that might mean. I really didn't."

"So, you still say that your intent wasn't to kill either Charlie Evans or Darcie Puckett?"

Tim shook his head fervently. "No, no, absolutely not. All I wanted was to teach him a lesson. To embarrass him the way he embarrassed me. And I took it too far, I know that. I made a horrible, horrible mistake. But I was thinking... if I tell you the source... if I tell you where I got the drug from... then I can get a reduced sentence, right?"

Olivia raised an eyebrow. "You're not here to make bargains, Tim. That's not how this works. You'll be lucky—very lucky—to get charged with anything less than attempted murder. But if you tell me what you know, that might help my decision."

Tim wavered. He clearly wasn't sure if it was worth revealing the information, but one glare from Olivia made him cower.

"Okay. Okay, I'll talk. But I just ask one favor. A phone call. Just one. That's what I'm supposed to be granted, right? Just one call?"

Tim swallowed anxiously. Olivia sighed, knowing he was entitled to it.

"All right, then. Make your call, and then we'll talk. One of the officers will supervise you."

"Thank you, thank you so much," Tim said, rising from his seat and rushing to the door. As the officer clapped the cuffs back on him and led him to make his call, Olivia wondered if she was wasting her time. She needed leads on Darcie's murder or Charlie's dubious company, not drug lords that doled out killer pills. But a lead was a lead, and for the sake of a little of her time, she was willing to wait and talk to Tim. After all, who knew? Perhaps he'd lead her straight back to one of her old cases or give her a lead that would topple an entire circle of criminals. It was worth a shot at least.

But Tim didn't return for some time. Olivia kept checking her watch, wondering what the hell he was up to. She knew he had his mother to take care of, so perhaps he was in contact with her, but he was wasting a lot of time. What the hell was taking so long?

When he eventually returned with his head bowed, Tim seemed different again. He was sullen, and his eyes carried a fear that hadn't been there before. Olivia studied his face, wondering what his deal was. She was certain there was something she was missing—something he wasn't willing to give up to her so easily.

And there was a question—why had he been so willing to tell her the truth? He hadn't even attempted to cover his own back, to lie to her, to pin his crimes on someone else. She had yet to meet many criminals who did that for no reason.

So, the real question was, whose back *was* he covering?

Tim cleared his throat, refusing to meet Olivia's gaze. He murmured something under his breath—something she didn't quite catch.

"Can you repeat that please, Tim?" she asked, leaning forward to hear what he was saying better. Tim finally looked up, forcing himself to meet Olivia's eyes. His voice trembled as he spoke.

"It was me. I killed Darcie Puckett."

CHAPTER NINETEEN

Why the hell would he confess?

OLIVIA KNEW THAT WHATEVER HAD HAPPENED DURING Tim's phone call had triggered him to confess, but something inside her told her that it couldn't be true. What motive did he have? He'd already told her that he intended to embarrass Charlie by drugging him, and that had nothing to do with Darcie.

And what's more, he couldn't explain to her how he'd done it. When Olivia pressed him for answers, he threw his hands up in the air and said, "I've given you my confession. What more do you want?"

She'd even pressed him to see if he wanted to wait until his lawyer was present, but Tim refused. He just kept repeating over and over. "I killed her. It was me. I killed her."

Olivia drove back to the motel to pick up Emily, who would be just as shocked as she had been about Tim's confession. Olivia was so sure that he was lying to her that she would have bet her life on it. It just didn't make any sense.

Whatever had happened while he was on the phone had caused Tim to turn his story around. Olivia knew she needed to investigate the call, but for the moment, Tim wasn't her problem. While he was safely tucked away in custody, she had no reason to keep an eye on him. What she needed now was to get out there and find out the truth.

Emily was waiting for her with their things outside the motel. She jumped quickly into the car and looked at Olivia expectantly as she drove off.

"How'd it go?"

"Well, I figured it would be like you said—that nothing much of interest was going to happen. But the weirdest thing happened."

"Oh?"

"At first, he was pressing hard for a deal. He said he'd tell me where he got the drugs in exchange for immunity. And then he changed his tune and said he wanted to make a phone call instead. I thought he was going to contact a lawyer or something. But the second he came back from the phone call, he confessed to everything. Not just to drugging Charlie, but to killing Darcie."

"*What?* How is that possible?"

"The thing is… I don't believe him. He probably didn't even know Darcie. He worked for Charlie for years, before he was even dating Darcie. It doesn't make sense for him to want her dead."

Emily chewed her lip. "Maybe it was part of his revenge plan? Hit Charlie where it hurts and kill the person he loves the most?"

"Maybe. None of this really makes sense," Olivia began, "and I don't know if he's smart enough to pull it off. He wouldn't explain to me *how* he killed Darcie, and I'm pretty sure his story won't add up regardless. I'll have to check over eyewitness statements and see if we can place him on the scene, but I'm sure we'll draw a blank. And besides... he's already told us his version of the truth in full. Why would he then refuse to tell us how he killed her? Something isn't right. We need to keep digging."

"Should we really be focusing on this? If we have a confession, then it's technically case closed. And remember… we're supposed to be trying to figure out what Charlie has been up to at Infinity."

"This is a murder case, Emily. We can't just assume we have the answers until we have real proof. I'm not giving up until we do," Olivia said, gripping the steering wheel hard. "I got in contact with Darcie's family on my way to pick you up. They said they'd be willing to speak with us. They're in town to identify the body anyway, so they've agreed to meet us at the station to talk."

"Alright. Let's give it a few more days," Emily conceded. "But then we need to get back on track."

Olivia nodded. "I know. I just… I don't like the idea of leaving this case as it is. Something is very wrong, and I can't quite put my finger on it. If we can just find that one missing piece, I'm convinced everything will fall into place."

"I sure hope so."

They drove in silence the rest of the way. Olivia wasn't sure if she was imagining it, but she thought Emily seemed a bit off with her. Was she in over her head with this murder case? Was she upset that they still hadn't gotten any farther into uncovering the financial crimes Infinity was suspected of? Olivia couldn't be sure without asking her directly, but it didn't seem like the time or the place to spark that conversation.

Olivia knew she could be headstrong—especially recently. It had been a long time since she had felt so strong, so sure of herself, and she was finally finding her feet again. She didn't like the idea of not following her hunches or speaking up about what she believed in. But she also didn't ever want to undermine Emily or make her feel like she was treating her as someone lesser. Emily was one of the smartest people she knew, and she wondered whether she'd ever truly appreciated that. Olivia hoped that Emily knew just how much she respected her. When they had a minute to talk, she'd make sure to tell her.

The back room where Olivia had agreed to meet Darcie's mom and sister was quiet when they arrived. It was a small area like a living room, with a few couches and a coffee table arranged in a circle. Olivia presumed it was used in situations exactly like this—interviewing people in a comfortable, private environment rather than in the harsh coldness of an interrogation cell.

She recognized both of them right away. Darcie's younger sister was the spitting image of her, and their mother was just like an older version of them both. Both of them had the same signature fire-red hair cascading down their shoulders, and both of them appeared to be swallowing back tears. Olivia and Emily approached them respectfully, offering their hands for a handshake.

"Special Agents Olivia Knight and Emily Boyd," Olivia said solemnly. "We're so sorry for your loss, Ms. Puckett."

The older of the two women nodded. "Thank you," she whispered. She took a deep, shaky breath, as if barely pulling herself back from the precipice of a breakdown, and finally looked up at Olivia. Her eyes were the same brilliant, verdant green as her daughter's, but they were rimmed red with tears. It was obvious that she'd been crying all morning.

"Can I offer you anything?" Emily asked. "Water? Tea?"

"Some water would be great," she rasped. Emily nodded to Olivia, who immediately got up and walked over to the fridge on one side of the room. She pulled two bottles out and set them on the table for the Pucketts.

They were silent for a few moments. Olivia wanted to give Carla and Rosie the chance to speak first. Rosie, Darcie's younger sister, swallowed, her eyes on her lap.

"Must have been some party you went to," she whispered. "I always told her to stay away from those people. I knew that one day she'd wind up in trouble. I just… I never thought… I never thought we'd get a call saying that she'd been murdered."

"It's awful," Emily said gently. "Do you think you could explain to us what you mean? You said that you knew she'd wind up in trouble… what gave you that impression?"

Carla sighed. "Darcie was always so social. She'd always go out dancing, out finding adventures, making new friends… sometimes she'd find herself surrounded by the wrong crowd. When she started dating Charlie… well, it's safe to say that neither

I nor Rosie approved. We warned her. We said that a cocky man like him wasn't worth the trouble. But she never listened."

"So, you disapproved of Charlie?" Olivia asked. Rosie scoffed.

"That's an understatement," Rosie said with deep contempt in her voice. "Darcie knew how we felt about him. As far as we were concerned, it would take a lot to welcome him into our family."

"Absolutely not. That boy reminded me so much of their good-for-nothing father," Carla added with a sniff. "He wasn't worth her time, but I guess she was enticed by the fact that he was rich and he spoiled her rotten. That's not how I raised her to be... but we can all be enticed by shiny things, can't we?"

Olivia nodded in understanding. She could see how Darcie might have been drawn into the world of beautiful people—a world of money and fame and constant gratification. She never wanted for anything with Charlie at her side.

Except perhaps for happiness.

"Do you have any idea who could have done this to her?" Olivia prodded. "Anyone she might have had a bad history with? An ex-boyfriend, perhaps?"

Carla shared a glance with Rosie, who shook her head. "I can't think of anyone," she said. "Darcie was so kind to everyone. She wouldn't have hurt a fly."

Olivia nodded. "So I've heard," she said. It was typical for family and friends to believe that their loved one was a perfect angel, but this was beginning to feel like a broken record. Was Darcie truly the kind, generous person everyone said she was? "I actually had a chance to meet her. Before..." she cleared her throat. "She was friendly and kind. It seemed like she was destined for great things."

"She was," Carla nodded, tears welling up in her eyes. "She really was."

Olivia looked over at Rosie. The young woman's face held just as much pain and grief as her mother's, but there was something else there too. Something like a secret she was trying to prevent from bursting out. She was staring off into the distance, like she wasn't really there at all.

"Rosie?"

"Hmm?" She blinked and came back to reality.

"Is there anything that you could tell me… maybe any secrets that Darcie confided in you? Something she might not have told your mom?"

"You can't ask me to break my own sister's trust," she said, almost pleading with Olivia. "That's not fair."

"I know, and I'm so sorry. But we need your help to solve this case if we want to get justice for her."

Rosie held her breath and looked nervously between her mother and Olivia, but still didn't say anything. With no other card to play, Olivia took a deep breath and decided to pry open the vault that she typically kept locked down in a case like this. It would hurt, she knew. But there was no other choice—and they were running out of time.

"I know exactly how you feel, Rosie," she finally said. "My… five years ago, my own sister was murdered. I miss her every day, even now."

The two women stared at her with rapt attention as if captured by her confession.

"If I'd known that—that I'd never see Veronica again, there's so many things I would've done differently," Olivia went on. "And for years, I told myself… if there was something, anything I could have done to find out who did that to her, I'd have done it. But I didn't know. I was in the *FBI*, and I felt completely powerless to help the investigation. It wasn't until just a few months ago that the case finally closed. We found new evidence and took down the killer. And that's why I'm asking you now, Rosie. I don't want it to take five years to get justice for your sister. I don't want you to have to suffer the way I did. I want to help. It's the least I can do, for Darcie. So please. If there's anything…"

Now the dam broke; both Carla and Rosie were staring at her with tears flowing down their cheeks. Olivia was barely holding back her own, too.

Rosie wiped her face and nodded. She looked back up at Olivia, a new light of determination in her eyes.

"I don't know if this will help, but… it might be something," she started. "She told me to keep it a secret, but I guess it doesn't matter now."

"What was it?"

"I think she was seeing someone else. Someone she'd met through Charlie's circles, but not a business guy. She said he was just an ordinary guy. He was sweet and funny and made her laugh, which Charlie certainly never did."

Olivia raised an eyebrow. She wasn't shocked at the revelation that Darcie was having an affair, given all that she'd heard, but she was certainly interested to know who the mystery man was. If she'd decided to tell her sister about him, then he must have been important.

"She strayed from Charlie?"

"Charlie's a bad guy," Rosie said defensively. "He was a womanizer from the beginning. He cheated on her more than once, and I think after a while, she decided to give him a taste of his own medicine. I don't think she intended to start a real affair, but then feelings got involved."

"Do you know the name of this guy?"

Rosie shook her head slowly. "No. She was very private about it. I guess she wanted to make sure that her secret stayed a secret."

"Would it have been Bishop?" Emily asked. "I understand the two of them were very close."

Rosie shook her head and gave a slight chuckle through a sob. "No… they dated a little in middle school, but that never worked out because Bishop found out he's gay."

Olivia's eyebrows raised. That was somewhat of a surprise but made sense, considering his interview.

"But if anyone will know who the guy is, it's Lucy," Carla added. "She tells Lucy everything. Even the stuff she refused to talk to us about."

Olivia nodded. It made sense that Lucy might have known about the affair, though she hadn't mentioned it during her interview. Was she respecting her dead best friend's privacy? Or was there another reason she'd hidden the affair from Olivia and Emily?

"I think we need to give Lucy a call," Emily said. Olivia nodded. If the affair was confirmed, then Olivia had yet another motive for Charlie to have killed Darcie. Or perhaps the man involved in the affair had a part to play in his lover's demise…

"Is there anything else you can think of? Anything at all?" Emily asked.

Both women shook their heads, their red hair dancing back and forth in tandem.

Olivia smiled gently at Carla and Rosie and handed them her card. "Thank you for your time. If there's anything at all I can do, please let me know. Once again, we're very sorry for your loss."

"Thank you, agents," Carla said, but she was already looking far off into the distance, like she was numb to what had happened. Rosie stood up and helped her mother to her feet, and the two of them leaned on each other as they shuffled out to the hallway. They needed each other. Olivia knew all too well how it would turn out if they didn't have each other for support.

She was already pulling up Lucy's contact information on her phone when a voice got her attention.

"Agent Knight?"

She turned back to see Rosie lingering in the doorway. "Yes?"

"Does… does it ever get any easier? Losing her?"

Olivia took a deep breath. "I… to tell the truth, I don't know if it does. All I know is you can only take it one day at a time."

Rosie nodded and turned away.

Emily placed a sympathetic hand on Olivia's shoulder. "You okay?"

Olivia sighed and shook the emotion out of her head. "Yeah. I'm okay."

On a certain level, she wouldn't ever really be okay, but right then, she had to be. Because she still had a killer to hunt down.

Olivia punched Lucy's number into the phone. She picked up almost immediately, as though she had been waiting for the call.

"Lucy, you're on speaker," she announced.

"Have you found anything yet?" Lucy asked desperately in place of a greeting.

"Maybe. I'm going to need you to be fully honest with me, Lucy. I know you're a loyal friend and that you likely didn't tell us this to protect Darcie's memory… but I need to know the truth. Was Darcie having an affair? Was she going to leave Charlie Evans for someone else?"

Lucy was quiet for a moment on the other end of the line. She drew in a small breath. "Yes," she said after a moment. Olivia nodded.

"All right. And can you tell us who the man involved was, please? It might be important."

Lucy swallowed. "I don't want to get anyone in trouble…"

"This could be a lead to our killer, Lucy," Emily chimed in. Olivia was surprised that she was participating so enthusiastically in the interrogation but grateful for it. "We need anything you can give us."

Lucy sighed. "His name is Harry. He works on the *Astoria*. I think Charlie was starting to suspect their relationship… but I'm not sure. Darcie didn't tell me much."

Olivia shook her head. She'd known there was more to Darcie's relationship with Harry than he had let on when she spoke to him. And now, his fight with Charlie only made more sense.

What Olivia didn't know was what had happened after Harry left the room, leaving Charlie and Darcie to their argument. Had Charlie become aggressive and done something to hurt her? Olivia recalled the bruising on Darcie's wrist, like someone had grabbed her hard. Was it Charlie who had done that to her? Or was she still missing a piece of the puzzle?

"I appreciate you being honest with us, Lucy. Is there anything else you haven't told us?"

"No, I swear. I'm sorry I didn't say anything. I wanted to, but I didn't want to betray Darcie. And Harry's a good guy, too. I didn't want to throw him under the bus and get him in trouble with Charlie."

Not for the first time, Olivia furrowed her brow in frustration. What was with all the secrets? All the lies? Why wouldn't anyone just tell the whole truth?

Lucy paused. "Between you and me, I don't trust Charlie. I never liked him much, and the things Luke has told me about him… he's not a good person. I don't know whether he would ever hurt Darcie. But if he did … I don't think I would be shocked."

Olivia sighed. "Okay. Thank you, Lucy. I appreciate your time."

"Please let me know when you find something. I'm driving myself insane waiting for news. I just… I just want justice."

"I know," Olivia replied. "Me too."

Olivia ended the call with a deep sigh. So, if Harry and Darcie were having an affair, then that changed Harry's significance in the investigation.

"How the plot thickens," Emily said. "The bosun."

Olivia nodded. "I thought something was up with his story. It doesn't shock me in the slightest, but it does mean that we need to talk to him again. He might not have lied directly, but he failed to tell us what was really going on with him and Darcie… which means that he might be hiding other things from us. If we want answers, he's our next stop."

"Then let's go," Emily said, nodding to the door.

"Let's."

They met with Harry at the dock, close to where the *Astoria* was moored. It was still cordoned off with police tape; as the analysts scoured every inch of the ship, Harry watched them with detached interest. He seemed like he was very far away, right up until the moment when Olivia tapped his shoulder to get his attention. He turned to her with a sad smile.

"Good afternoon," he said with a timid nod. He looked like he hadn't slept in a long time, and Olivia found herself taking pity on him. But then she reminded herself that he had lied to her in a murder investigation. He wasn't someone she should be feeling sorry for.

"Do you know why we're here?" Olivia asked him pointedly, hoping to coax some information out of him without having to poke too hard. Harry dug his hands deep into his pockets and fought off a sigh.

"I can guess. I suppose someone told you that Darcie and I were having a secret affair?"

"Something like that."

Harry smiled ever so slightly and nodded. His gaze turned to the floor. "It's true. We were together. Or at least, I wanted us to be. I never really knew where Darcie stood on the whole thing. She told me she loved me, and yet she stayed with Charlie. And just when I thought we were finally getting somewhere… someone snatched her life away."

He paused, wiping a tear from his cheek. "I loved her. She's the only woman I've ever loved. And I don't think I can forget a woman like her in a hurry." He blinked several times. "I did lie a little to you. Not just about the affair, but about the problem with the engine…"

Olivia's eyes flared. "You *what?*"

"It's my fault the engine wouldn't start. I was the one who sabotaged it from the beginning."

Olivia was apoplectic. "You sabotaged your own ship? And let me guess, you never called in the Coast Guard either."

His entire body cringed, and he looked deflated. "No, I didn't. Don't tell the captain. Or Mr. Evans. But I just… it seemed like a good idea at the time."

"You have one chance to explain yourself, Harry," she growled. "I've already made one arrest in this case, and I don't mind making more."

He nodded nervously and licked his lips. "It's just… I figured that if we were stranded out there, then the killer wouldn't be able to get away. I happened to be checking the engine anyway when you made your big announcement, and I thought… well… the only way to stop them from getting away was to keep them on board. I was just trying to help."

Olivia closed her eyes and took a deep breath. She gestured for him to continue.

"So, I cut the engines and pretended like the problem was something very hard to fix. No one had any reason to doubt me, considering I'm the expert. I stalled for as long as I could. But as the night went on, I began to realize it wouldn't be so simple. I knew that it wasn't a problem that would be solved overnight, that you needed extra help to try and figure out what happened to Darcie… and so I switched the engines back on and got us back to shore."

"You're damn lucky that I'm not going to bring you up for obstruction of justice," Olivia growled. "What the hell were you thinking? We could have found evidence much quicker if you hadn't pulled that stunt. We could have used the Coast Guard's help."

Harry gulped. "You're... not going to charge me?"

"I haven't made my decision yet," she told him. "Are you going to cooperate?"

He nodded fervently. "I've told you everything I know. I swear, this is the truth. I don't know whether I did a bad thing or not... but I only did it out of love for Darcie. And I figured that none of that was important to your investigation, so I left it out. I'm sorry. I should have been more honest. But I guess I'm not thinking clearly. Love and a broken heart do funny things to your head."

Olivia handed him her card. "Stay in town. We'll be in touch later."

"We're so sorry for your loss," Emily added gently. "Thank you for telling the truth."

"I hope it helps," Harry said glumly. His gaze returned to the moored yacht, the place where he'd lost everything. As Olivia and Emily walked away, Olivia felt a pang in her heart for him, despite her anger at him.

"Poor guy," Emily said, voicing Olivia's thoughts. "I think maybe he got a raw deal out of this thing with Darcie... I guess affairs never end well."

Olivia nodded. "You can say that again. But this leaves us at another dead end. If Charlie knew about the affair, as we suspect he did, it strengthens his motive. But until we get some more evidence, we don't have enough to charge him."

"Let's hope the analysis from the *Astoria* gives us some more information," Emily said. "Where to next? I hope you have some ideas."

Olivia chewed her lip. "There's only one other person that I think had a strong enough motive to want her dead."

"Congressman Atkins."

Olivia nodded. "I wouldn't mind having another word with him. I want that awful man to know that I'm on to him. Even if he didn't kill her, he certainly did something bad. If I can prove what he was up to, I can bring him down too."

A small smile showed up on Emily's face. "Then let's take him down."

"Really?"

"Absolutely," Emily nodded. "I'm so sick of all these gross men trying to mess with women's lives and getting away scot-free. Trying to force a woman to have sex with him so that she could keep her job? It's disgusting. I want to see him fall from grace."

Olivia smirked. "Me too. Wanna pay him a little visit?"

"I think we have to. We've got some time to kill while they process the scene. Might as well spend it taking down a scumbag like him."

They grinned at one another as they set off for Olivia's car. The tension she'd imagined between them seemed to have gone completely. As she started up the engine, she reached out and squeezed her best friend's hand.

"I'm so glad we're doing this together," Olivia said. Emily smiled back.

"Me too. Now, hit the road. We've got some politicians to mess with."

CHAPTER TWENTY

ONGRESSMAN ATKINS HAD INSISTED ON MEETING IN A public place, which Olivia didn't mind. What she did mind was that he had picked one of the swankiest restaurants in Virginia Beach—the kind of place where food portions were tiny and the prices were high. Olivia was sure that he'd picked it to make her squirm, to make her back off when she realized that she'd be footing the bill. But Olivia was willing to throw a few hundred dollars at getting the answers she wanted. It even gave her a chance to wear her nice dress again.

When Olivia and Emily arrived at the restaurant, David Atkins was already waiting for them at their table. He offered them a smug smile as they sat down in silence, not bothering to make any small talk with him. Olivia appraised the menu, but she could barely concentrate with such an awful man sitting across from her. She didn't want to be in his presence any longer than she needed to be, but if it took her all night to shake some answers out of him, then she was willing to wait. After all, she had nowhere better to be.

With wine and food ordered, Representative Atkins stared down the two women. He sat opposite them as though at an interview. Olivia nodded to the empty chair beside him.

"No Rebecca tonight?" she asked. He smirked.

"Let's just say, she won't be joining me for dinners any longer. We've mutually decided to part ways."

"How sad," Emily said, and Olivia almost laughed out loud at the sarcasm in her voice. It was unlike Emily to be that way, but she was enjoying seeing the sassier side of her friend. Atkins sniffed.

"Yes, well, these things happen. Especially when you discover you can't trust your own wife."

"Are you sure it wasn't the other way around?" Olivia asked with a raised eyebrow. She leaned closer to the congressman. "Don't play us for fools, Mr. Atkins. We have all heard about your little proposition to Darcie. You tried to force her into a sexual relationship with you."

Atkins's expression didn't waver for even a moment. "It can hardly be described as *forcing* someone if they have a choice. I simply asked her if she'd like to take our relationship to the next level."

"That's not what we heard," Olivia fired back, glaring at him. "You tried to force her to have sex with you in order to keep her job."

Atkins scoffed at her. "That's quite an accusation you've made there, Agent Knight. It's like I said. There's no law against two consenting adults having sexual intercourse."

"There is if it was a condition of continuing her employment with you," Emily said. There was an edge to her tone indicating she was ready to snap at any moment. Atkins scowled at her.

"I think you'd better be more careful about what you're saying. I would hate for there to be consequences in your career for speaking to me like this. If you dare go public…"

"*Dare* to?" Olivia cut in, her eyebrows raised. "If you have nothing to hide, then a little public slander wouldn't do you any harm, would it? I think you're scared of what we might say, congressman, because you know that we know the truth."

Atkins said nothing, chewing the inside of his cheek. Olivia knew that he was guilty of that much, at least. There was no way he could deny it. He sipped his wine, keeping a steady eye on Olivia.

"I know the law," he said darkly. "And I know my rights. You've got nothing on me. Nothing at all."

"Oh, but that's not true at all," Olivia replied, her voice equally sharp. "You see, I know the law pretty well too. You may look at us like a couple of young women, not so different from Darcie… but we're agents of the *Federal Bureau of Investigation*. We're not just here to ask questions and blindly believe whatever you feel like telling us. We're a lot smarter than you're giving us credit for. We know how you view women. We know you think we're all just pawns in your game. But we're not. We're players too. And with every single word you say, we're getting closer to our answers. And if you want to play dirty… then we will too."

Atkins had the sense to look a little afraid. Out of the corner of her eye, Olivia could see that Emily had the barest shadow of a smile on her face. Olivia leaned back in her chair, keeping her gaze steady on the congressman.

"It's a little convenient that the woman you tried and failed to entice turned up dead very shortly after she rejected you," Olivia pressed. "Very convenient that you're talking about divorcing your wife when she finally had the guts to stand up to you. I'll bet she has all sorts of secrets she'd be willing to tell us. And after the way you've treated her over the years, no doubt she'll be very forthcoming. So maybe you'd like one last chance to tell the truth before we find it out from someone else."

Atkins was squirming in his seat. Olivia stared him down, determined to make him as uncomfortable as possible. He finally tore his gaze away from her.

"I'm not a killer," he snapped. "I'm just a man. A man who wanted something and didn't get it. Is that a good enough answer for you?"

"Tell us what you did," Emily snarled. "Tell us what you did to Darcie."

"Nothing," he hissed. "I told her that if she wanted to continue her employment, then she would consider my proposition… but that was all. I didn't lay a hand on her. I didn't try to force myself on her, or grab her, or anything like that. But she was practically begging for it, the little flirt. All this time she's been sucking up to me, getting me to take her to all the expensive places in town, trying to get on my good side. And then when I finally gave in to her, she acted like *I* was the one who was out of line. How the hell do you explain that one, agents? It's not my fault that the girl was a slut."

Olivia didn't react at all. She knew exactly how Atkins would respond to the accusations. He'd pin it all on the young, ambitious woman who dared to dream of having a career. He'd blame it on her good looks, her irresistibility, her audacity to be so nice to him.

Olivia knew that their victim wasn't perfect. No one was. She knew that she'd had affairs, been unfaithful to her partner, flirted her way through life, and left a trail of broken hearts behind her. But that didn't mean that she'd asked to be propositioned by a much older man as a condition of her employment. That didn't mean that she'd asked to be mistreated, to be threatened, to be humiliated. Even if the congressman wasn't a killer, he was a bad man. Olivia could see that in him from the beginning. And now, with his full confession laid out in front of him, she might not have found her killer, but she had taken this man down a few notches.

"How gracious of you to be so honest with us," Olivia said quietly. "We're so pleased that you finally had the guts to tell the truth. What you did was illegal, congressman. And now that we know the truth, we'll have grounds to open up an official investigation into your office for practices of sexual harassment. And when the media gets ahold of that…"

It was at that moment that the food arrived. Atkins stared at his plate in horror, completely thrown off by their takedown of him. Emily picked up her knife and fork.

"Mmm. This looks great," she announced, as though their entire conversation hadn't just happened. Olivia dug into her food too.

"Makes a change from diner food," she said with a smile. Emily and Olivia devoured their meals while the Congressman sat blankly staring at the table, unable to eat a single bite. The moment Olivia and Emily were finished, they stood up from the table and called over a waitress.

"He'll handle the bill tonight," Olivia said with an enigmatic smile. She glanced back at Atkins. "We'll see you in court, congressman. Enjoy your luxuries while you can. You won't have them around much longer."

Olivia and Emily threaded their arms through each other's and left the fancy restaurant behind, riding the high of their success. Sure, they still didn't have their killer, but they had a win. Olivia couldn't stop smiling. She glanced over at the marina and felt a tug at her heart.

This one was for you, Darcie, she thought.

The following morning, Olivia was up and raring to go early on. Emily took a little more convincing to get out of bed, but once they were both up, they had plenty to discuss.

"All right, so still no results from the lab, but I do have a few leads we can chase down," Emily announced. "Last night I couldn't sleep, so I went searching online for some leads, digging into the backgrounds of all our players here. Social media was mostly a dry well, but I did find something worth pursuing."

"Please be good news," Olivia implored.

Emily turned her laptop to show Olivia the page she'd kept open since the night before. "I found an anonymous forum for people to vent about any person, place, or thing that reaches their ire. As you can imagine, a lot of the content is… pretty predictable, given the way the Internet is. But there is a surprising amount of content on the site that isn't necessarily extremely racist or horrible."

"Well, that's good," Olivia said.

"Look here at all these posts about Charlie Evans and Infinity over the last few months," Emily went on. "It's under a username that doesn't give away the identity of the person, but I think the person posting might have been Tim. It's a safe bet, given how angry he was. And the dates of the posts seem to line up with when he would have left the company."

"Okay... so what do these posts tell us?"

"Well, for one, that his anger was directed at Charlie only. He didn't seem to have any quarrel with Luke or any of the other directors and higher-up employees. He took it personally, and he blamed Charlie. Look, it says here... *Charlie Evans is a low-life scumbag who only cares about money, money, money. He has no interest in protecting the rights of his employees. In fact, if he had it his way, we'd all be slaves to him.*"

"Damn. He really hates him, doesn't he?" Olivia said, raising an eyebrow. Emily nodded.

"Like I said, he's particularly fixated on Charlie. Which means he could have wanted to lash out at Charlie by hurting the woman he loved. And he has confessed as such. But none of it lines up with his first statements at all," Emily said.

"Is that so unusual in this case?" Olivia pointed out. "I'm starting to feel like nobody told the truth in their first statements."

She knew Emily was on to something though. Something had changed when Tim had taken that phone call. His whole story had turned on a dime, and now he was confessing to a murder, when before he'd been so adamant about the fact that he'd only meant to drug Charlie that he'd been willing to take a deal to give up his drug dealer.

"We know that he didn't mean to drug Darcie at all, right?" Emily asked. "The glass was meant for Charlie, and she happened to drink half of it. But he'd pre-planned everything else that night. Why suddenly change directions and kill her when he realized she was so intoxicated? It just doesn't make sense."

Olivia considered it and nodded. "I think you're right. But therein lies the issue. He's made a confession. If he's covering for someone, he has to have a good reason why. Maybe someone has something on him or has threatened him." She tapped her lip with the pen she was holding in her hand. "We need to figure out who he spoke to on the phone. Before he made that call, he was just about ready to tell me everything. He seemed to think there was plenty in it for him if he did, so why backtrack?"

"Because whoever he spoke to on the phone told him to," Emily concluded. "So, it must be someone who has power over him … and probably someone he trusts."

"Let's go down to the station and talk to him. We can try and figure out if the online account actually belongs to him. And then we can go through the call logs and see who he called."

Olivia and Emily headed straight to the station to get answers. When they arrived, Tim was looking a little worse for wear. He was rocking back and forth in the holding cell, just like last time, and he'd clearly had another sleepless night. He looked away when Olivia showed her face.

"I have nothing more to say at this time," he said, as though he'd rehearsed it. Olivia frowned and showed him the screenshots she'd taken of the forum.

"That's your right. But since you've already apparently confessed, you've got nothing to lose here. We're curious to know if this account belongs to you, under the username *AngryMobInfinity*. Sound familiar?"

Tim said nothing for a moment. "No comment," he added eventually. Olivia let out an irritated sigh.

"This isn't the time to be playing games with us, Tim. We're trying to get to the bottom of this. A woman is dead."

"I know. I killed her."

"I don't believe you."

Tim shrugged, his back turned to her in his cell. Olivia felt unnaturally angry. Tim's confession was the one thing holding them back. She was so close to the truth, she could sense it. She knew if they could just break down Tim's lie and get beyond it, they would finally have some answers.

"Tim. You've got to be honest with us."

He whirled around on them. "I am being honest with you. It was my drugs that got into her system. And after that, it was all too easy to throw her off the side."

"But why would you ever do that?"

Tim opened his mouth to say something, but nothing came out. He turned his back on Olivia again and slumped his shoulders. "No comment."

Olivia was certain he was lying to her. That was the only explanation. And yet there was no way to force the truth out of him. If he never spoke to her again, it still wouldn't change a thing for him. He was going to prison regardless. He didn't need to be honest with them now. Whatever his reasons were for hiding the truth, he clearly wasn't budging.

And that was going to be enough to ruin everything.

Olivia was about to say something else when her phone rang. She sighed and picked up the call quickly.

"Agent Knight here."

"This is Dr. Lee at the ME's office. You should come and see us. We have some information from the autopsy and the crime scene analysis that might interest you."

Olivia shared a glance with Emily, and without another word, they turned out of the cell and left Tim behind.

CHAPTER TWENTY-ONE

A S SOON AS OLIVIA AND EMILY ENTERED THE DOORS OF the Virginia Beach Medical Examiner's Office, they were greeted by Dr. Mara Lee, the head crime scene investigator on the case who was waiting for them in the lobby. She was a slight woman with short bobbed hair and glasses. She wore a white lab coat over a simple shirt and pants, but she somehow managed to make the whole ensemble look classy. She smiled as she shook Olivia and Emily's hands.

"Thanks for coming so quickly. With any luck, I'll have something useful for you," Mara said, a sympathetic tilt to her voice. "Follow me."

They followed her down a few hallways and entered a back room that looked like every other morgue Olivia had ever been in. Everything was sterile, white, and clean. She supposed it would feel odd for things to be bright and colorful when dealing with such morbid subjects.

Mara led them over to the table where Darcie's body lay. It was always difficult seeing a victim of a murder, but Olivia felt sad for the young woman on the table in particular. She had so much going for her, so much to live for. She looked quite different under the harsh, cold fluorescent lights. Her face was bruised beyond recognition and stained with blood. Mara caught Olivia looking and nodded to her.

"Yes, as you can see, it was quite a bump to the head she received. I have determined that as the cause of death. However, I don't believe that a weapon was used to cause this damage. I think the head trauma was caused by her head hitting the hull. We found traces of her blood on a railing. We believe that she fell from one of the higher decks, tumbled over, and crashed her head on the metal railing below, which instantly cracked her skull. There was no water in her lungs, meaning she was dead before she hit the water."

"Jesus," Olivia murmured. She thought back to the heavy splash she'd heard.

"So, if she hit her head on the way down... then she could have fallen in by herself?" Emily asked.

"I think it's likely that she was pushed. To get a hit like that to her head, I think there had to have been some momentum behind her, more than her simply tripping and falling over the railing. She has some bruising to her ribs, too, which makes it look as though she was pushed violently, possibly into the railing on the upper level. Perhaps then she toppled over, but again, I think she might have been pushed a second time, simply judging by how hard she must have hit her head on the way down."

"So, whoever did it didn't just attack her once and then regret it," Olivia mused. "It wasn't just a spur of the moment that they tried to backtrack on. They pushed her and then pushed her again to finish the job."

"That would be my guess," Mara said, nodding solemnly. "But it seems that she was subjected to quite a lot of violence that night. In addition to the bruising to her ribs and the head trauma, you'll notice that she was clearly grabbed several times. Not only is there bruising around her wrist, but there also appears to be some bruising to her upper arm, as though someone grabbed her there and whirled her around. I don't know what kind of trouble your victim was in, but it seemed like she might have been on the receiving end of some serious abuse."

Olivia thought back to Charlie and his undeniable anger. She certainly thought he was capable of grabbing her hard. And then she thought about the Congressman. He'd been clear to state that he hadn't laid a hand on her; but he'd lied before, and he could lie again. Maybe there were people she hadn't even thought of yet who were willing to lay hands on Darcie to get what they wanted from her… she certainly seemed like she had been a woman in demand.

"What about the rest? Did you check the drugs in her system?"

Mara nodded. "I did. It was a match for the drug that Charlie Evans also consumed. I'm not exactly sure what it is—it's not anything common, that's for sure. We're running some further tests at the lab. But whatever it was, I think it would have had quite an effect on her body. I imagine that it would have made her feel woozy, almost as though she were drunk, but it might have had other effects too. Often, powerful drugs can enhance feelings of anger or sometimes even amplify sexual impulses. It's possible that the drug played a part in what happened to her."

Emily nodded. "Maybe she spoke differently to the killer than she might have normally. Her inhibitions were lowered, and she told him her true thoughts."

"Not exactly an excuse to kill someone though," Olivia said stiffly. "Although I've had similar theories all along. I think maybe the fact that she was intoxicated influenced the killer. But then again, we've been assuming this was pre-planned. We had an anonymous tip telling us that something might happen at the party, after all."

"But it seems like a crime of passion," Emily pointed out. "Shoving someone isn't a well-thought-through action, and it's not something that someone often does if they've thought their actions through. There are certainly easier ways to kill someone than shoving them off a boat. Would a fall from that height have made her drown?"

Mara shook her head. "Not unless she was submerged in the water for several minutes. If she knew how to swim or even tread water, she could have easily survived. Had she not hit her head on the way down, she'd likely still be alive today."

Olivia considered this. Mara was right. Whatever had happened to Darcie, it was starting to look more and more like it wasn't a completely intentional act. Perhaps the killer had intended for her to die, but they'd gotten pretty lucky if that was the case. The more Olivia thought about it, the more it seemed like it could have been just the heat of the moment… or even a complete accident.

It didn't help much when considering their suspects though. Olivia was still wary of Charlie and Atkins; they both seemed like they could be impulsive enough to do something on the spur of the moment, and both had a significant motive for harming her.

But it also made Olivia think about Tim. He kept insisting that he was the killer, and yet she hadn't figured out a way to make it make sense. Now, maybe she had an explanation. Was he simply caught up in the moment? Did he see Charlie's girlfriend stumbling around in a vulnerable position and decide that she should die to make Charlie suffer?

It still didn't ring true to Olivia. Not when Tim refused to say why or how he'd killed Darcie, and not when he'd changed his story so quickly. But it did make her feel a little less sure of herself. The whole case had so many threads to pull that she didn't know which to let go of and which to hold on to for dear life.

"Is there anything else you can tell us? Any evidence left on the body of who the killer might be?" Emily pressed. Mara sighed, shaking her head.

"No, I don't think so. Anything that might have been important likely got washed away when she fell into the water, and after that, it wasn't preserved in the room you had her stored in. I appreciate you doing what you could to ensure continuity of evidence, but there's nothing more I can really do in this situation."

"Thank you for your help," Olivia said, shaking Mara's hand once again. "If you find anything else, please don't hesitate to call us."

"Will do. Good luck with your investigation. I hope you can find some answers for this young woman's family."

Olivia felt a little deflated as they left the room. They still didn't have a full picture of the night, and it was beginning to frustrate her. She needed to be able to sort the truths from the lies. She needed a way to place where everyone was at Darcie's time of death…

And then it hit her. Reaching into her bag, she pulled out Devyn Ward's phone. It had been ringing all night on the *Astoria*, so she'd shut it off. She'd almost forgotten that the woman had documented a lot of the night through pictures. Olivia smiled, turning it over in her hand.

"Bingo," she murmured. She turned to Emily. "I think we need to look through these photos. I'll bet that we can piece some of the night together if we look closely at the pictures and their time stamps. We might even be able to figure out whether it was possible for Tim to have killed her based on what we find here."

Emily's face lit up. "This might be the breakthrough we've been looking for. Let's go sit in the car and have a scroll."

They headed back to the car and slid into the back seat together to look at the pictures. There were a lot of them to get through; Olivia had already done a quick scan of a few, but not close enough to get answers. She knew that they needed to be meticulous if they were going to find the answers they wanted.

They started from the beginning of the night. Devyn had photographed each guest as they got onto the *Astoria*. Olivia scrolled through the familiar faces as each of them arrived. Charlie and Darcie looked surprisingly cozy at the beginning of the night as they greeted the guests, which Olivia hadn't been expecting. It certainly hadn't stayed that way.

"Looks like Luke and Lucy showed up separately…" Emily noted as they looked through the pictures. Olivia sighed.

"Poor Lucy."

They continued to look through the images one at a time. As the party built up, the pictures got harder to analyze. With more guests in the picture, it was harder to spot the important faces among them. However, it seemed as though everyone started the party in good spirits. Darcie was pictured talking to many of the guests, laughing and joking with them. Charlie was often at her side, but after a while, he disappeared from the photos. He only reappeared when he and Angus made their speech together, and he was already looking a little drunk.

"This must have been before he was spiked though," Emily pointed out. "So, he lied about how much he drank."

"Surprise, surprise," Olivia said, rolling her eyes. She continued to scroll through the pictures until she saw one of interest. Olivia paused, staring at the picture intently.

"Are you seeing what I'm seeing?"

Emily nodded. In the background of the picture, Charlie and Luke were standing together, talking with their faces close together. Charlie's back was turned, but by the look on Luke's face, the conversation had taken an angry turn. Olivia raised an eyebrow.

"And both of them swore blind that they barely saw one another. Looks to me like they talked about something pretty serious," Olivia observed.

"Maybe they were arguing over Darcie. Seems like that was the theme of the night."

"You're not wrong, but it doesn't prove much. So, they spoke to each other. It doesn't really give either of them more of a reason to have killed Darcie."

"That depends, doesn't it?" Emily challenged. "She pit them against each other before. Maybe she was doing it again."

Olivia hadn't considered that. She kept looking at the picture, wishing it could tell them more of a story, but the picture wasn't even good quality, and without context, it meant almost nothing. Olivia sighed.

"I guess we should keep searching."

It wasn't until a while later that Olivia saw something else of interest. She paused her scrolling to examine the picture, her heart thumping slightly.

"This is weird…"

"What?" Emily asked. Olivia knew why she was confused: neither Charlie nor Atkins—their two main suspects—were even in the photo. No, this was someone else entirely. Someone they'd previously overlooked.

In the picture, Angus Greenfield could be seen exiting a locked storage closet. Olivia immediately recognized it as the room where Bishop had stored away the checks brought to the party by the guests. It struck Olivia as odd that he would be in there. After all, the checks were being directed to charity. Why would he need to be anywhere near them in the middle of a party?

Was he skimming off the top of Bodymind Worx?

And then there was someone else in the picture that made the whole thing come together. Someone who changed what the photo might mean...

Standing close by was Darcie. Her lips were parted as though in shock, and her eyes were trained on Angus leaving the safe room. Had she come to the same conclusions that Olivia had? That Angus might be doing something he shouldn't?

Olivia pondered what that might mean for Darcie and how her evening had ended. Olivia's heart was racing hard.

"If he was stealing from the charity funds... and Darcie saw him doing it..."

"Then maybe he tried to keep her quiet," Emily jumped in. "Maybe things got heated between them. She told him to put the money back, or she threatened to tell someone what he'd done..."

"And at this point in the night, the drugs had made it into her system. She might have been more confrontational than normal..."

"So, she started a fight she couldn't finish," Emily concluded. She let out a breath. "This is a huge assumption to make based on a photograph. We're making up our own story here, for all we know..."

"Or we're spot on, and we just need evidence to back it up," Olivia countered. It was a long shot, but it gave them something to aim for. After all, it might be throwing another potential suspect into the mix, but it opened up the investigation. They'd been running dry on Charlie and Atkins for a while.

Was Angus the guy they were after?

"Let's not get ahead of ourselves here," Emily said. "We don't know that he was stealing, and we don't know that Darcie suspected him either."

"But, bear in mind, the time stamp was around five minutes before we heard her go overboard," Olivia pointed out. "Look, there we are in the picture, dancing…"

"I guess if it was him, then this picture puts him close to the scene. And if we're right about what he did, he has a motive to want her dead," Emily said quietly. "He certainly has the ability, being a fighter and all—it could explain the bruises. But what about Tim? Can we see him in any of these pictures?"

Olivia frantically flicked through a few of the pictures, looking for signs of Tim. She hadn't seen him in any of the pictures so far, and she was starting to get worried that she wouldn't.

And then she saw it. There was a picture of herself and Emily pushing through the crowd of people toward where Darcie had gone overboard. And there, tucked right into the corner of the picture with a tray full of drinks, was the man who claimed to have killed her, his hands full with a tray of hors d'oeuvres.

"He's right there. Tim was still at the party," Olivia said. "He was right in the thick of it serving snacks."

"Which means he couldn't possibly have killed her. He couldn't be in two places at once," Emily added, her eyes widening.

"He's lying to us. But why? We still have no idea why." Olivia threw her hands up in frustration. "Who is he covering for? Damn, we didn't figure out who he was on the phone to while we were visiting him. We got distracted by Dr. Lee's call…"

"It doesn't matter for now; we can cover that later. Now that we know Tim Sweeney wasn't the killer, we need to find out what was going on in that picture with Darcie and Angus. Something doesn't seem right in that picture, does it?"

"I guess there's only one way to find out the truth," Olivia said with a decisive nod. "We need to talk to Mr. Greenfield and see if he'll give up any information."

"We'll have to go back to DC and see him in his office. If we leave now, we should get there in time to talk to him today."

Olivia nodded, already scrambling into the front seat of the car. Emily got in the passenger seat and without a word, Olivia began to drive them back to Washington DC, toward the man who might have been the culprit the entire time.

Olivia only hoped they were one step closer to justice.

CHAPTER TWENTY-TWO

B Y THE TIME OLIVIA AND EMILY REACHED THE CITY, Olivia was beginning to doubt herself. Was the picture of Angus and Darcie really enough to make her believe that he could be a killer? The picture looked suspicious because they were looking for things to be suspicious about, but to anyone else, it would seem like quite a stretch to assume there was anything amiss. Were they about to accuse an innocent man of murder?

Olivia told herself to snap out of it. It was her job to ask questions, even uncomfortable ones. It was her job to look where no one else did and make bold assumptions. If Angus was innocent, then he'd have no problem answering her questions, right?

It was that thought that propelled Olivia inside the tall, glass skyscraper that housed the headquarters of Bodymind Worx. She recalled his past career as a high-profile MMA fighter and presumed he had millions in prize winnings and endorsements to fund a place like this. But even then, this place seemed a little much.

The entrance opened into a large gym area, complete with high-end exercise machines and full racks of weights. Various posters on the wall were emblazoned with Angus Greenfield's smiling face, giving off catchy slogans in bright colors about the importance of physical and mental health. A few people were scattered around the gym, working out or chatting—mostly teenagers and young people, Olivia noticed. To their right was a pair of massive rooms containing a full-size basketball court and an Olympic swimming pool, complete with extensive locker rooms on the outer wall. To their left was a staircase with a sign pointing to a library above them and a movie room above that.

Emily whistled. "Fancy digs."

"You're telling me," Olivia nodded. "I have to say, this is not what I was expecting when I pictured a charity…"

"Do you think we've got the wrong place?" Emily asked, but just as she did, they spotted the man himself emerging from one of the elevators. He still had his cheery smile from the other night and was dressed in a tight workout shirt and joggers. Just like Charlie Evans's outfit, though, Olivia could tell it was very pricey.

He smiled and waved to some of the employees, and they were equally friendly in return. They seemed like his friends rather than his employees. Even the kids working out seemed to know him on a personal basis. Any other time, Olivia might have thought that was a positive thing, but it only made her think of how tight-knit rich people could be. The party on the *Astoria* had shown her that much, and it felt very much as though she were mingling with the elite once again. She'd never really known rich people to be charitable unless it was within the public eye as a PR stunt, and it made her uneasy to see so many clearly wealthy people under one roof in the name of charity when clearly, it was the last thing on their minds.

When Angus spotted Olivia and Emily standing near the reception area, his smile faded a little, and he blinked in shock. Olivia smiled, feeling satisfied. She'd wanted to catch him off guard; she hadn't announced that they'd be coming. She didn't want to allow him time to fabricate some story to make her go away—not with her mounting suspicion of him and his questionable lifestyle.

"Hello, ladies! I wasn't expecting to see either of you again," Angus said with a wide smile. "Have you come with good news? Have you found out who hurt our poor Darcie?"

"Not yet," Emily said with a tight smile. She was clearly growing weary of these people trying to butter them up, trying to make out like they were innocent when most of them were busy hiding all their lies. "We were hoping to speak with you today—see if we can pick your brains about something."

"Well, of course, but…" Angus made a show of checking his watch and frowned. "I'm actually on my way to a meeting. I wish you would've called ahead—"

"We won't take up much of your time," Olivia said, her smile unwavering. "And if necessary, we can wait until you're done. It's important."

Angus looked a little uncomfortable at the sudden bombardment, but he forced a smile onto his face and nodded. "Well, then, I'm sure I can make a little time. I'd be glad to help, of course. Not so sure what you could possibly want with me…"

"Why don't we go to your office? I'm sure you'd prefer to keep a conversation as… *delicate* as this… private," Olivia said pointedly. Angus was no longer smiling as he nodded again.

"All right. Follow me."

Angus took them up to the top floor of the building. As they stepped into his office, which spanned the entire floor, Olivia couldn't help thinking how needlessly grand it was. It was sparsely furnished—the kind of minimalism that celebrities and high rollers loved to think made them relatable and cool—but nothing in the room could possibly have been labeled anything other than priceless.

"It's very nice up here," Olivia said pointedly as she took a seat at Angus's desk. "Love your art."

He let out a low chuckle, though he didn't seem to find the comment very funny at all.

"Well … we all have to treat ourselves from time to time, don't we?" he said. "My good friend Charlie made some donations as a kind gesture when we partnered up. You know, I was never really an art guy. Didn't get it. But I've really come to appreciate it ever since I retired. It's so crazy what you miss out on when you're so busy training day and night."

Olivia nodded, content to just let him blather on.

"That's why I started this place, you know. I wanted to find ways to help kids get that balance. It's right here in our mission statement." He squinted and read the words from a plaque on his desk. "In order for man to succeed in life, God provided him with two means: education and physical activity. Not separately, one for the soul and the other for the body, but for the two together. With these means, man can attain perfection."

"That's quite eloquent," Emily replied, though Olivia was sure she was resisting the urge to roll her eyes. "Did you write that?"

He smiled. "Me? Oh, no. I think it was, uhh … who was it? The Greek philosopher guy."

"Plato?" Olivia offered.

"Right. Yeah, he was big on that. Did you know that Plato was a pro wrestler in his day? People think guys like us are just dumb meatheads, but we have substance too."

"Of course," Emily smiled through gritted teeth. "Now, let's get to it. Have you seen this photograph before?"

She leaned in and showed him the picture of him leaving the locked room at the party. He seemed to latch on to Darcie's face right away, making his eyes widen in shock. But he quickly shook his head.

"Well, no. I don't think anyone has really shared any pictures of that awful night, for obvious reasons."

"Can you describe to us what was happening in this picture?" Olivia asked. "Because it looks to us as though you were exiting the room in which all of the charity donations for the foundation were being kept …"

"Well … yeah, that is what was happening," Angus admitted with a frown. "I went in there to check that nothing was out of place and to count up how much we made. I know it sounds bad, but sometimes, I have to shake these people down for all they're worth. You know how these rich people are," he joked, trying his smile on them. "People just don't like to be as charitable as they claim to be. They really want a special ass-kissing just for them."

Olivia raised an eyebrow. *I think you might be among those people,* she thought, making a point of looking around the room.

"Do you know what time you left that room?" Olivia asked Angus. He blinked several times.

"I dunno," he shrugged.

"Well, the time stamp on this picture places this image around five minutes before Darcie went overboard at ten forty-nine. So could you please tell us what you did after you left that room?"

Angus blinked again. "I beg your pardon?"

"It's a simple question," Emily added with a sweet smile. We're just putting together a picture of where everybody was in the moments before the murder. Just to do our due diligence."

Angus narrowed his eyes at her, but it seemed that he had decided to believe her because he took a deep breath and furrowed his brow in concentration. "Hell, I dunno… I think I must have rejoined the party! Like I said, you've gotta kiss a few butts to make things work in this business. I was hoping to speak to a few guests about the size of their donations and see if I could push them to make a second."

"Right. It's just that… we can't seem to place you anywhere in these next photographs," Olivia countered, taking the phone from Emily and swiping through the next few photographs. "The reporter who took these took around twenty more pictures of the party scene between the time you left that room and the time when Darcie was found. You're not in any of them."

Angus's face turned pale. His shoulders appeared to tense up, and he clenched his jaw.

"I don't like what you're insinuating."

"We're not insinuating anything. Did you think we were?" Olivia asked innocently. It only made Angus swell further with anger.

"Don't play me. I know your game. You're trying to set me up!"

"We're simply stating the facts in front of us. We asked for your interpretation of the photograph, and we asked some questions based on your responses," Emily shot back, still managing to play it cool as Angus's anger became more evident. He clenched his fist and brought it down on the glass table so hard that Olivia was sure she heard it crack a little.

Anger issues, she noted.

"You come into my office, and you speak to me like I'm some sort of criminal! What the hell is wrong with you!" he cried out. Olivia threaded her fingers together.

"Not once did we say you were a criminal. But now that you mention it, it seems as though you have a guilty conscience. Is there something you'd like to tell us, Mr. Greenfield?"

"We noticed that you have a temper too," Emily said, poking him further. "Is that what caused you to grab Darcie Puckett that night? To shove her hard enough to send her to her death?"

"Enough!" Angus roared, his face screwed up in anger. "I won't hear this in my own office. I would never hurt a young woman. Nothing on earth could make me!"

"Unless she saw something you didn't want her to see," Olivia pressed. "In the photo, it looks as though she's caught you red-handed. Maybe she got a little bold with you. Confronted you and asked what you were doing in that room. And who could blame you for panicking? Maybe you just wanted to keep her quiet. Maybe you just wanted to show her what you were capable of. You are a big, strong fighting champion, after all..."

"You pushed her once. She hit the railing, bruising her ribs," Emily continued the narrative. "And then, you shoved her again. Only this time, she went overboard. She hit her head and she died on impact. Must have been some shove that you gave her..."

"This is sickening," Angus snarled, shaking his head in disgust. "I thought you had your man! You arrested that other guy! Why am I suddenly being attacked like this? Who do you think you are?"

"We're just here to bounce off of you a bit. See how you respond," Olivia said with a slight smile. "You seem to be a little worked up, Angus. Is that because we're getting close?"

"I want you out of my office *now!*"

Olivia stood up from the table. Angus's response was exactly what she'd hoped for. It got them one step closer to proving that he might be capable of killing Darcie. "We're sorry to have taken up your time, Mr. Greenfield. You can head off to your meeting now."

Angus turned bright red, but Olivia and Emily didn't stick around to see his face transform. They got in the elevator together, and as soon as the doors were closed, they exchanged a look that said everything they were thinking.

He's acting like a guilty man.

Of course, they still needed more proof. The photograph had been enough to send them in the right direction and shake him up a little, but there were still pieces of the puzzle to put together.

"Where to next?" Olivia asked Emily. She chewed her lip.

"I hadn't really thought that far ahead. Maybe we need to talk to Charlie again. He knows Angus best. And if anyone was going to cover for him—"

The doors to the elevator opened, and Olivia's mouth almost dropped open in shock. Standing waiting for the elevator was Luke Shaw, Charlie's business partner. He looked as shocked to see them there as Olivia felt. Thoughts whirled around inside Olivia's head. Didn't Luke say that he wasn't really involved in the Washington branch of his company? Olivia had assumed he'd be on his way back out to LA …

But here he was, clearly on his way to see Angus. But what for? If he had taken a backseat in the company, didn't that include the formation of the foundation? Angus seemed to imply all night that it was him and Charlie working in collaboration.

Which begged the question … why was Luke the one standing in the lobby of Angus's office building?

"Um, hi, Agents," Luke said, nodding awkwardly to both of them in turn. "I wasn't expecting to see either of you here today."

"We could say the same about you," Olivia replied, smiling and cocking her head to the side. "I thought you'd be headed home by now."

Luke shifted from one foot to the other. "Ah, well, you know how work can be… I guess I've been lured back in since I'm in the area. I thought I'd maybe get a little more involved in the foundation, give something back to the community…"

"I see," Olivia said, staring Luke down. It was a well-formulated response, but Olivia wasn't sure it was true. According to his own words, he'd barely set foot in Washington since he and Charlie fell out over Darcie. It seemed odd to her that mere days after Darcie's death, he was suddenly lingering around town. Not even to make amends with his grieving friend, but to conduct business? Something wasn't sitting right with her.

"I was glad to hear that you arrested someone," Luke said, clearing his throat. "We all want justice for Darcie. I'm sure you've got the right guy. You did a great job with the investigation. And all that crap he spun about doing it for his family? I don't believe a word of it."

Olivia narrowed her eyes at him. How did he know about that? Olivia was sure it wasn't public knowledge. Tim had confessed that he had a grievance with Charlie after he was fired due to his family… but how would Luke know that? He hadn't even been there when they were told."

Olivia's blood ran cold. Was Luke hiding something from them? She watched him closely, and she was sure she could see a sheen of sweat on his forehead. It wasn't a warm day, so were they making him anxious?

What the hell did he know that they didn't?

"Well, I'm… heading up there," Luke said. Olivia stepped out of the elevator, shortly followed by Emily.

"Right, well. I guess we'll see you around," Olivia said pointedly. Luke hesitated, like he was going to say something, but at the last minute, he simply got into the elevator and pressed the button for the top floor, leaving them behind.

"Something's not right," Olivia mused as they watched the elevator rise. "We're still missing something…"

CHAPTER TWENTY-THREE

"MR. SWEENEY... WE KNOW YOU'RE NOT TELLING US the truth. We know you didn't do it."

Tim pressed his lips together as if they were glued shut. Olivia sighed and looked at Emily. She was clearly at the end of her rope with Tim as well. Olivia took out the reporter's phone and showed him the picture of him at the party.

"You see this picture? This places you at the party at the time when Darcie was killed. There's no denying it. That's you, right there. You couldn't possibly have had time to get there, kill her, and get back. It's not physically possible. You may have been responsible for her being drugged, but you were not the person who sent her overboard. So how about you stop lying to us and tell us the truth?"

Tim finally seemed to realize that he'd been busted; his eyes widened a little, but he still didn't say anything. Olivia drummed her fingers on the table irritably.

"There's a reason you couldn't explain how or why you did it, Tim. Because you didn't do it. What we can't seem to understand is why you would claim that you did. Has someone blackmailed you into doing this? Has someone threatened you if you don't cover their back?"

Tim still said nothing, avoiding Olivia and Emily's gazes and keeping his eyes firmly focused on the table. Olivia could tell that he was scared, that he had something on his mind, but she was now convinced that he wouldn't talk no matter how much they shook him up. She needed to rely on his facial expressions to give her answers. Fortunately, he was an expressive young man, and Olivia could read him like a book.

"There must be something in it for you," Olivia mused. "For you to own up to a murder you didn't commit. Something must have convinced you to do it. How about that phone call you made the other day? Because it's interesting... your story changed the moment you came back from making that call. Who promised you something in exchange for your confession?"

Tim's silence spoke volumes as his expression wavered. Olivia could feel that she was getting closer and closer to answers, even if Tim wasn't directly giving them. She decided that she would push him to his breaking point if necessary.

"I think someone did. I think that whoever you spoke to on the phone said that they would give you something. Something important to you. We already know the lengths you'd go to for your family... that you got yourself fired because you were trying your best to care for your mother. But you knew you were going to prison for poisoning Charlie Evans and Darcie Puckett. You've been aware of that all along. You knew you wouldn't be able to work to get money for your mom's treatment or be around to give her care in person... so you did what any person would do, right? You made a call and made arrangements to have her looked after... but I think you paid a heavy price in return, didn't you?"

Tim's lips were pressed so tightly together now that it was like he was physically having to force himself to remain quiet. It only spurred Olivia on, making her certain that she'd got it right.

"Twenty-five to life in prison for murder... that's a hefty charge. And yet you were willing to take it on because you were promised the one thing you care about: safety for your mother. Whoever you bargained with promised to cover her healthcare, maybe, to make sure she was fed and watered in your absence. Maybe they even offered to give her the best care money could buy. And anyone willing to offer that must be pretty wealthy in the first place. Am I getting warmer?"

Tim's discomfort was growing by the second. Olivia could hear his shallow breathing, smell the sweat radiating off his skin. Even without saying a word, he was giving himself away. She knew that she was close to the truth.

"You must have friends in high places. No, not friends... but someone willing to bargain with you. What about Charlie Evans? He could definitely afford to foot those medical bills. The two of you have had quite a turbulent history too. He fired you, you poisoned him, and now... well, is there more to the story? I wonder... did he ask you to take the fall for him? Did he strike a bargain with you to make things even between you?"

Tim looked up for the first time during the interview, and Olivia could see that she wasn't going down the right path. He didn't seem so shaky now, and the fact that he was making eye contact told Olivia that her assumptions were wrong. She chewed her lip.

"Alright, not Charlie Evans then." She paused, thinking back to her brief conversation with Luke at the charity building. He'd known about Tim's family. He'd known more than he should have. Olivia stared Tim in the eyes, hoping to intimidate an answer out of him.

"Does the name Luke Shaw mean anything to you?"

Tim swallowed and looked away again. Olivia smiled to herself. Bingo.

"All right, now we're getting somewhere. Luke... the man who was in love with the victim but was pushed aside by her. The man who played second fiddle to his best friend. Now, I guess that gives him the motive to want her dead, doesn't it? Did he tell you any of this, Tim? Did he confide in you before he asked you to take the fall for him?"

But something wasn't quite right. Tim was squirming at the mention of Luke, and yet Olivia still didn't feel like she'd hit the nail on the head. Did that mean that Luke wasn't their killer? That somehow, he was involved in the whole mess, but he wasn't the man she was looking for?

Olivia chewed her lip. She had one last piece of ammunition to use, and now it was time to bring it out. She leaned forward in her chair, closer to Tim.

"Now, we can do this part the easy way or the hard way. Because I can check this information anyway. But I want you to tell me. If you help me with this, I'll see what I can do to help you, okay? A nod will do."

Tim hesitated before nodding. Olivia continued to stare him down.

"The phone call you made … I want to know if I'm right about who you got in contact with. As I said, I can check, regardless. But I want to know from you. Did you make a phone call to Luke Shaw?"

There was a long pause while Tim considered how to answer. But then, very slowly, he nodded. Olivia let out a satisfied sigh. Finally, they were getting somewhere.

"Thank you, Mr. Sweeney. I think you've been a big help today. Thanks for being so chatty," Olivia said dryly. She and Emily stood to leave the room, and Tim was taken away by an officer back to his holding cell. As Olivia was walking, she pulled out her phone and called Luke's number. Her heart was thudding with every ring, but he didn't pick up. She tried his office instead after quickly researching it online.

"Hi, you've reached the LA branch of Infinity, how may I help you?" answered a cheery receptionist.

"This is Olivia Knight with the FBI," Olivia said, going straight in there. "I'd like to speak with Luke Shaw, please. I've been unable to get ahold of his cell."

"I'm sorry, Mr. Shaw isn't available at the moment," the woman responded, sounding for all the world like a robot. "Should I tell him to return your call?"

"You can try," Olivia murmured. "Although I don't think he's likely to call me back."

As the call ended, Olivia and Emily exchanged a glance.

"Convenient that he's gone missing, isn't it?" Olivia said.

"It's almost like he knows we're on to something," Emily agreed. "After we saw him heading to see Angus, he must have panicked a little."

"Which means that he's got something to hide," Olivia added darkly. "I think they both do. I'll bet anything that's why they were meeting in Angus's office to talk about what they'd done. But I bet they're counting on Tim not talking. They clearly offered him a lot to keep him quiet, so they won't be expecting him to betray them. It's a good thing he's not very good at hiding his expressions."

Olivia paused. "I think our best bet now is to hope that the analysis of the scene gives us something good. We need proof that either one of them was on the scene."

"We're nearly there. I can feel it," Emily said. Olivia sighed. "Let's hope so."

CHAPTER
TWENTY-FOUR

W HEN OLIVIA AND EMILY WERE CALLED BACK TO THE
docks to get the analysis, Olivia's heart was racing
hard in her chest as they made the drive back down
to Virginia Beach. It all came down to what they were able
to find onboard, and according to the phone call, there were
definitely some things of interest for them to look at.

The *Astoria* was still in the harbor where it had docked
after the party, cordoned off by police tape. Several analysts and
officers were milling around, discussing what they had discovered
on board. Dr. Lee was among them, and she beckoned them
toward her.

"Thanks for joining us, agents. Come on board."

Olivia and Emily stepped onto the *Astoria*; Olivia felt a little
strange returning in the daylight to the place that had presented

them with such a complex case. Never before had Olivia been so suspicious of so many people, but she hoped that now she would be able to get some answers—answers that would finally lead to justice for Darcie's death and maybe even help them unturn the other mysteries they had not yet solved.

"Let's first go to the murder scene," Mara started, leading them up to the top level where Darcie had fallen. When Olivia leaned over the railing, she could still see splatters of Darcie's blood on the hull that hadn't been washed away yet.

"You can see where Darcie hit her head, right there on the lower railing. We also found her fingerprints on this railing where we think she tried to cling on before she was shoved overboard. We found several other sets of fingerprints of guests there, too, but none of note. Of course, people were touching the railing all night."

"Is there anything at all that points to who the killer could be?" Olivia asked hopefully. Mara shook her head.

"Not that anyone could find so far. It's like I said, there are a lot of fingerprints here but not much else to go on. And since you were still out at sea for a couple hours afterward, all that evidence got completely contaminated. But we did find something interesting in the room that was locked. We had to break the lock to get in, but it was worth it. Come on, I'll show you what they found."

Intrigued, Olivia and Emily followed Mara across the deck to the locked storage closet where the checks had been stored. The room that Angus had been seen leaving in the photograph. Olivia felt a flicker of excitement. Whatever was in there was likely incriminating to anyone who had been in there. Perhaps Darcie had known that, and it got her killed.

"I'm not sure if this was what you were expecting to find, but feel free to take a look inside," Mara said, using her gloved hand to open the door.

"It looks like a storage closet to me," Emily said.

Mara nodded. "And to the average person, it would. But look here," she pointed. In the lower corner, tucked behind a mop and bucket, was a tiny keypad mounted to the wall. "We spent ages looking at this, finding the combination, trying to brute force it open. As you can see above us, there are slight metal shutters embedded into the wall."

"A false wall?" Olivia frowned.

"Exactly," Mara nodded. She stooped low and typed a code into the keypad. "It took hours of trial and error, but we finally got the code. You won't believe this."

With a metallic clang, the wall began rising right in front of them like a garage door, and when Olivia saw what was waiting inside, her eyes widened in shock.

"Well, this wasn't exactly what I was expecting," she murmured.

The closet had opened up into a surprisingly large storage room with shelves lining each wall. And on each shelf, there were boxes and boxes full of pills.

Olivia couldn't be sure what they were just by looking at them, but she doubted very much that they were standard over-the-counter drugs. She stared at the cache in horror. There must have been hundreds of thousands of dollars' worth stashed in the small room. Was this the secret that Darcie had uncovered? Was this discovery what had gotten her killed?

"That's a … a lot of drugs," Emily said, stepping into the room to get a closer look. Each plastic baggie must have contained at least a hundred pills, if not more. They were bursting at the seams. Olivia couldn't recall a time when she'd ever seen so many pills stashed in such an ordinary place.

Mara chuckled. "That's one way of putting it."

"Someone was running some kind of operation, clearly," Emily mused. "But who? There were plenty of people who had access to this room. The captain, the bosun, Charlie, Angus …"

"Maybe they were all in on it. I mean, surely the captain knew what was going on in his own ship?" Olivia pondered. "But I don't see how this links to anything else we know. This has just opened an entirely new can of worms. It could explain why Angus might have wanted Darcie dead if she found out what was stored inside… but the rest? It doesn't seem to add up at all."

"I might be able to help you there," Mara said. "There may be a link to the rest of your case after all. The drugs found in here are a match for the ones found within the victim's body and in Charlie Evans's. We also found the glass that was poisoned, and the drug residue inside matched up with these as well. Additionally, we matched the fingerprints on the glass to Tim Sweeney, who served the drink, but that's beside the point. What I'm trying to say is that it's likely Tim got the drugs he used *after* he boarded, not before."

"Somebody gave him the drugs to use," Olivia said. "So, someone at the party clearly wanted Charlie dead too… it explains why Tim was so unaware of what the drugs were capable of. He said he only hoped to embarrass Charlie, to humiliate him like he was after he was fired. Perhaps whoever gave him the drugs convinced him to do it and didn't tell him what the drugs were truly capable of…"

"And if Charlie had ingested all of the drug, he might not be here today," Emily added. "If that's the case, are we looking at two attempted murders now? Darcie *and* Charlie? This opens up so many questions. Does that rule Charlie out as Darcie's killer if he was a target himself? And who would want Charlie dead?"

"I can think of a few likely candidates," Olivia replied. "Luke would have stood to gain a lot from Charlie's death. A possible second chance with Darcie, full ownership of their company, his biggest rival out of his way. I guess it would make the most sense for it to have been him. And then there's the fact that he was the person that Tim called. We know already that he's been up to something." Olivia turned to Mara. "What else can you tell us about the drug? And do you know who accessed this room during the party?"

Mara nodded. "The drugs in this room are extremely dangerous. They're not your average party drug. They have very strong psychoactive chemicals in them, meaning that even the most controlled person would likely feel the effects of whatever this pill is. It could cause a complete imbalance in their neurochemistry, causing them to be extremely susceptible to rapid mood swings—possibly an increase in aggression, an overload of emotions, and even an altered state of mind."

"You mean like hallucinations?"

"Possibly," Mara nodded. "I imagine that if consumed with alcohol, the effects would be even stronger. That's likely why Charlie was so out of it after consuming the drug. The residue in the glass he drank from suggests that one of these pills was crushed up and put into the drink. It was extremely lucky for him that he didn't take the full dose. Drugs like this are so strong they could induce seizures or even a heart attack."

Olivia was suddenly reminded of the drugs she'd found during her time investigating the Grim Reaper in prison. His drugs had been similarly horrific, relative to ordinary drugs. They had been cut with all sorts of harmful substances, and Olivia wouldn't be surprised if the little white pills in the bags before her were just as bad.

But they had disrupted the Reaper's operation. Hadn't they?

"We need to know who these belonged to," Olivia murmured. She turned to Mara again. "Any ideas?"

"Well, according to the fingerprints we matched up, several people entered the room on the night of the party. Charlie Evans was one of them. Angus Greenfield was also in here, which you already knew, I believe. And then the final person who entered the room was Luke Shaw."

Olivia took a moment to wrap her head around the facts. All three of them were the main suspects in their case now, and knowing that all of them had been in the room at some point was important. That meant that they were all aware of what was being stored inside, and none of them had done anything to report it. That meant that they were all in on it. And if they were all working together, then wasn't it possible that any one of them could have shoved Darcie over the railing to protect their secrets?

But the question still remained… who had told Tim to poison Charlie? Who had provided the drugs to him and then forced him to take the fall for it? All signs pointed to Luke in that instance, especially since he'd now suddenly fled town. He was looking more and more guilty to Olivia by the minute. She couldn't believe that he hadn't been on her radar sooner, because in the light of day, he looked as guilty as any of the others.

"Three men… all of them connected by Darcie… and now by the drugs as well," Olivia muttered to herself. "They all have a motive to want her dead, and one of them has a motive to double-cross one of his teammates. That same person enlisted someone else to do his dirty work for him in order to get away with attempting to kill his partner. But then the other victim was also affected by his plan, and it ended up with her dead."

Olivia shook her head. There was a lot going on between the suspects and the victim… or should she say victims? Charlie could easily have wound up dead too.

"We need to find Luke," Emily stated, voicing Olivia's own thoughts. "I don't think there's a world where he isn't guilty of something here. We need to get him to talk, and maybe we can take him and the others down for good."

Olivia nodded, but her mind was still whirring. So much was still unexplained. What were they doing getting involved in drugs? Presumably they were selling them, which might explain their profit margins, but why did they need to do that when business was going so well? Was it greed, or something more?

Or was Infinity all a fraud from the beginning? Just a front to push these drugs? And how did Bodymind Worx fit into everything? They'd seen the facility themselves—clearly, there was some element of real good work the charity did. But was that the true nature of both organizations?

Had they just stumbled upon a massive drug ring by accident?

Whatever their reasons were, Olivia could at least bring the three of them in for questioning based off of their knowledge of the drugs alone. And then, once she had the three of them in custody, maybe she could break them down even further and figure out the true parts each of them played on the night that ended Darcie Puckett's life.

"We should bring them all in," Olivia said. "I'll contact the LA field office to bring in Luke. The other two should be easier to bring in. I still can't make sense of what's going on here, but I think the three of them are all involved, and I think whatever they're up to, they're in it together. Even if one of them chose to betray the others…"

Mara chuckled. "The lives of the rich and famous, huh? You couldn't make it up."

"Thank you for your help, Mara. Is there anything else we should know?"

"Unfortunately, there's not much else. Everything we've found has been completely contaminated. We'll keep investigating and keep you posted, but I'm not sure how helpful it'll be."

"Thank you." Olivia turned to Emily, heaving a sigh. This case was beginning to exhaust her. It felt like they hadn't stopped for even a second to breathe.

"We're so close," Emily insisted, reaching out to squeeze Olivia's arm. "Let's keep up the momentum. We're going to take them down once and for all."

CHAPTER TWENTY-FIVE

IT DIDN'T TAKE LONG TO ROUND UP CHARLIE AND ANGUS. Charlie was in his penthouse suite still recovering from his brush with poison when Olivia showed up with the police to arrest him. On the other side of the city, Emily was making an arrest of her own by taking Angus in, which she was more than happy to facilitate.

But the problem they'd been left with was Luke. They had informed the Los Angeles field office that he was an active suspect in a murder case, but it seemed that Luke had disappeared entirely. It made Olivia simmer with anger. If only they'd realized it a little sooner, before they had him running scared, they could have taken him down easily. *Why would an innocent man go on the run?* Olivia thought.

But still, having two out of the three in her custody was a good start. She wanted to talk to them both, but separately, to try to sift through the cracks in their stories and shake out the truth, one way or another.

After both men had been taken into police custody, Olivia rejoined Emily, and they grabbed some well-earned coffee to prepare them for the evening ahead of them. They were waiting to hear back from Sam with one key piece of information.

The online account that Tim had made to publicly complain about Charlie had been on Olivia's mind for a while, so she contacted Sam. As the resident computer expert of their team, she knew that if anyone could hack into the account and mine some gold from within it, it would be him. But that process would take some time.

She planned to postpone her interviews until she knew what was in the account. With any luck, they'd crack it open and find some incriminating private messages. And since Tim had been the one to plant the drugs, she thought maybe it would lead to a trail of where they'd come from.

Olivia's shoulders were aching from the stress of the last few days, but the coffee in her hand was warm and creamy. It soothed her a little as she drank it, despite her heavy eyes and tired mind. Emily looked equally content as she sipped her drink, like she'd been waiting a lifetime to enjoy a hot beverage.

"What a week," Olivia said, rubbing at her shoulders. "We started with tax regulations and now we're trying to deal with a murder and an attempted murder."

Emily smiled. "I have to say, though, this is way more exciting than I thought it would be. I'm usually so holed up in paperwork that I never get to make arrests."

Olivia chuckled at that. Seeing things through Emily's eyes, it wasn't so bad. And she did have to admit, this was a lot more exciting than tracking down corporate fraud.

"Do you ever wonder… why?" Emily asked.

"Why what?" Olivia asked curiously. Emily heaved a sigh.

"Why people choose to make their lives so complicated? How hard can it be for people as rich as these guys not to deal drugs and get themselves into trouble?"

"Money can't buy happiness, I suppose," Olivia shrugged.

"But that's the thing. All of this is in pursuit of even *more* money. Money for money's sake," Emily said. "They're already living the lives most regular people dream of. Living it up with fancy yachts and all that stuff. Why even bother with the drugs? Why even put your career and status at risk to pressure your subordinates into sex? It just baffles me sometimes. They could've had perfect lives. But instead, they chose to make trouble, to wreck everything within moments. Whoever killed Darcie... was it really just two shoves that ended her life? Unplanned? If so, then how do people ever put themselves in a position where they do that to someone? Why can't people just... live their lives?"

Olivia offered Emily a smile. "You know what? I don't know. It's impossible sometimes to know why people do things. Maybe they're bored. Maybe they just don't know any better. Or maybe they can't help themselves. We're lucky that we've never had those kinds of impulses... but how many times have people hurt you, and you wished you could find a way to make them feel what you felt? Not because you want them to suffer, but so they see life through your eyes and experience what you experienced. Imagine taking that a step further. An eye for an eye. Revenge."

Emily sipped her coffee thoughtfully. "I just could never understand that. Sure, I've been angry before. And sure, I've hated people through and through... but it's never crossed my mind to do the things these people have done. Isn't it crazy to think that nearly everybody on that yacht had a supposed motive? That enough of those people were deemed capable of murder? It's like it's inside every single one of us... an impulse waiting to come out. It scares me half to death to think about that."

"Ah, Emily. I don't think you need to worry about that."

"Yeah? Why's that?"

Olivia's mouth twitched into a smile. "Because you're a good person. One of the best I've ever known, actually. And you say it's an impulse in all of us, waiting to come out, but I don't think you've ever had that in you. You're one of the good ones."

Emily's head cocked to the side as she took in what Olivia was saying. "You know what? That's weirdly one of the nicest things anyone has ever told me."

"What, that I don't think you're capable of ever being a murderer?"

Emily gave her a coy look. "Well, that you know of."

Olivia burst out laughing, and Emily joined in too, with her reserved little giggle. It felt good to finally have something to laugh about. It felt like weeks since Olivia had had anything to really laugh about. With Brock away and the case to work on, things had been weighing heavily on her. But laughing with Emily just made the whole load seem a little lighter.

"I'm so glad we're doing this together," Olivia said with a smile at Emily when they managed to stop laughing. "It's nice to work with someone on my level. Someone who cares as much about getting the case solved as I do. You're a really good partner."

"Thanks, Olivia. That means a lot. Maybe even more than you telling me that I'm incapable of murder."

That set both of them off laughing again. It was a lame joke, but it was just what they needed. A break from the darkness of the world they were immersed in. A break from the horrors people were capable of committing. Sometimes, laughter was all Olivia needed to escape for just a little while.

But there was always something ready to take Olivia back to reality. She felt her phone vibrating in her pocket and knew it must be Sam. She quickly picked up the call as she finished off the dregs of her coffee.

"Please tell me you have something good for us?"

"I've got something very good for you, Olivia," Sam said cheerily on the other end of the line. "Something very juicy indeed."

"Well then, spill the beans, yeah? We've been waiting for this."

"All right, calm down, I'm getting to it. I managed to hack into the account. I'll take praise and thanks later—not exactly hard when this guy clearly thinks *password123* is a safe password to use…"

"Was that really his password?"

"It may as well have been, it was so obvious. Anyway, I won't tell you what it actually was. What's *much* more interesting is what I found on the account. There were several messages back and forth with another anonymous user. Tim had been in contact with a few other former employees of Infinity who had been fired for stupid reasons, but not much came from the messages I found there. The most recent messages, however, told me a lot. He was talking to someone from within the company."

"A current employee?"

"More like one of the higher-ups. They promised Tim that they could help him get revenge for what happened to him. They promised him a payout, too, but I think that was meant to be given to him after he completed the job. Tim didn't ask any questions. He didn't seem to care why someone else might want to make a fool of Charlie. He literally just took up the offer right away. So, he made a plan to get hired for the yacht party, which clearly worked. And then he arranged to meet the person he'd messaged on board to be handed the drugs. From there, it was down to him and… well, you know the rest."

"So, did you figure out who the person was that he was messaging?" Olivia pushed, her heart racing. She was certain she already knew the answer, but the evidence would give one final blow to her suspect. It would topple their entire alibi, and they'd finally be getting somewhere.

"I didn't get a name from the account, but I did trace the IP address back to the Infinity office in LA. Does that help at all?"

Olivia smiled to herself. *Luke.* She really had him now. There was no denying that he was guilty of attempting to kill Charlie now. Maybe once she let him know that he was busted, he'd confess further. Perhaps he was the one who killed Darcie, after all.

"Thank you, Sam. I think we've got what we need."

"I hope that was helpful. Good luck. I hope you take these people down once and for all."

Olivia ended the call with a gleam in her eye. Emily leaned forward hopefully.

"Well?"

"Luke supplied the drugs," Olivia filled her in. "He arranged with Tim before the party for him to spike Charlie's drink. Luke must have known how powerful the drugs were—possibly enough to kill a man—which means that he likely not only wanted Charlie dead but that he also tried to hire someone to do it for him."

"What a sicko. I can't believe we didn't see it in him," Emily said, shaking her head.

"Me neither. But it's not over yet. We still have to actually find him. And given what we know now, it's no wonder he made a run for it."

"We'll find him," Emily said firmly. "He's not going to get away with it. And once we loosen his lips a little, we might be able to take down the three of them for good. Their operation, their fraudulent activity, the whole thing. No matter who killed Darcie, they've all got a lot to answer for."

"I'm really going to enjoy sending these jerks off to prison," Olivia added with a gleam in her eye. "We're so close to a win now, I can almost taste it."

"When this is over, we are definitely going to deserve a beer," Emily said with a grin.

Olivia's heart panged a little. She sounded like Brock at that moment. But this moment wasn't about him, Olivia reminded herself. It was about her and Emily and the hard work they'd done to take three criminals down—four when she counted Tim in there too, and five when she considered the report she'd filed against David Atkins for sexual harassment. Five dangerous men were going to be off the streets because of the two of them, and that was a joy that couldn't be replicated. It felt damn good, and they were owning it.

In that moment, the world was theirs for the taking.

CHAPTER TWENTY-SIX

"OLIVIA... WHAT ARE YOU DOING? IT'S LIKE ONE IN the morning."

Emily was straining her eyes as she emerged from her bedroom to see Olivia sitting up on the couch in her apartment, furiously scrolling through a bunch of documents. It took Olivia a moment to process that Emily had said something to her before she glanced over with a weary smile.

"Sorry, did I wake you?"

"Kinda, yeah. You type like a maniac. Why are you on your laptop at this hour? I thought we agreed to approach the case with a fresh mind in the morning."

"We did, but I'm not very good at that. I had a few brainwaves and I had to follow them before they disappeared into the night."

"Like what? Other than button bashing, of course?"

"I wanted to look through the files from Luke's computer. Ever since they were seized for evidence yesterday and sent our way, I've been desperate to do a deeper dive. I figured that I might find something to trace the drugs further back, or maybe to explain the fraudulent activity that we suspected within the company. We always assumed that Charlie was the one making all the moves since he owned the majority of the company. Who could have expected that Luke was the mastermind behind it all?"

"I wouldn't go as far as to call him a mastermind," Emily countered wryly. "He sort of shot himself in the foot, like, multiple times. His trail didn't even have time to go cold before we caught up to him. It's, like, still lukewarm."

Olivia chuckled. "I like that analogy. But whatever way we look at it, the scales are tipping more toward Luke being the brains behind the operation now. Which kind of makes sense when you think about it. Charlie never did seem like the sharpest tool in the shed… and he was too busy partying and arguing with his girlfriend to really get involved in company matters. My guess is that Luke did most of the heavy lifting, and then Charlie enlisted Angus to help make their operation bigger. It's just a guess, but if I can find anything in these files, then we'll be well on our way to getting answers."

"Well, I'm awake now. I guess three hours is enough sleep to go on, right?" Emily said a little grumpily.

"I mean, it can wait," Olivia offered. "We still have an FBI team scouring in California for him."

"Nah, you're right. The sooner we crack this, the sooner it's over. And then I can sleep for a full day if I want to," Emily said, stifling a yawn as she walked over to turn the lights on. They both winced at the harsh light, and then Emily joined Olivia on the couch to look over her shoulder at the laptop.

"Does Brock usually let you get away with this?" she asked.

Olivia frowned. "I don't know what you mean."

Emily scowled back. "I think you do. All these late nights, working yourself to the bone when you haven't stopped all day. I don't know how you can possibly function like that."

"It works for me. I guess insomnia has kind of screwed me up the past few years. I find it easier to get to sleep when I'm bone tired. Which I definitely will be once I've scrolled through all of these documents."

Emily managed a smile, but Olivia could still see a twinge of concern on her friend's face. She sighed and forced a smile.

"You don't need to worry about me," Olivia said. "I'm fine. Better than I have been in a long time, actually."

"Are you just saying that to shut me up?"

"No, I swear I'm not. I really am. My family is starting to come back together. I'm working past everything that's happened to me over the last few years. I've got my friends watching my back…"

"Even now that Brock is away?"

"*Especially* now that Brock is away. I just got to spend a week with my best friend for the first time in forever. What more could I ask for?" Olivia asked with a gentle smile. Emily looked a little unconvinced, but she smiled back, clearly too tired to take the conversation much deeper.

"As long as you're not running yourself into the ground."

"Don't worry. The case won't suffer. I do a lot of my best work when I'm tired. It lets me think a little more freely."

"I wasn't concerned about the case," Emily clarified, raising an eyebrow in warning at Olivia. She chewed her lip and turned her attention back to the screen.

"Noted. But hey, if it makes you feel any better, I think I'm close to finding something good here."

"Explain?"

"Well, I'm currently looking through some of the company financial statements, and there's a regular payment into a charity fund here. It got me thinking about a few cases I've worked in the past, where charities have been used as a cover-up for redirecting funds elsewhere. I'll bet that these 'charity payments' will lead us to one account… which will then lead us to the offshore accounts you were convinced Infinity was using. I'll have to make some calls in the morning and see what we can find."

"I mean, if you're right, that would make our case airtight," Emily stated.

"Exactly. And there's more. The company has also been redirecting money to a private bank account. I checked the name of the account, and it belongs to a Hugo Lewis. A little research told me that he's Luke's cousin. So I wondered what that was all about and dug a little further; it seems like criminal activity might run in the family. Hugo has previously been jailed for lower-level fraud … *and* he served a few years for possession of drugs."

"You think that maybe this cousin is the source of the drugs? Or perhaps their dealer?"

"It's entirely possible," Olivia agreed. "I think he's definitely involved. He's clearly not that good at what he does if he's been caught before, so I say we bring him in for questioning about his cousin's crimes. It might help to build up a case against Luke for when we eventually track him down … *and* it might get a dealer off the streets."

"That's got to be a good thing, especially with the stuff they're dealing. If it's the kind of stuff we found in that secret room, then we're going to have a hell of a lot of people getting sick in this city."

Olivia nodded solemnly. "I've seen it before. Months ago, when I was working the Grim Reaper case, everyone was suffering. I can understand how people get roped into taking drugs. They're looking for an escape, just looking to feel better … but it's getting more and more dangerous out there. No one can trust their sources anymore, and new drugs are being invented all the time. It makes me sick. People profiting off the suffering of ordinary people, as if they're not rich enough already."

"It's like you said, though. Maybe the company isn't doing as well as it claims to be. Maybe the whole thing really is just a front for the drugs," Emily pointed out. "And we know for a fact that these men are just plain greedy. They want everything. The money, the parties, the fame, the women—they want it all. It seems like they'll do just about anything for their own gratification. How many men did we meet over this week who were willing to do bad things just to be with Darcie? They're insatiable. It's a sickness."

Olivia nodded. She couldn't have agreed more. She'd never understood those kinds of people, and yet she was constantly surrounded by them. More often than not, it was those kinds of people that she worked to take down. It wasn't the poorest of the poor getting involved in crime just to get by. It was the richest of the rich just trying to get farther ahead than they already were.

"They'll regret what they've done when they're spending the rest of their lives behind bars," Olivia said. "They'll wish they never messed with us in the first place."

Emily finally raised a real smile. "You bet they will. We make a good team, don't we?"

Olivia smiled back. "I really think we do. Maybe when Brock comes back, you can kick him out of his apartment. Move to Belle Grove and work with me."

Emily gave Olivia a mischievous look. "I'm not sure that would work. Then where would you get your eye candy from?"

Olivia blushed deeply. Emily grinned, hopped off the couch, and headed back to her bedroom. She flicked the light off on the way and snuggled back under the covers.

"Go to sleep now, Olivia," Emily urged. "We'll finish this tomorrow, I promise."

"You're no fun. Brock would let me stay up."

"Brock would do anything for you, Olivia, and you know it. Me? I run a tighter ship. Laptop off NOW!"

With a sigh, Olivia set down the laptop on the coffee table and headed to the other bedroom—the bedroom that had once been her own—and sidled into the bed there. She wasn't expecting to fall asleep, but the promise of the morning's excitement had her drifting off faster than she had imagined.

"I'll be glad when we don't have to deal with this guy ever again," Emily mentioned to Olivia as they made their way to Tim Sweeney's holding cell. They were about to conduct their final interview with him to try and persuade him to give up the information he had. They knew a lot more now, thanks to Sam and his deep dive into Tim's account. But he'd been evasive all along, only giving up what he wanted to give up. But fortunately, after making a phone call to one of his loved ones that morning, Olivia and Emily had some ammunition to get him talking.

"Hopefully he'll be a little more forthcoming today. After all, the information we have is going to give us an upper hand," Olivia said.

Tim was waiting for them in the interrogation room, his lips pressed tightly together as though to say, *"I'm not telling you anything."* Olivia sighed into her seat opposite him. She was hoping to get the interview over and done with as quickly as possible. Then, she could shift her focus to the more important part—charging the real villains in this criminal conspiracy.

"Good morning, Mr. Sweeney. I think I should tell you that it's very much in your interest to talk to us today," Olivia started with a knowing look at him. "We may have some information that you would be interested in … and I think it might be enough for you to tell us what you know."

Tim raised an eyebrow. Olivia was beginning to get good at interpreting his facial expressions. This one said something like, *"Yeah? Try me."*

Alright then, Tim. I will, Olivia thought.

"We already know who you called the other day, and we've managed to hack into your personal accounts to give us a clearer picture of what you've been up to," Olivia said. "You had promised to tell us the source of the drugs you used to poison Charlie Evans, but you never actually told us in the end, did you? After that phone call you had with Luke Shaw, you clammed up on us. Fortunately, we didn't need you to tell us, because now we know. Luke Shaw was the man you were working with all along. He convinced you to give the drug to Charlie after he saw the things you were posting online. He didn't tell you what would happen to Charlie if you went along with it, but you jumped on the opportunity to hurt him. Which landed you here, didn't it?"

Tim still hadn't said a word or made a single sound, simply staring at the wall behind Olivia's head. She continued.

"We think Luke Shaw fully intended for you to take the fall for what you did, even before the two of you cut any sort of deal. I think he was relying on the fact that you'd be caught and that you wouldn't give him up to the police. But when Charlie didn't end up dead, and Darcie did instead … that changed the game. When you spoke to him on the phone, he must have been desperate. He was looking for a way to cover his back. So, he told you that he'd take care of your family if you took the fall for the whole thing. Your confession to killing Darcie was never a convincing one, but you stuck with it because you felt like you didn't have another option, did you?"

Still nothing from Tim. Olivia cleared her throat and continued.

"You were worried about your mother and what might happen to her if you angered Luke. So, you've stayed silent this entire time, even though you never intended to truly hurt anyone. While you're not responsible for one death and one near miss, you're taking the blame. It's admirable what you're willing to do for your family, Tim. But what are you willing to do for your wife?"

Tim's head snapped up, and his lips parted as though he was about to shout something at her. Olivia knew she'd finally hit a nerve. Not once had he mentioned that he was married, but Olivia had done some digging to find his family and hear what they could tell her.

And that was when she hit the jackpot.

"Your wife sends her love," Olivia said gently, keeping steady eye contact with Tim. "And she wants you to know... that you finally did it. She's finally pregnant."

Tim covered his mouth in shock, his eyes softening as he took in the news. He stared at Olivia, trying to figure out if she was tricking him, but she shook her head. "No, I'm not lying to you. She wanted to tell you herself. Except you wasted your phone call on Luke Shaw. She's going to have a baby. *Your* baby."

Tim was sobbing softly behind his hand, his entire face pained as he realized what that meant for him. He would be in prison while his child was growing up. He wouldn't be able to hold his baby or be there for his child's first steps. Olivia knew it was cruel to tell him that, but she needed him to talk. She needed the last pieces of the puzzle to fall into place.

"If you want to be there for your child... you can't do life in jail. We don't want that for you," Olivia said gently. "Not when you didn't intend to hurt anyone. Which is why you need to tell us the truth. Make a statement against Luke Shaw. We're so close to taking him down. Once we've caught him, we're going to need all the evidence we can get to fight him and his expensive lawyers. You know it's the right thing to do, Tim—for you and for your family. We can make this a lot easier on you … if you'll be honest with us."

Olivia watched as Tim's entire face transformed. He was slowly but surely coming to the realization that if he ever wanted to be able to do his duty as a father, then he needed to give up his act and tell them the truth.

"Please, Tim."

He looked up at Olivia, who gave him an encouraging nod. He took a deep breath, his lips parting once again. Olivia held her breath in anticipation.

"Luke Shaw gave me the drugs. He handed them to me when I got onto the *Astoria* that night," he finally admitted, the words coming out in such quick succession that they nearly tripped over one another. He looked up at Olivia then, his eyes wide with intensity. But he wasn't trembling. He wasn't avoiding her gaze. He was finally telling the truth. "I didn't know what was in those drugs, I swear. I wouldn't have done it if I did."

"So, Luke informed you in advance that he'd be providing you with the drugs?"

Tim nodded. "Yes. He set it all up and told me to contact Charlie about working that night as a waiter. He said he'd make sure Charlie got me on board. I … I think some part of me felt guilty before it happened, because when Luke warned me that there would be FBI at the party, I did some research and slipped an anonymous tip about the party to you." He nodded to Emily. "I'm sorry. I hope I didn't frighten you."

"You … *you* sent the poem?" Emily asked, blinking. Tim blushed.

"Yes. I've been working on some creative outlets lately. I thought it was a perfect opportunity to try it out."

Olivia tried to hide her smile by pressing her lips together. She didn't want Tim to see her amusement and back off at the last moment. He turned back to Olivia.

"I'm willing to make a full statement against Luke Shaw, in exchange for immunity. I have to be out of here as soon as I can. I need to see my child. I need to be a good dad."

Olivia nodded encouragingly. Despite how wrong Tim's actions had been, she didn't think he was a bad person. Just a man down on his luck. He certainly wasn't the person she wanted to see in jail most in this case.

"I don't know that I can offer immunity. But we'll see about community service or something. You still committed assault."

Tim nodded fervently. "That's fine. That's fine. I can deal with that."

Olivia's phone began to ring in her pocket, and she saw that the call was coming from the agent leading the Los Angeles office field team in search of Luke.

"Can you finish up here?" Olivia asked Emily, who nodded as Olivia left the room. She could feel the excitement building inside her as she picked up the call.

"Knight here."

"We've got him," said the agent. "Luke Shaw has been placed under arrest."

Olivia grinned. It was finally coming together. In no time at all, they would have the whole thing wrapped up neatly with a bow.

"That's what I like to hear," she crowed. "How did you catch him?"

"He attempted to board a flight out of the country. TSA flagged him, and we were able to take him into custody from the airport. We'll be transferring him back to DC shortly. Then he's all yours."

"Thank you. Tell Luke I look forward to speaking to him. It's going to be a real pleasure."

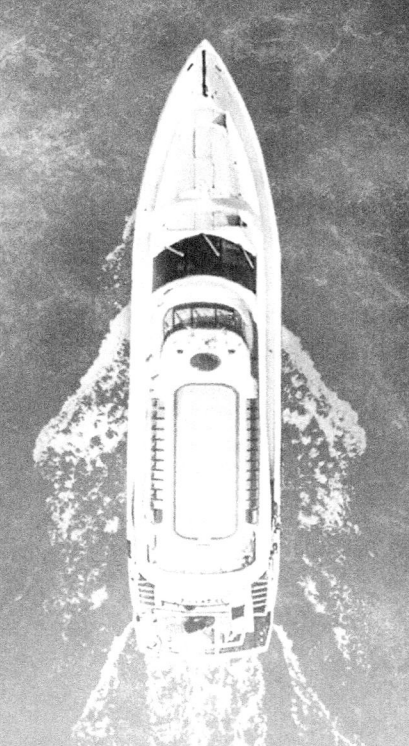

CHAPTER TWENTY-SEVEN

"**W**ELL, MR. EVANS. IT'S GOOD TO SEE YOU AGAIN. You look a little better than the last time we spoke," Olivia said as she sat down opposite Charlie Evans. He scowled at her, his arms folded over his chest.

"You can't do this. You've held me here for almost forty-eight hours now. You shouldn't be allowed to do that."

"I can, actually, given the circumstances," Olivia replied with a pleasant smile. Charlie didn't return it. He glanced at Emily, nodding to her.

"You... you seem much more reasonable," Charlie offered. "Are you going to allow this to continue? You both must know by now that I didn't kill Darcie."

"Yes, we know that much," Emily nodded. "We don't think you're responsible for your girlfriend's death. At least not directly."

"What is that supposed to mean?" Charlie snarled. He leaned forward across the table, his handsome face made ugly by the sneer that sat upon it. "Look here. I have a very, very good lawyer. I will make sure he takes you both down for this. You've got nothing on me. You just said yourself that I didn't do it. So, why am I still being treated like a caged animal?"

"Because you may very well become one soon," Olivia said darkly. "We're not charging you for murder, Charlie. We're charging you for just about everything else under the sun. Money laundering, tax avoidance, drug trafficking, possession with intent to distribute... should I continue, or have you heard enough?"

"What the hell are you talking about?"

"You know very well, I think," Olivia said. "We found your secret room behind the storage closet on the *Astoria*."

"I swear, I didn't know—"

"No more lying," Olivia snapped. "No more half-truths, no more secrets. We have your fingerprints in that room. We know you've been in there."

Charlie shook in rage but fell silent.

"You and Mr. Shaw may not have seen eye to eye for a long time, but there was one thing you both always agreed on, wasn't there?" Olivia pressed. "And that was that you wanted to make as much money as humanly possible together. You went into business together to get rich, to get drunk, and to get women. You might have fallen out about the latter two things, but money was always at the core of your relationship."

"And you were willing to do anything to make it and keep it, weren't you?" Emily added, scowling in disapproval at Charlie. "You kept money offshore in accounts to hide your undeclared income, which is very handy when you're buying and selling drugs. That's not exactly the sort of thing you want to write about in your tax papers, is it? And since your only legitimate business isn't doing half as well as you like to claim in public, your offshore accounts have kept you from falling into debt. On top of all this, you've been double-dipping into Infinity's accounts, defrauding investors, and skimming off the top... isn't that right, Charlie?"

"Not to mention that your tax payments are lower due to your small legitimate income, the only thing you ever declare to the government," Olivia went on, raising her eyebrows. "You might look rich when you're partying every weekend and showing off your bling, but none of that came from a successful business. It came from your drug distribution network."

"And what's more, you've been maintaining your status by only trusting a small group of people. That's Luke and Angus, presumably," Emily continued. "Which explains your high turnover of staff. But you know, they say to keep your friends close and your enemies closer, Charlie. Perhaps if you hadn't fired Tim Sweeney, none of this would have happened in the first place."

"You alienated your staff so much that they were willing to do anything to take you down a peg, the way you did to them. You had no regard for them or their livelihoods, and you found any excuse to toss them out of the company like yesterday's trash. Well, it came back to bite you, didn't it? It was Tim, your former employee, who opted to come aboard your yacht and risk everything to spike your drink, to humiliate you the way you humiliated him."

"But it didn't all go according to plan," Emily said, "because that drug you consumed was designed to kill you, Charlie. Did you know that? Did you know you were being poisoned by your own stash of drugs? And did you know that it was your business partner who set out to have you killed in the first place?"

Charlie looked too shocked to speak. He clearly had no clue that it was Luke who'd instructed Tim to spike his drink. Of course, the rest wasn't news to him, but knowing that he'd been betrayed by his inner circle? That had to sting.

"I don't think he will ever forgive you for being with Darcie," Olivia said. "She broke his heart when she threw him under the bus, told you about their flirtations, and blamed it all on him. But he loved her too much to hurt her. So, he turned his attention to you—the man who always got everything he wanted. Maybe you looked down on him one too many times. I don't know. But whatever went down between the two of you, it was far too much for him to handle. He wanted the business for himself, and the girl too. If only it were that simple."

Charlie frowned after the whole truth came to light. "Wait... you came here to tell me that not only did *I* not kill her, but he didn't either? So why are you sitting here, rubbing it in my face that my best friend wanted me dead?" Charlie spat. Emily rolled her eyes.

"We're just making sure you know exactly why we're sending *you* to prison for life. But at least you'll have your buddies there too," Emily said coldly. "And I'm sure that Angus will tell you all about his role one of these days."

"I have no intention of going to prison," Charlie growled. "You think you can take me down? You think you can mess with me?"

"Yes," Olivia said simply. "We do. But don't worry. We have plenty of evidence to back up our claims. We'll be sure to bring it along to your court case. But until then, I guess this is goodbye."

Charlie's eyes widened as an officer entered the room, ready to take him away for good. "You're under arrest, Mr. Evans," he started.

"No," Charlie said firmly. "I won't allow you to do this to me! Get your hands off me!"

"Don't make this harder for yourself," Emily said as Charlie struggled against the man's vicelike grip. "Who knows? If your lawyer is as good as you say, you might even get a few years knocked off your sentence."

Charlie was screaming obscenities as he was carted away by the officer. Olivia sat back in her chair and puffed out air.

"Wow. He's really not used to having the tables turned on him, is he?" Olivia said, feeling a little smug. Emily returned her comment with a grin.

"That should take him down a peg or two," she said brightly. "So. Who do we want next out of the golden trio? Angus or Luke?"

"Let's save the best until last. I think Angus is the one we want to speak to next."

Emily nodded to the officer who was standing at the door; he disappeared for a moment to bring in their next interviewee. When Olivia saw him coming through the door, she felt a stab of anger that she hadn't been expecting. After everything that had happened, this was going to be the hardest of all of them.

Because what it came down to was that Angus was the reason everything had fallen apart in the first place. He was the reason they were about to take down a branch of a drug trafficking ring—

the one who'd finally blown open the case of Darcie's murder. Olivia was about to have the full truth, but at the cost of a young woman's life. That didn't feel worth it to her.

Olivia tried not to lash out in anger as Angus sat down opposite her. It didn't feel nearly as satisfying to be speaking with him as it had with Charlie. Charlie was a bad person through and through, but he wasn't a killer. At least not directly.

"Feeling a little calmer today, Angus?" Emily asked him, her voice ice cold. But it didn't seem to provoke him today. Instead, Angus bowed his head a little, avoiding eye contact with them.

"I should apologize for my prior behavior," he said. "My therapist says I need to work on that."

"Smart therapist," Olivia said, trying not to betray her surprise at his response. She narrowed her eyes at him, wondering whether he was trying to gain their sympathy, but he still wouldn't look at them.

Emily cleared her throat. "We're charging you today for many things, Angus, including money laundering, drug trafficking, and multiple counts of fraud, but the thing we're most interested to know is… why did you kill Darcie Puckett?"

He shook a little bit in his seat, and a single tear fell down his cheek. The big man didn't even resist, didn't even angrily protest his innocence. It was strange seeing such a powerful, muscular man, his face so damaged by years of combat sports, nearly reduced to tears as he sat in front of them.

"We'd like to give you a chance to explain your story, Angus," Olivia said. "Otherwise, we have to go where the evidence leads us. And right now, that's putting you behind bars."

He still couldn't bear to look at them. Was it because he'd come to terms with what he'd done, and he was ashamed? Was it because he planned to lie? Olivia wasn't sure until he opened his mouth and a small choking noise escaped. And that's when Olivia was sure that something had gone all wrong for Angus the night of the party.

"I didn't want to kill her. I didn't want to hurt her," Angus said, his voice strained with emotion. "I liked the young woman very much. But she was always so nosy. Charlie had insisted on keeping our operations secret from her because he knew she wouldn't approve. In fact, he was sure that she would have felt morally obligated to turn us in. And that was the last thing any of us wanted. So, we kept her in the dark."

There it was. Olivia wished she was surprised, but at this point, she no longer was. Darcie had been a good person after all, an innocent life lost in the mess of these men.

"Did you think she ever suspected the three of you were involved in something like this?"

Angus shook his head sadly. "I don't know. Maybe. We were so careful never to let her find out."

Olivia leaned forward. "But she found out anyway, didn't she?"

Angus swallowed. "I... I thought she did. I *knew* she did. I came out of the storage room, and she was standing right there, looking at me. Wide-eyed and wild. I'd never seen her that way before. She looked... she looked terrified of me."

"So, you tried to silence her."

He glared angrily at Olivia, but took a deep breath and tried to calm himself.

"So, I chased after her," he clarified. "Tried to calm her down. She was inconsolable. She was babbling at me, saying things I could barely understand. She was out of her mind, talking about losing everything. She said she was going to lose her job, she was going to be alone in the world, she'd have nobody to love her once the world found out... I don't think even she knew half of what she was saying, looking back. But I was so sure she was talking about *me*, talking about what she'd seen. I thought that she was going to turn us in to you, knowing there were FBI agents on board. I thought she was going to take us all down on her sinking ship."

A stone sank in Olivia's stomach as the final pieces clicked into place.

Angus swallowed. "Now that I know more... I think she must have been drugged up and talking at least some nonsense. She never got like that, never drank to excess or anything like that. And I didn't know what she was capable of. She was flailing around, acting all crazy... so I shoved her. I thought it might keep her away from me. She crashed against the side and hurt her ribs.

And then when that sank in, she turned to scream at me. And so, without thinking… I just pushed her again."

His eyes filled up with tears now, and he stared at his hands, as if finally realizing for the first time what he'd done. "I don't know what came over me…"

The room was silent. They all sat there in the knowledge that Darcie had died for nothing. If Angus hadn't let his anger get the better of him, they might never have discovered any of this vast conspiracy in the first place. They might have gotten away with it all, and Darcie would still be alive. She died for nothing other than the madness of men who were drunk on riches and power.

And that made Olivia furious.

She shook her head slowly at Angus, and he had the decency to lower his head in respect.

"She shouldn't have died. I didn't think… I didn't think that she would. I didn't think she'd go over the edge. I thought… I thought I could just keep her quiet," he murmured. Then he shook his head. "I really just wanted to give back to the community. But Charlie was my friend, and he helped me manage my money. I never meant to get caught up in all of this…"

Despite his sorrow, Olivia didn't feel an ounce of sympathy for him. He'd given in to his clear anger issues and killed a woman just to maintain his own lifestyle.

But it would have been better if he were like any of the other killers Olivia had taken down. Killers that hurt people out of their own sadistic desires. This was just a man who'd been driven to monstrous things in a split-second decision… and he would regret it for the rest of his life.

Angus finally raised his head so he was looking Olivia in the eye. He swallowed, a single tear dripping down his leathery cheek.

"I deserve this. And for what it's worth… I'm sorry. I thought I was a better man than this."

Then, with that, Angus stood up and offered himself up to the officer at the door, who took him away without another word. Olivia felt herself deflate. Taking a man like Angus down should have felt like a win, but the circumstances were too grave for her to feel like celebrating. She offered a tired smile to Emily, who squeezed her shoulder gently as their final interviewee of the case was brought in to speak to them.

CHAPTER TWENTY-EIGHT

LUKE SHAW STILL DIDN'T LOOK LIKE THE CUTTHROAT businessman they'd discovered him to be. He didn't look like the mastermind behind all of the trouble that had ensued in the past few weeks. As he sat down opposite Olivia and Emily, he looked completely neutral. Not angry, not upset, not scared. Nothing. Olivia wondered if Luke was actually a psychopath, so unbothered by everything that had happened that he felt no need to express any emotions about it.

"So. It was *you* who orchestrated this whole mess," Olivia started. She folded her arms over her chest. "Are you pleased with yourself?"

Luke shrugged slowly. "I think it would be much more pleasing if you hadn't caught me."

"Sucks for you then. We know exactly what you've done."

"Okay. Then tell me," he countered. "What do you know?"

So it was a challenge he was after. He had no idea what they had in store for him. And Olivia was happy to deliver.

"We suspected Charlie all along of foul play. We were even willing to make him our main suspect after Darcie died. He was always the more obvious fall guy for this whole thing. But you flew under our radar for a while. And even now, with all the evidence we have stacked up against you... I still don't understand what pushed you so far. You wanted Charlie dead, for what? For daring to love the same woman as you? For being the one that she wanted instead?"

There was a fire behind Luke's eyes that she hadn't seen before. Or maybe she just hadn't been looking for it. And then there was the cruel smile that played on his lips, the kind of smile he didn't seem capable of having. And yet, all along, he'd been playing with them. All along, he'd been one step ahead of them.

But in the end, it hadn't mattered. They had him in their grasp, and they weren't letting him go now.

"She was supposed to be mine," Luke said through gritted teeth. "She would have been mine. Charlie was the one thing standing in our way."

"She chose *him*. She had the opportunity to be with you. She had you wrapped around her little finger, didn't she? But she didn't want you enough to leave him. So, she stayed and you ran off to form a little revenge plan, right? You dated Darcie's best friend, hoping she'd find out about your secret affair and have her heart broken. But when that didn't work, you turned on Charlie."

"He took everything from me," Luke snapped. "All our life... he's always come first. Women always flocked to him first. He was the handsome one—the one that everyone wanted to be around. He didn't have a single brain cell in that head of his, but he acted like he ruled the world. He always thought he was smarter, but I showed him. I double-crossed him, and he had no idea. He would have died not knowing why if things had gone according to plan. But everything got messed up in the end. At least now he knows how much I hate him. At least now he knows that I was the better man."

"A better man? I wouldn't say that," Olivia said cuttingly. "And since you're both going to prison for a long, long time, I don't think it really matters at this point, do you? No one will know the difference between you when you're living in a cell. I guess you'll have plenty of time to reflect on what you've done, though. You won't be leaving prison for a very, very long time."

"It was worth it," Luke snarled. "It was worth it just to let Charlie know how much I despise him."

"Well, we're glad you seem to think so," Emily said. "Good luck with that."

By the time the room had been cleared of all three of their culprits, Olivia and Emily sat for a long moment in silence, reflecting on what had just happened. A simple party had led to them taking down a lot of men who had dipped their fingers into a lot of criminal pies. They were the worst of the worst, and now they were dealt with for good. It was a good day for them.

And yet, it was bittersweet. Olivia thought of Darcie. She had seemed so bubbly, so full of life… and she'd been so unaware. After all their wondering about what she'd done, it turned out that she really was innocent. She'd had a good heart, and her peers had trampled all over it. Perhaps she hadn't been perfect, but she certainly hadn't deserved what happened to her.

None of these men cared about her, not truly. All of them were willing to sacrifice her to get what they wanted. And in the end, she lost her life simply for being in the wrong place at the wrong time, as the men in her life tried to destroy each other.

"At least we got justice for her," Emily said after a long time. "That's what we're here to do."

"Yes," Olivia said quietly. "It's the least we can do. At least something good came out of this in the end."

CHAPTER TWENTY-NINE

"CHEERS TO US!"
Olivia smiled as she clinked her beer bottle against Emily's. After they wrapped up all the loose ends of the case, they headed back to Emily's apartment for a celebratory drink.

"Cheers!" Olivia said, and they both swigged from their bottles with appreciative sighs. Emily sunk low in her chair, and Olivia grinned at her.

"I don't think I've ever seen you so relaxed," Olivia mused.

"Oh, believe me, I'll be back to my tightly-wound self by tomorrow," Emily replied with a smile. "And I'll bet you'll be exactly the same."

Olivia chuckled. She was right. By the time morning came around, Olivia would likely have found something else to occupy her mind with, to use as a distraction from the life she lived. Already, her mind was straying back to her family and the promises they'd made to her, as well as to Brock on his mission in New York. While they'd been running around looking for clues, it was easier to forget that she was a real human being with a life of her own. During cases like these, she got lost in the stories of other people, taking on their lives and problems until it felt like she was truly a part of them.

But that was over now, and she was left with reality. It was easy to get bogged down by that, but when she glanced up at her friend, she smiled. Her life could be pretty turbulent sometimes, but at least she had good people in her life. Emily had been one of the most consistently good things in her life for a long time. Sure, they had drifted apart a little when she moved away from the city and out to Belle Grove, but Olivia had felt like she needed a new start. She had felt like she needed a little time to get her head in order and process all of the crazy things that had happened to her.

She'd lost so much over the past few years. Her sister, her mother for a while at least, her sense of self, and sometimes even her sanity. And when someone had broken into her new home and shattered her sense of safety, she'd lost a piece of her happiness too. Olivia knew that life was all about overcoming obstacles, no matter who you were as a person. But sometimes it did feel as though she was given more hurdles than most.

And that had made her life harder. It had made her withdraw from her friends and family, the people she'd cared about most. Even after Brock brought a new light into her life, she still shied away from the people who had shaped her past—scared that she had left all of them behind for good.

And yet, here she was, sitting with her best friend and sharing a beer. It was almost like nothing had changed, even though everything had. Olivia watched her friend fondly and realized that in their time apart, Emily had changed too. It was in small ways, but it was noticeable. Just like Olivia, she was more confident and surer of herself; she wasn't so afraid to speak her mind. She was still the same kind, selfless, purehearted woman that Olivia had always known … but she was still growing.

And Olivia hadn't been around to see it.

"Em?"

Emily looked up with curiosity. "Yeah?"

"Do you ... do you think I've been a bad friend to you?"

Emily's smile turned into a confused frown. "Olivia ... where is this coming from?"

Olivia took a deep breath. "I guess it's crossed my mind a few times over the past week that we've been together. I know that we haven't spent that much time together lately. This past year, it's kind of felt as though we've always been far apart. We went from being roommates to barely speaking and ... and I worry that I haven't been a good friend to you. We've both changed so much, and I haven't been around to watch you thrive. And I just ... well, I'm sorry about it. I'm sorry that I've missed so much. I'm sorry that I've missed out on *you*."

Emily listened to Olivia with a frown resting on her face. Then, she got up from her chair and joined Olivia on the sofa, resting her head against her shoulder. "Olivia ... oh, Olivia. You're worrying over nothing. Again."

"I am?"

"Like you always do," she chided.

"You don't ... you don't think I've abandoned you?"

"Of course, I don't." Emily sat up straight and looked her friend in the eye. "Look. It's perfectly natural in adult friendships for there to be dry spells. If I had a kid tomorrow, you wouldn't expect me to be hanging out with you every other day, would you? It's not natural. We grow up and our lives take different paths and we have to make room for new priorities. And that's just in normal circumstances. For you, it's ... different."

"What do you mean?"

There was sadness in Emily's eyes as she looked at Olivia. "When you left the city... you were broken, Olivia. I saw you change in the years after your sister died and your mom disappeared. Those things would be enough to make anyone go a little crazy. But when you said you needed to get out of the city, I totally understood. I didn't take it personally when you left our apartment behind and said you needed space. How could I? You were hurting in ways that I couldn't even imagine. How could I blame you for needing some time to figure all that out?"

Olivia didn't realize she was crying until Emily reached out to blot a tear from her cheek. She sniffed, her throat suddenly tight with emotion. She hadn't been expecting to get emotional, but hearing Emily's thoughts had taken a toll on her. Emily laid her head against Olivia's shoulder once again.

"I guess I did mourn our friendship a little when you left. Not because I thought it was over, but because I knew it was changing. It still felt like we were kids back then, when we were living together, having wild weekends together, talking for hours every single night when we got back from training or from work… and I was clinging to that feeling for a long time. That feeling of just having fun and not taking life too seriously, even in a line of work like this. It just felt like we were freer back then. But I knew that even though you were trying to put on a good face for me, for Sam, for everyone… you were really suffering. I knew that at some point you'd have to figure that part of yourself out. We had to grow up at some point. So, when you left… I guess I said goodbye to a past version of myself too. But look at us now! Just because things are different, it doesn't mean they're not good."

Emily's face softened. "The other night, when you told me you were the happiest you'd been in a long time… I knew you meant it. And I didn't take offense, by the way. I didn't think you were, like, implying that your life was better since we moved farther apart. I just know that things aren't so hard for you anymore. And that's what I wish for you, more than anything."

Olivia couldn't speak without bursting into tears, so she laid her head against her friend's and closed her eyes. She was filled with so much emotion that she could barely hold it back. Emily had proven to her once again that she was a perfect friend—that she was the kind of person that Olivia would always be able to rely on. And above that, she was always going to be around, no matter how much things in their lives changed.

"I've missed you so much," Olivia managed to say eventually.

"I know. I'm very miss-able."

Olivia giggled and Emily swung an arm around her shoulder, locking them into their hug. She let out a long sigh.

"I've missed you too," Emily admitted. "This week has been ... well, it's been crazy, but it's been good just being back with you. I'll never take our friendship for granted ever again."

"Me neither. And I'm going to come up to the city more often. I want to see more of you and Sam. It's about time we got the gang back together."

"Exactly. And you know, we'd love to meet Brock properly," Emily prodded, giving Olivia a pointed look. Olivia rolled her eyes with a laugh.

"He's just a friend."

"For *now*."

"Well, yes, for now... and for always, no matter what. So, yes, I'll bring Brock along to meet you guys. I think Sam would appreciate a little male company."

"Oh, I don't know about that. I think he kind of likes having two female friends at his side all the time. I think he thinks it makes him look desirable."

The pair of them exchanged a look before bursting out laughing. And there it was again. That feeling of elation that Olivia had so sorely missed. The feeling of laughing with her friends without another care in the world. She'd found it in Brock, and she'd rekindled it with Emily. It was exactly what her life had needed to get it back on track, to make her feel normal again. And now that she'd been reminded of the feeling, she never wanted to let it go again.

It was a few beers later, while Emily was putting on a movie, that Olivia realized that she needed to figure out her next move. Where was she going to stay, anyway? With the case over, she should be heading back to Belle Grove, to the place she'd called home for nearly a year. And yet, she didn't feel like she was ready to go back there. She knew it would feel different without Brock there too. She couldn't go back to her own home because it wasn't safe there, and Brock's apartment still felt off-limits while he wasn't around. She could go and stay with her parents, especially now that she had patched things up with them, but that felt strange too. She couldn't actively live with her parents when she still didn't fully trust them.

"Emily?"

Her friend glanced up at her again with a knowing smile. "I know what you want to ask me. And the answer is *yes*. You're welcome to stay here for as long as you like."

Olivia's throat felt tight again as her emotions returned, washing over her body like a tidal wave. "Are you sure?"

"Olivia, this used to be your home too. Your bedroom is still practically the way you left it… although I kind of use it as a dressing room now… but the point is, it's there for as long as you want it. I know that when Brock comes home you'll feel more comfortable going back to Belle Grove. But with everything that happened at your house, I wasn't going to allow you to go back anyway. You should stay a while. It'll be fun!"

Olivia smiled sheepishly. "You're sure?"

"Of course, I'm sure! We can have movie nights and Taco Tuesdays and go jogging together every morning…"

"You hate tacos."

"Well, I couldn't think of anything else that sounded fun," Emily said with a grin. "But seriously, it'll be just like old times. You'll be closer to work too. And hey, maybe we can work another case together in the meantime."

Olivia smiled again. "I think I'd like that."

"Good, then it's settled. I do have one condition of you being here though… you have to take out the trash."

Olivia groaned. "Aw, man, really?"

"Really. Ever since you've moved out, I've had to do it myself, and it *sucks*. I think I was sadder that I'd have to lug out my trash bags every day than about you actually leaving, you know…"

"Hey!" Olivia said, throwing a pillow in Emily's direction, making her laugh once again. And just like that, Olivia felt herself settle back in. She was beginning to realize that home wasn't about the place where she stayed. It was about the people she surrounded herself with. And until Brock was back for good, Emily was the closest thing to home that she had.

As she sipped her beer and lounged on the sofa, she felt good. She felt like a little change for a few weeks would be healthy for her. She didn't have to worry about being found there, or have constant reminders of Brock's absence back in Belle Grove. She could finally relax a little and just *live*.

She would still miss Brock, of course. While he'd been away, she'd missed being able to talk to him about every single little thing. She'd missed being able to delve into cases together, and she'd missed the downtime they shared. When it was just the two of them alone together, it was like everything clicked into place. Everything made sense with him at her side.

And now, she felt like half of her was missing. Working with Emily had been great, but it wasn't quite the same. She and Brock were so different, and yet it made them the perfect team. She missed that. It had barely been a week since he left, and she couldn't wait for him to return home.

But until he did, it was time to get a grip on herself. It was time to learn to be without him. And she was proud of what she'd achieved during her case with Emily. She'd taken charge, led the way, and found the answers herself. She'd worked hard, as she always did, but she had also learned to function as an individual again. Being joined at the hip with Brock had its perks, but she reminded herself that she didn't *need* him. She was strong with him, but she was even stronger alone.

She was more powerful than she'd ever been before.

EPILOGUE

OLIVIA WOKE UP TO THE SOUND OF HER PHONE RINGING. It took her a moment to realize where she was. It was like waking up in an old memory when she took in her surroundings and saw her old bedroom in Emily's apartment. But when she came back to the present, she remembered that things were different now, and that getting a call in the middle of the night wasn't part of the norm.

With a groan, she sat up and glanced at her phone screen. A jolt shot through her heart. Why would Jonathan be calling her at this hour? Surely any of their cases could wait. What could be so important for him to call her now? Had something happened to Brock?

She fumbled for the light switch in the bedroom as she answered the call.

"Knight."

"Knight … are you sitting down?" That was unusual. Jonathan never bothered with pleasantries.

Olivia blinked, trying to adjust to the light in the room. "Um… well, I'm in bed, sir. It's three in the morning."

"I know. But I have something you need to see."

Olivia's heart skipped several beats. She hadn't been prepared for bad news. Not when things were finally going well for her. She took a deep breath.

"What's going on?"

"We have a situation. I just sent you an email of a message the Bureau received."

"Okay. Give me a second …"

She pulled out her laptop and immediately went to her email, feeling sick to her stomach as she saw the forwarded message from Jonathan. It didn't feel any better when she saw the video clip attached to it.

"What is this?" she asked.

"Watch it," he instructed her.

Olivia swallowed and clicked on it, terror consuming her entire body. When the file opened, she saw immediately what Jonathan had been so horrified by.

In the video, a man was tied to a chair. He had a hood over his head, but she would recognize him anywhere. Olivia held her breath, unable to look away as the scene unfolded. Then, as the sound of a whip cracked across his back, he cried out, and Olivia covered her mouth in horror.

"Brock…" she whispered.

The room he was being held in was dark and nondescript. Olivia had no idea where he could possibly be, but she got the feeling he was far from home.

His cover must have been blown, she thought.

Tears welled in Olivia's eyes as she watched the video unfold. Someone continued to beat him, clearly relishing his cries of pain. Olivia didn't want to watch, but she couldn't look away. The clip wasn't very long, but it felt like it lasted for hours.

And then they ripped the hood off of him, and all doubt was gone. Brock sat there, with a black eye and bruises all over his body, his hair messed up and his cheeks swollen, and his mouth was stained with blood. He looked in such pain that he couldn't even raise his head to the camera.

"Your precious FBI agent won't last long in our hands," came a voice from off-screen. The voice had clearly been altered for the purpose of the video, and Olivia felt a shiver run down her spine. She recalled The Messenger doing the same thing all those months ago to hide his identity. Was this the work of the cult again?

"If you would like to see him alive, then you will pay a price," the voice continued. "You will bring two million dollars to the coordinates that we disclose. You have one week. Should you fail… then the next video you receive from us… will detail his death."

The video ended, and Olivia began to tremble. This couldn't be real. Not Brock. Not the person she cared for most in the world. She felt faint, like she might collapse if she tried to stand. Though the video was over, she could still hear the echo of Brock's cries and feel the shiver running down her spine at the sound. She could still see his beaten and bloody face.

If they didn't do something, he would die. If they didn't work fast, she'd lose him.

And she couldn't lose him.

AUTHOR'S NOTE

Thank you for reading *Murder on the Astoria*, book 5 in the *Olivia Knight FBI Series.*

We particularly enjoyed planning and writing this one! We thought it was different and fun... or maybe we just have summer vacation on our mind and want to be by the water! :D

Our intention is to give you thrilling adventures and an entertaining escape with each and every book. However, we need your help to continue writing this new series. Being indie writers is tough. We don't have a large budget, huge following, or any of the cutting edge marketing techniques. So, all we kindly ask is that if you're enjoying the books in the Olivia Knight series, please take a moment of your time and leave us a review and maybe recommend the book to a fellow book lover or two. This way we can continue to write all day and night and bring you more books in the Olivia Knight series.

We cannot wait to share with you the upcoming thrilling adventures of Olivia and Brock!

Your writer friends,
Elle Gray & K.S. Gray

P.S. If you want to read more awesome books while you wait for the next Olivia Knight book. Please, checkout *Pax Arrington Mysteries and Blake Wilder FBI Mystery Thrillers*

P.P.S Feel free to reach out at egray@ellegraybooks.com with any feedbacks, suggestions, typos or errors you find so that we can take care of it!

ALSO BY
ELLE GRAY

Blake Wilder FBI Mystery Thrillers

A Pax Arrington Mystery

ALSO BY
ELLE GRAY | K.S. GRAY

Printed in Great Britain
by Amazon

22977755R00130